more than friends

more than friends

New York Times Bestselling Author
MONICA MURPHY

More Than Friends
Copyright © 2016 by Monica Murphy

Cover design © Hang Le byhangle.com
Interior Design and formatting by

E.M.
TIPPETTS
BOOK DESIGNS

www.emtippettsbookdesigns.com

everafter ROMANCE

chapter one

Amanda

I'm cruising on my bike, contemplating everything Livvy just told me. How her mom was so mad when she discovered Livvy had spent the night at Ryan's house, she grounded her and took away her phone. Livvy is seriously going to lose her mind being grounded for so long, unable to see Ryan unless we're at school. That won't be enough for her. When it comes to Ryan, it feels like nothing is ever enough for her.

At least I'm not in trouble like she is.

Liv's going to stress out over Ryan, though. Over those hours when she's not with him and he could possibly be up to no good. She worries about him all the time. I get it—sort of. He seems to play games, and that must get exhausting.

Truthfully, I wouldn't put up with that crap. But I'm not Livvy.

Thank goodness.

The wind blows through my hair as I make a right into my neighborhood, turning the wild strands into a tangled mess. Not that I care. There's no one I'm hoping to impress. It'll just be Sunday night dinner with the family, as usual. I'm not even sure if they're home yet. Dad mentioned something about going to Home Depot to pick out fall flowers for the yard, and Mom said something about shower curtains and Bed, Bath & Beyond.

Bleh. I'm glad I made my escape when I did.

My house slowly comes into view and I smile to myself. I might not live in a giant mansion in a fancy neighborhood like my new so-called friends, but our house is nice. Small and on the older side, but it's cute, with a pretty front yard and a big porch with a white swing…

Oh. Crap. There's someone sitting on the swing. His arms are spread out along the back of the wooden frame, his gaze locked directly on me, like he knew I was going to appear at any second.

It's Jordan Tuttle.

My heart is racing as I press gently on the brakes, taking him in, my gaze roving over every single tiny feature that makes him Jordan. I want to slow down the moment, revel in the anticipation of finding *him* waiting for *me*. He rises to his feet, runs a hand over his thick, perfect hair almost nervously, and a shuddery breath leaves me.

The memory hits me, socks me in the stomach and leaves me aching. I remember what it felt like, having those hands on me just last night. His mouth on mine, the words he whispered in my ear. It wasn't a dream. It wasn't something I made up inside my head, because seriously, I was starting to wonder if I really was losing my mind when it came to Jordan Tuttle.

But no. Jordan is real. He's in my life because he *wants* to be here for some crazy reason. And now he's waiting for me, his hands on his hips, the faintest smile on his face as he continues to watch me.

"What are you doing here?" I ask as I make my approach, hopping off my bike so I can roll it up the front walkway.

We meet in the middle, Jordan stopping just in front of me. "Nice way to greet me."

I frown, worried I was doing everything wrong. He had a way of making me feel like that. "How should I greet you?"

"Like this." His hand is suddenly curled around my nape when he pulls me in for a too-quick yet somehow lingering kiss. My lips tingle when he pulls away, and by the smug expression on his face, I know *he* knows the effect he has on me.

"Jordan," I chastise, stepping away from him and nearly tripping over my stupid bike. Luckily enough, he catches me by the elbow, steadying me before I fall over like an idiot. "What if my parents are inside?"

"They're not." He grabs the bike from me, nudges the kickstand down and sets it in place on the sidewalk a few feet away from us. "Where've you been?"

His confidence makes me crazy. He's so sure of himself, and I wish I had even an ounce of his self-assuredness.

I don't. Not even close. He lives in another realm. I'm just a lowly peon compared to His Majesty, Lord Jordan Tuttle.

"I went over to Livvy's," I tell him when I realize he's waiting for my answer. As usual, my mind wanders when I'm in his presence. "I wanted to make sure she's okay."

Jordan frowns. "She is, right?"

"Oh yeah, her mom just grounded her for life." When he sends me a *come on* face, I readjust. "Fine, she's grounded for a couple weeks. No phone. No Ryan."

"It might do her some good, the no Ryan thing," he mutters.

I say nothing. I don't understand the relationship he has with Ryan. They're friends. Then they're not. They're teammates always, and that's something Jordan has to deal with no matter what.

"What are you up to right now?" I ask, hoping to change the subject.

He smiles. Reaches out to tuck a wayward strand of hair behind my ear. I feel that innocent touch all the way down to my toes, which are currently curling in my battered white Converse. "I want to take you out."

My mouth drops open. "In public?"

The frown is back. It's not fair, how attractive he still is despite the scowl he's currently wearing. "Of course in public. What the hell, Mandy."

I shrug, my cheeks burning with embarrassment. "We haven't actually been seen together."

He grabs my hand and pulls me in close. My body immediately goes hot and I wonder if he has some sort of powerful force field I can't resist. "I want to change that."

My gaze meets his and I can't look away. He's so sincere. So serious. "What happened between us last night was…"

"Real." He kisses me again. Another brief brush of lips on lips, yet I'm decimated. Shaky all over when he pulls away. When my ex Thad kissed me, I never felt like this. Ever.

Never.

Ever.

Never.

"Maybe we were just caught up in a moment?" I ask tentatively. It's like I'm always waiting for the bomb to drop. For the joke to be on me. No one in a million years would ever match me with Jordan Tuttle. Not even me. So what's his deal? Why is he so persistent? I don't get it.

I like it, but he also scares me. I don't want to get hurt.

I don't want my heart to be broken.

"Every time I'm near you, I get caught up in a moment." One side of his perfect mouth tips up in this semi-smile that is absolutely adorable. I wish I had my phone out so I could snap a pic of him. "Maybe we need to give this a try and see if all we ever experience together is one giant moment."

"That's impossible." The words are out before I can stop them and I slap my hand over my mouth, my eyes wide as I stare up at him.

Jordan actually laughs, shaking his head. It's a rare sound, but wow, is it amazing. "Nothing's impossible if you want it bad enough."

I drop my hand, gaping up at him. "So are you saying that you want—*me*?"

"Yes." He dips his head, his mouth hovering above mine. "I do."

HE TAKES ME to a coffee shop that's tucked into a corner of a strip mall, an elegantly trendy place that looks totally out of place considering its location. He's not the only one who's heard of the place, though. It's so crowded I practically have to fight someone to snag a suddenly empty table.

"Your mocha." Jordan sets it on the table and drops into the chair across from me, scooting it in so his knees bump against mine.

"Thank you." I turn my legs to the side, not necessarily wanting to touch his legs. Then again, I sort of want to tangle them up together. Preferably with no clothes on.

My cheeks go hot, betraying my thoughts, and the slow smile that curves Tuttle's perfect lips tells me he has suspicions.

"We could go back to my house if you want," he suggests in that velvety smooth voice of his. I swear it ripples across my skin and settles into my bones, staying there. Reminding me that he exists.

Like I could forget.

"No way." I shake my head quickly, bringing the cup to my lips and taking a careful sip. It's not too hot. In fact, it's perfect, much like the guy who's sitting with me, and I sort of hate this stupid mocha for its perfection.

But I can't hate my drink for too long because it tastes so good.

"Why not?" He reaches across the table, his fingers dancing across the top of my hand for the briefest moment. "No one's home."

That's the problem. I don't do well in Tuttle's presence, especially when we're alone. I tend to become careless. Reckless. I do things that I would never do otherwise. That sort of behavior is completely unlikely me.

And dangerous to my well-being.

"I have to be home by dinnertime." I sit up straighter, my fingers clutched around the smooth, hot paper cup that holds my coffee. "No matter what, I can't escape our Sunday family dinner."

A dark brow rises. "You have dinner with your family *every* Sunday?"

I nod, a little embarrassed. "It's the only time we're together, you know? There's always something going on. Soccer practice, volleyball practice, band—" I clamp my lips shut for a brief moment, mentally crossing band practice off the list. It's hard to break the habit when you've been going to band practice for the last five years of your life. "Either my mom is working or Dad's working, and Sunday evening is the only time we're all under the same roof."

He stares at me like I'm a rare, exotic animal that he's only noticing for the first time. Wonder, confusion, maybe even the faintest hint of disgust crosses his face. Like he can't believe that we'd be such a close family. Is family time a foreign concept to him?

I wouldn't doubt it.

"Sounds like something out of a movie," he mutters with a shake of his head before he takes a long drink from his cup.

"My family is close." I shrug, not willing to offer up any more explanation. He doesn't reveal too much to me any more, so why should I open up to him? "We're weird, I know."

"I never said you were weird." His gaze lingers on my lips for a beat too long, and I wonder if he's thinking about kissing me. I know I'm thinking about kissing him. So much that my lips are tingling. "Most everyone I know has shitty parents."

He's right. Most everyone I know has bad parents too. "Guess I lucked out?"

Jordan nods, his gaze meeting mine once more. "Guess so."

I change the subject and we talk about school. Homecoming is happening this week and king and queen nominations are tomorrow. Nominees will be announced Tuesday morning and lots of activities are held throughout the week, including way too many pep rallies, a parade and finally the big game Friday night, followed by the annual homecoming dance.

"You'll be nominated," I say with all the assurance I feel, because come on. It's Jordan.

He makes a face. "I don't want to be."

"Please." He has to be full of crap. "You love it."

"Not really." He waves a dismissive hand as if he can make the subject magically disappear. "Are you playing in the powder puff game?"

It's my turn to make a face. "Um, I don't think so."

"Why not?" He tilts his head to the side, appearing thoroughly confused. And thoroughly adorable. "You should."

"No thanks." Only the popular girls play. It's the female version of the big homecoming game, and all the girls wear the football players' jerseys, paint their faces and basically run around on the field like idiots trying to catch a ball. All while the football players wear the cheerleaders' uniforms and too much makeup, jumping up and down while risking junk exposure. "It's totally sexist."

"You really think so?" He hesitates, his gaze dropping to the table before he blows out a breath. "And to think I was going to let you wear my jersey."

I'm gaping. I can feel my mouth hanging open and I'm sure I look ridiculous, so I do my best to force it shut. "You were not."

"I totally would. All you have to do is ask."

I sort of hate how he throws it into my court. Shouldn't he offer? Why do I have to ask?

"You never let a girl wear your jersey," I whisper, not knowing if that's really true but guessing it must be. My chest suddenly feels heavy, and it's like I can't breathe. He puts too much on me, too much importance on this—*thing* between us. And it is so equally terrifying and wonderful all at once, I'm tempted to pinch myself to make sure I'm not dreaming.

"Yeah, well, I've never found someone worthy before." He drains his coffee, crumples the cup between his fingers and turns around, tossing it into a trashcan with ease.

"And I'm worthy." My voice is full of sarcasm.

"Amanda, you've been worthy for months. You've just been fighting it." His gaze meets mine, deep blue and deadly serious.

I can't think of anything else to say, sooo… "I should go home."

"No way I can convince you to come back to my house?" His expression is completely neutral, but I see a faint glimmer in his gaze—and it reminds me of hopefulness.

Surely I must be seeing things.

"I can't," I say regretfully. "But maybe you should come with me to my house. Have dinner with my family." Mom would be mad that I'm bringing an unexpected guest, but she'd get over it. I would love for my parents to meet Jordan. He's so good-looking and smart and rich and…

My stomach sinks. He's too smart. And too rich. He'd take one look at our shabby house with the ratty old couch and the walls that need paint and the kitchen that needs updating and he'd *know*.

He'd know I'm really not worthy of him. And then he'd leave me in the dust.

Jordan makes a face as he stands, reaching across the table to grab my empty cup. "No thanks. I'm not the bring-home-to-family-dinner type."

I say nothing as he tosses my cup in the trash. Instead, I follow beside him quietly, letting him guide me out of the shop with his hand pressed against my lower back. No way can I react to his touch or his closeness. He makes me feel vulnerable and unsure and I constantly second guess myself in his presence. In fact, the entire ride back to my house we remain quiet, the music playing softly, and I wish it could drown out my thoughts.

But it doesn't. Instead I keep sneaking looks at Jordan while telling myself what we're doing together is nothing. *We're* nothing. I sit up straighter and think of the many ways I can tell him that whatever the heck we're doing, it's never going to work.

Maybe if I keep coming up with excuses, I'll eventually believe them.

The moment he stops the Range Rover in front of my house, I open my mouth, ready to throw some lame this-won't-work line at him. But he doesn't even give me a chance. Instead, he's eagerly reaching for me, like he knows I'm about to drop some it's-not-you-it's-me bomb. He pulls me into his muscular arms and presses his mouth to mine, silencing any and all protests I was about to unleash on him.

I lose approximately two hundred brain cells in the ninety seconds he thoroughly kisses me, and when he finally pulls away from my lips, I open my eyes and stare at him as if in a daze. His lips are damp and his hair is a mess—I think I might've done that, I have no clue—and his eyes are extra bright as he watches me. He even nods, like he's pleased with his kissing results, and his smile is soft as he slowly releases his hold on me.

"See you tomorrow, Mandy."

I practically collapse against the passenger door. "Okay," I squeak, blindly reaching for the handle so I can open the door. I stumble out of the SUV and slam the door, turning to smile and wave at him as he starts to pull away.

Maybe we can make this work. Maybe we can be a real couple. Amanda and Jordan.

Jordan and Amanda.

Hmm, Amanda Tuttle does have a nice ring to it...

I frown. Okay, now I'm getting just a *little* out of control.

chapter two

"**O**h, God. You don't know anything, do you?" Livvy says as she slips into my car, slamming the door so hard I wince. She turns in her seat so she's facing me fully. "I can see it in your eyes. You're so oblivious."

"I'm oblivious to what exactly?" I can admit I'm in a Tuttle-induced haze. I sat through dinner last night staring off into space, which infuriated my father for some reason. Probably because I wasn't talking much, and I'm usually the one they beg to shut up. When the family dinner ordeal was finally over, I locked myself away in my room and ransacked my closet, trying to find something cute to wear to school tomorrow. Something to make a certain boy drool…

But then I remembered it was Homecoming Week, which meant there were themed days where we dressed up. I couldn't remember what Monday's theme was and I couldn't be bothered to look it up or ask anyone, so I chose a pair of my favorite jeans that make my butt look pretty good and a navy blue T-shirt—our school colors are blue and white—with a low V-neck. Maybe Tuttle would stare at my chest when he saw me wearing it.

I mean Jordan. *Jordan* might stare at my chest. And that would be awesome.

"I don't know how to tell you this," Livvy says, her voice breaking through my thoughts and reminding me something awful is about to go down. I meet her gaze, noting the sympathetic look she's sending me. And I also notice her eyes are rimmed with red and her cheeks are blotchy. Like she's been crying.

Uh oh.

"What's going on?" I ask when she still hasn't said anything. I don't like how she's looking at me. Or the way she's sniffing. This can't be good.

"I figured you'd already seen it."

"Seen what?" Now she's just irritating me, and I think she knows it.

"Um, can I show you something?" She tilts her head toward the center console where my phone is sitting.

I almost forgot her mom took her phone away, so I grab mine, enter the password and then hand it to her. This is such a major show of trust, letting her into my phone. Crap, I wouldn't even let Tara, my ex-best friend, into my phone, and I'd known her forever. But Liv and I have become especially close since school started, and I'm so grateful for her friendship. Without her I'd be lost, and I think she feels exactly the same about me.

Livvy bends her head, nibbling on her lower lip as she opens the Instagram app and starts scrolling. "My mom didn't take away my laptop and she forgets I can still text and see Instagram on there." I glance at the clock on my dash, worried if we sit here for too much longer we'll be late for first period.

When she hands me my phone and I stare at the photo she pulled up for me to see, I realize in an instant I don't care if I'm late for school. My stomach pitches and rolls almost violently, and I slap my hand over my mouth, frightened for a moment that I might throw up all over my lap and my phone.

It's a photo of Ryan—Livvy's boyfriend—and Tuttle, along with Em and a girl I remember Tuttle talking to one night at a party he was having. The one who's name he couldn't remember, yet he knew she'd given him a blowjob, which is the epitome of tacky.

All four of them are close to each other. Em is in Ryan's lap. Tuttle and the skank are wrapped around each other, all of them smiling at the camera, which I think Em is holding, snapping a selfie to immortalize forever.

"I think I'm going to be sick," I mumble, causing Livvy to snatch my phone out of my hands before she's shoving at my shoulder.

"Get out of the car! Puke on the lawn! Hurry!"

Her suggestion is totally valid. I scramble out of the car and bend over, resting my hands on my knees as I wait to throw up my toast and coffee breakfast all over the strip of dying lawn that divides Livvy's house from her neighbor's. But nothing comes up and I realize the longer I stare at the yellow lawn, the more unfocused my vision gets.

God, this is so incredibly disappointing. And that's the worst thing. I'm furious at myself for actually believing I had a chance with Jordan Tuttle.

Clearly I was delusional.

"I didn't want to tell you like this!" Livvy is yelling from the car. I stand up straight and watch her warily, noting the sadness in her eyes, how her face looks ready to crumple at any given moment. "I was kind of hoping you would've caught the photo on Em's feed, though honestly, I don't know which way to find out is worse."

"Em posted this?" Oh. My. God.

That *bitch*.

"Yeah." Livvy nods and sniffs. "Last night."

My blood is immediately boiling. Whenever there's something bad happening, Em always seems to be behind it. The girl is toxic. Poison. She's also Livvy's former best friend.

I don't trust her as far as I can throw her.

"I was with Tuttle yesterday," I say as I get back into the car, my mind going over everything that happened yesterday. What time he dropped me off at my house—around five—which gave him plenty of time to go somewhere else with Ryan and end up with the girls.

"For how long?" When I tell her, her mouth turns grim. "He could've left you and ended up with Ryan and Em and whatever her name is…"

I want to believe he would never do that to me. Every tiny molecule that makes me into who I am literally aches for that to be the truth.

But maybe…maybe it's not. Maybe he did leave my house to go meet another girl. He is a known player. Who am I to him, really? He says a bunch of stuff, and it all sounds good, but maybe he says the same thing to lots of girls.

"The photo looks recent. Not like her and Ryan have known each other that long, but you know what I mean. Maybe it's from another time when they were together?" she asks almost hopefully.

"Please. This was taken last night." I'm going with that. It's almost easier to believe the absolute worst right from the start. Gets the painful part over with, you know?

"You really think so?"

Glancing in Livvy's direction, I see the shock etched all over her face. She doesn't want this to be true. She'd rather believe it was an old photo and Ryan is innocent. Of course she feels that way. He's her boyfriend. She just recently gave up her V-card to that guy. He's sort of a douche, but a hot douche, so I can kind of understand her attraction. Sort of like how Tuttle's a hot douche too.

Disgusted with my Tuttle-filled thoughts, I hit the button to shut off my phone's screen and drop it into the center console cup holder. "If this didn't happen last night, then they were probably together very, *very* recently."

Liv says nothing and I stare out the windshield, my fingers curled tight around the steering wheel. I need to start the car and drive to school, but it's like I'm paralyzed. Going to school means facing Tuttle, and he's suddenly become the last person I want to see.

"What are we going to do?" Livvy whispers hoarsely. "I don't know what to say to Ryan. I don't want to look like the jealous girlfriend—he hates that sort of thing. But I don't know how else to handle this without confronting him."

Ugh. Proof again that Ryan is a total jerk. He runs hot and cold with Liv, especially before they officially got together. "You're allowed to be the jealous girlfriend. He has his hands all over Em, yet you're supposed to be his girlfriend," I remind her, heavy on the sarcasm.

"They've hooked up before," Livvy says.

"Who cares? He's with you now. Or at least he's supposed to be." I turn the key in the ignition almost violently, pressing my foot on the gas so the car's engine revs up, loud and rumbling. I thought hearing it would bring me some satisfaction but so far, no go.

Livvy is watching me in shock, with her mouth hanging open and her eyes wide. "Um, are you okay?"

"Of course I'm not okay," I bite out as I put the car into reverse, glance over my shoulder and back out of the driveway. I do it so fast that when I put the car into drive, my tires squeal as I pull away from Livvy's house.

I don't want to go to school. I don't want to face the whispers and the rumors and stupid Tuttle's handsome face. He'll tell me it was all a misunderstanding, and if I stare into his eyes for too long, I'll probably agree with him. Forgive him. Forget all about that girl cozied up next to him.

How I wish I could go back to yesterday. Sitting with him at the coffee shop, listening to his sweet words and not savoring them enough. Oh, and I can't forget that amazing kiss in front of my house. For all the time we've spent together these last few months, we've never really taken it very far. The most we ever did was the night I discovered my now ex-boyfriend having sex with my now ex-best friend…

My entire body goes warm at the memory. We hooked up that night and took it pretty far, but not too far. I didn't give him every piece of me. Thank goodness.

That's what I keep telling myself.

Thank goodness.

THE BELL RINGS and I shoot out of my class as fast as I can, staring straight ahead as I exit the doorway and turn left when I normally turn right. I'm moving against the crowd, since everyone's either making their way toward the cafeteria or the parking lot, and I do my best not to make eye contact. No one pays me any attention anyway, which is a good thing.

But then again it infuriates me. It's like I don't even rate, and I've been with the most popular boy at school, not that anyone really knew this. Though I'm sure if anyone did see me with Tuttle they probably thought we were working together on a class project or whatever. No way could he see anything in *me*.

Ugh. I'm actually pissed people aren't noticing me when I don't want them to notice me. I make no sense.

I blame it all on Tuttle.

The crowd thins as I make my way farther down the hall and that's when I spot her. Liv is standing close to Ryan, laughing up at him after he leans in close to her ear and whispers something.

My stomach twists and I fight the disappointment that wants to take over me. I knew she'd cave fast.

"Amanda!" she shouts when she spots me, and she waves me over after we make eye contact. I approach them slowly, my feet feeling like they're encased in cement instead of my worn-out Converse. "Hey, you," she says cheerily when I stop in front of them.

Ryan flicks his chin at me in that boy way that's supposed to be a greeting. I say nothing in return, just send him a withering look. Like she can sense what I'm about to do—say something rude to him—Liv grabs hold of my arm before I say something ugly and leads me away from her boyfriend.

"Please don't give me any crap," she starts, and I shake my head, cutting her off.

"So you believed him." My voice is flat and I send her an accusatory glare.

Livvy sighs as we stop on the opposite end of the lockers. "I believe him because he's telling me the truth. The photo was taken at a party late last summer. Before I came back from my dad's, and when he was with…" Her voice fades and she wrinkles her nose. She doesn't want to say the same so I supply it for her.

"Em?" I raise both brows and she rolls her eyes.

"Yes. *Em*. It's an old photo. He swore up and down he was being one hundred percent honest. He hasn't been near Em since we've been together." She leans in close, her voice dropping. "You should believe Tuttle too. That photo is old. And I know he's totally into you."

I hate how my body reacts just hearing someone else say his last name. I'm pretty sure it's not normal. "Why should I believe him? So he can go out and do something like this again? Because it'll happen, I can almost guarantee it. Some other girl will come out of the woodwork full of half-truths and make him look bad, and I won't be able to trust him. Or worse, he'll cheat on me. Remember, he doesn't do relationships."

"Is that what you really believe?"

I whirl around, my heart dropping when I see Tuttle standing in front of me looking stupid gorgeous clad in dark jeans and his football jersey. He also looks really angry and…hurt?

No way.

"That girls will always be a problem for you?" *For us?* "Yes."

"You don't think I can be faithful to you." He's not asking a question. He's just stating the obvious.

"You've never had a girlfriend before." I lift my chin, trying my best to appear strong. I don't like having him so close. Temptation sweeps over me, urging me to take another step forward and wrap my arms around him. But I fight the impulse and win. "I'm guessing there's a reason for that."

"Right, because I fuck every girl I see. I can't control myself." The lack of emotion in his voice and on his face is unnerving. When he crosses his arms, he looks intimidating. I take a step back.

"I never said that," I start, but Ryan speaks over me.

"Come on, Amanda. Are you really going to be such a bitch?"

I turn on him, ready to tell him where to shove it, but I don't have to.

Tuttle is on him in an instant, his hand curled into the front of Ryan's shirt, pinning him against the metal lockers. The locks rattle and shake when Tuttle shoves him again, stepping closer so they're in each other's faces.

"I don't *ever* want to hear you call Amanda that again." He twists Ryan's shirt tighter and Ryan curses under his breath. "Tell her you're sorry."

"Jesus, she's treating you like crap, and you still act like this?" The locks rattle once more as Tuttle pushes Ryan yet again, and his gaze meets mine. "Fine, I'm sorry. I'm sorry!"

Tuttle lets him go with one last shove and then turns to face me. His handsome face is a mask of ferociousness, and his eyes are so hot I swear they singe my skin when he looks at me.

"You can think whatever you want," he says between clenched teeth. "Believe what you want. You know how I feel."

"No, I really don't know," I throw back at him, my voice shaky. I'm not one for violence, but watching Jordan push Ryan against the lockers in defense of me was all kinds of hot. My entire body is tingling and the urge to throw myself at him for a job well done must be some sort of instinctual reaction. "You've never told me."

Our gazes lock. Never waver. Ryan and Liv slink away. A few people pass by us, but Tuttle doesn't even notice. Neither do I.

"I thought I showed you. I thought that was good enough." He takes a deep breath. Exhales loudly. "Guess not."

That's the last thing he says before he brushes past me, his shoulder bumping into mine as he goes by. I turn to watch him walk away, shocked and annoyed that he left me wanting more. Left me feeling bad, like I should chase after him, full of apologies. But I don't. I refuse to play his head games. He'll only end up hurting me.

Better to stay safe and alone versus getting burned.

chapter three

Liv stayed after school to watch Ryan practice—gag. I'm so disappointed in her. She forgave Ryan way too easily, but she did point out yet again that maybe I was the one being stubborn.

Maybe she's right. I don't know, nor do I care. My decision is made. Ever since Tuttle pushed his way into my life, things haven't been right. I know I'm the one who sort of fell on him at his party last summer after the Thad and Tara fiasco, and that really my life was thrown into complete turmoil after that unpleasant incident. Yet he's the one who continues to confuse me. Brings drama into my life. Drama I don't want or need.

After lunch I have AP English with Tuttle, and I sit in my usual spot at the front of the class, refusing to look back at him. My neck remains warm the entire period. I could feel his eyes on me, watching me, staring at my nape. I totally regret wearing my hair in a high ponytail.

When the bell rings, I bolt out of class so fast I run into the edge of a desk on my way out. That probably caused a major bruise.

But at least I didn't have to talk to Tuttle. See his face. Look into his eyes.

Instead of driving straight home after school like I normally would, I go in search of a job. It's time for me to grab hold of my life and control it. I need money. Lots of it—and all for college. Working a part-time job after school and during the weekends wouldn't make me much, but it's a start.

I pull into a shopping center parking lot and walk from store to store, asking if they were hiring. Asking for applications. Most of them told me to apply online, especially the chain stores, and I knew I'd never hear back from them. I need to find a local store, a place that's run by the actual owners versus a management crew hired by corporate. But those types of businesses are getting harder to find.

So when I stop in front of Yo Town, a relatively new frozen yogurt place located at the far end of the shopping center, I'm thinking it might have strong possibilities.

Pushing open the door, I walk into the chilly shop, noting how clean it looks. A vaguely familiar teenage boy sits on a stool behind the counter with his back against the brightly painted wall, his head buried in a book. So buried, I really can't see his face at all, just a shock of light brown hair sticks up above the open book, his lanky body hunched over as he reads.

"Um, hi?" I say after I clear my throat.

He startles, nearly dropping the book to the floor, but he catches it just in time. I recognize him immediately. Blake Stephens. He's a senior. Quiet. Studious. He's in most of my advanced classes, just like Tuttle.

I've maybe spoken ten words to him the entirety of our high school life.

"You're Amanda Winters," he says after an uncomfortable moment of silence.

"That's me." Lame, lame. Yikes. "So, hey. Are you by chance hiring right now?" I ask.

Blake jumps to his feet, coming to stand directly across from me behind the cash register. "We are. I can put in a good word for you, too."

I laugh nervously, noting how closely he examines me. His rapt attention is kind of creepy. "That's awesome. Can I have an application, please?"

"Yeah, sure." He reaches beneath the counter and hands over a standard job application. I take it from him with a faint smile, thank him for the pen and clipboard he also hands me then go sit at one of the small table so I can start filling out the application.

I'm concentrating so hard on making sure all of my answers on the application are correct, I don't notice at first what's playing on the flat screen TV hanging on the nearby wall. But then it slowly dawns on me that he's watching a kid movie on the Disney Channel.

He must've seen me stare at the TV because he says, "My parents keep it on Disney so the kids are entertained."

I turn to look at him. "Your parents own this place?"

"Yeah." He ducks his head and shuffles his feet. "I hate frozen yogurt."

This time my laugh is for real, and there's not a hint of nervousness in it. "So why do you work here?"

"Because they make me?"

I laugh some more and he joins in with a low chuckle. "Seriously, you don't want to work here?"

"Oh yes I do."

My gaze returns to the application and I work on it some more, wishing I'd prepared better. It's hard to come up with a list of references on the spot. I grab my phone and start scrolling through my contacts, stopping when I find my grandma's address. She's a great reference, though maybe I should tell her not to say she's my grandma. "I need a job."

"Not this one.'"

"Yes, this one would be perfect." The more he talks about me not wanting it, makes me want it even more. "What's so bad about working here?"

"Cleaning the place. The machines, the toppings bar, the bathrooms, the floor." He makes a disgusted face. "It's awful."

"I don't mind cleaning." I really don't. Mom runs a tight ship. We're always cleaning around the house every weekend, sometimes even after school. Mom always says, "Idle hands lead to idle minds," and I hate that quote, probably because it's true.

Not that I'm really sure, considering I don't keep myself idle for too long.

"Then you're crazy," he tells me with all the assuredness of someone who doesn't have to worry about his job, considering his parents owned the place. He was guaranteed a job for the rest of his life. Granted, no one wants to work at Yo Town when they're forty, but I'm sure Blake knows he can always work at the yogurt shop if he has to.

I'm almost done filling out the application when a buzzer sounds, alerting that someone's walked into the shop. I glance up to see a pleasant-looking older woman stop at the register to talk to Blake. Their features are similar and I'd bet money it was his mom. I drop my head when she catches me looking, concentrating instead on my application and hoping she doesn't think I'm a creeper.

"Are you applying for a job?" the woman asks a few moments later.

I glance back up to find her standing on the other side of the little table I'm sitting at. "I am. Blake said you were hiring?"

The woman's smile grows. "You know Blake?"

"We go to school together," I tell her, hoping she doesn't ask for any more details. I don't really know Blake at all.

"Mom, stop questioning her," Blake says from behind the counter.

She glances at him over her shoulder. "I have to question her if she wants to work for me." She returns her attention to me with a pleasant smile on her face. "Do you have a few minutes to chat?"

Excitement and nerves bubble inside my stomach. "Sure."

Blake's mom introduces herself as Sonja, and after a few minutes of chit-chat, questions about my (lacking) experience and inquiring exactly how I know her son, I've got the job.

That was way too easy.

"Can you start tomorrow after school?" she asks after letting me know I'll average 15 hours a week and the starting pay is minimum wage.

I'm shocked she'd offer the job so quickly and want me here so fast, but I recover quickly. "Yeah, definitely." I smile as we both stand, and shake her offered hand. "Thank you so much for taking a chance on me." Considering I've never had a job before, she was doing me a huge favor.

"I think we both lucked out." Sonja smiles warmly. "See you tomorrow, Amanda."

I check my phone as I'm walking back to my car and see that Liv has texted me what feels like five million times. Deciding I don't have the time to text back, I call her instead.

"Why are you calling?" she practically shrieks into the phone as her greeting. "We never talk on the phone."

"You sent me a thousand texts. I thought it would be easier to call," I say as I make my way to my car.

"Did you read my texts?"

"No." They were full of emojis and exclamation points so who knows what she's losing it over now.

"Oh my God." She sighs and it sounds shaky. "You'll never guess who Dustin is taking to the homecoming dance."

"Em," I say just to freak her out.

"Ew, no! He would never do that. Well, I don't think he would." She pauses for dramatic effect, and it works. "He's taking Brianne Brown."

Huh. "Is that really a surprise?"

She hesitates. "I guess, considering he snuck into my room last night and we made out."

"*What?*" Now I'm the one shrieking. "Are you freaking *serious? What about Ryan?*"

"I was mad." Her voice is small and I know she knows she messed up. "I just saw that photo Em posted. I couldn't believe it. I was so hurt and confused. And then Dustin showed up. Next thing I know we're kissing on my bed."

"Olivia." My voice is stern and I glance around, thankful when I find a bench in front of Old Navy. I sit and keep my head bent, hoping I don't see anyone from school. "You get mad at Ryan for being a supposed cheater when you're the one who—"

"Don't say it!" she pleads, cutting me off. "Please. You're right. I know you're right. I'm a total hypocrite, but I was so furious at Ryan and Em. The minute Dustin left, I cried. I felt so bad for using him, but I was still angry at Ryan too, you know? I've ruined everything with

Dustin. And Em. Maybe even Ryan."

"You always jump to conclusions." She's way too spontaneous. I plan everything so her spontaneity blows my mind on a regular basis.

"So did you," she points out. "Now you won't even talk to Tuttle and he practically beat up my boyfriend in defense of you."

"Right, because your boyfriend called me a bitch," I remind her.

"I'm sooo sorry he said that." Liv sighs. "This is all a total mess."

"I know. That's why I'm staying out of the drama. No more boys. I just got a part-time job. Between school, yearbook, filling out college applications and working at Yo Town, I'll be too busy for boys," I say, desperate to believe every word I say.

"Wait a minute. You got a job? At Yo Town? What's that?"

"A frozen yogurt shop," I explain. "Blake Stephens' parents own it."

"Who?"

Of course she doesn't know who Blake is. Poor dude. He pretty much keeps to himself. "He goes to school with us. He's in our class."

She's already forgotten about him. "I love frozen yogurt. Can you get me a discount?"

"I don't know. I didn't ask about that." Sometimes my friend can be a tad selfish.

"When do you start working there?"

"Tomorrow after school. I'll also work this Friday night and Saturday afternoon."

"Friday night? But you'll miss the homecoming game and dance! Can't you tell them you already have plans?"

Like I want to go to the homecoming game and dance now. Not when I know it'll just be one big Tuttle fest. I love football. I love how our team is slowly turning themselves around—and a lot of that is because of Tuttle.

Ugh, stupid Tuttle and his gorgeous face and perfect lips and irritating, smug personality. He is nothing but trouble. Trouble I don't need. I always thought he was gorgeous, but he's just a mythical creature. Someone who was in my advanced classes these last three years, though I never really talked to him. Someone I watched play out on the field while I sat in the stands wearing hideous, itchy polyester and an awful hat with a feather plume.

He wasn't real.

Well, now he is. And he's ruined everything. I can't watch football anymore, not if I have to work every Friday night. No more band, no more football and no homecoming dance.

There are worse things to deal with in life. Or so I tell myself.

"I already said I'd work the Friday night shift," I explain. "I can't back out now. I need this job."

"I'm going to miss you, Amanda. Who will I sit with during the game?"

My friend is so wrapped up in her own drama, all she can ever think about is herself. She really needs to work on that. Become a more thoughtful person.

"You'll find someone," I reassure her. "I'm sure you'll survive without me."

chapter four

"**H**ey Amanda."

I brace myself, my shoulders tight, my entire body tense. I'm afraid to turn and see who just said those two words. It could be anybody. Worse, it could be Tuttle. Considering I'm in English and he's in this class with me, I almost expect it to be him. Pushing his luck. Pushing himself on me.

I don't know if I have the strength to make him stop.

But here's the thing: when you want something bad enough, you start to believe it can be true. Like having Tuttle talk to you—you start to believe it's going to actually happen, even though you claim you don't want it to. I know Jordan's dreamy voice anywhere, and the voice that just said my name was definitely not Jordan Tuttle.

Turning, I blink in shock when I realize it's Blake Stephens standing in front of me. He's never approached me before in class. Ever. I don't even think we've ever locked eyes before, let alone said hi.

"Hi," I say, offering him a tiny smile. "How's it going?"

"Pretty good." He ducks his head and his shaggy hair hides his eyes for a moment before he flicks his head. "Thought I'd say hi, considering now we're coworkers."

"Right. Coworkers." I nod and continue to smile, kicking it up a notch when I spot Tuttle slip in through the door and head for one of the desks in the back row of the classroom. "My first official shift starts after school."

"You excited?" Blake raises his brows.

Um, not the way I'd phrase it, but close. "I guess so."

"It's going to be a thrill a minute." His expression betrays nothing, so I'm not exactly sure if he's joking or not.

"You really think so?"

"Nah, I'm just kidding with you." He nudges my arm with his elbow and I laugh. He watches me, pleased with my reaction or whatever, but then the smile slowly dies. I glance in the same direction he's looking to find Tuttle glaring at us from where he sits, his fingers gripping the edge of his desk.

Wait a minute. Is he...*jealous?* Of Blake freaking Stephens?

No. Way.

"Are you working after school?" I ask after I tear my attention away from Tuttle. I take a step closer to Blake, because yes. I'm a total bitch who wants to make a boy jealous. I'm petty and awful but I also sort of don't care.

Truthfully, it feels kind of awesome, knowing that talking to Blake is driving Tuttle insane. Most of the time Tuttle drives *me* absolutely insane and I'm certain he doesn't have a clue.

"Yeah, I'll be training you." Blake nods, his cheeks turning ruddy, as if he's embarrassed. "Thought I'd warn you now."

"It won't be so bad," I say, my voice soft. I don't want him to feel awkward or weird around me. Blake has always been quiet and shy. Crap, *I've* always been quiet and shy too. Blake is more my type of person than Tuttle could ever be. I need to remember that. "Hopefully I'll catch on quickly."

"I'm sure you will. During the weekends, my mom will probably schedule us together a lot, since it can get pretty busy," he explains, making a little face. "Hope you don't mind."

"I don't. I like staying busy. Makes the time go by faster," I tell him just as the bell rings.

Blake smiles, taking a few backward steps until he turns on his heel and settles into his seat. I return my attention to the front of the classroom, resting my linked hands on top of my desk, determined to get into attentive student mode. Mrs. Meyer starts talking and I try my best to pay attention, but I can't focus.

All I can think about is Jordan Tuttle sitting behind me. Watching me. What is he thinking? Does he hate me for cutting him out of my life? Probably. I doubt that happens to him much. He's the type of guy who gets what he wants, whenever he wants it.

"...and what that means is you'll be working on a group project together! Won't that be fun?" Mrs. Meyer ignores the groans that sound throughout the room. "Oh, come on, guys! This will be great. It'll be in teams of two, so the workload must be shared fifty-fifty."

Great. A group project. I hate them, mostly because I always end up doing all the work. I can be a bit of a perfectionist and a control freak, which means I'm super annoying to everyone I end up working with.

"Now, I normally would pair you up myself, but considering

you're seniors and should be able to figure who you like to work with on your own, I'm going to suggest you choose your partners. Don't leave anyone out! And don't fight over each other," Mrs. Meyer calls over the commotion that starts at her announcement. I turn and watch everyone scramble around in frantic search of a partner when I meet Blake's gaze.

"You want to be my partner?" he asks, pointing a thumb at his chest.

I part my lips, ready to say yes, when I hear someone speak from behind me.

"She's with me."

Slowly I turn to find Tuttle standing there, looking intimidating as crap with his arms crossed in front of his broad chest and a glower on his face that could slay a thousand dragons.

I try not to let him affect me, but I swear I feel my toes tremble in my shoes. "How exactly am I with you?"

His gaze lingers on mine, and damn it, I can't look away. "You're my partner."

"But you never asked me," I point out.

He looks ready to roll his eyes. Or walk away. He does neither. "Would you like to be my partner, Mandy?"

I hate it when anyone calls me Mandy…with the exception of him. He somehow gets away with it. "I don't think so."

Now he does roll his eyes. The desk beside me is empty and he drops his perfect body into the seat, tipping the desk onto its two front legs so he can lean as close as possible in my direction. "You're being ridiculous."

"No, *you're* being ridiculous, assuming I want to be your partner for this project." I hesitate, quickly looking away like a coward. "I don't,"

I say to the wall.

He's quiet for a moment, and amidst the growing noise and chaos of the room, his silence is completely unnerving.

"I mean it." I look his way when he still hasn't said anything. "I don't want to be your partner."

"Even after everything we've done together?" he asks, his voice deadly soft.

Of course, his question reminds me of all the things we've done together. And they are a lot. Mostly having to do with touching. And kissing. The boy can kiss like no other. He has this way of making me forget everything the moment his lips touch mine…

"*Especially* after everything we've done together," I say firmly. "This isn't going to work."

"Oh, this is fabulous. You two are going to be great partners together!" Mrs. Meyers exclaims when she stops in front of the both of us. She clasps her hands together, a giant smile on her face. "I love it!"

"He's not my partner," I start, but Tuttle sends me a look that renders me silent. My protest doesn't matter anyway because Mrs. Meyer is already gone, moving on to talk to someone else.

"Looks like you're stuck with me."

The smug smile stretching Jordan Tuttle's perfect lips makes me want to slug him.

I show up at Yo Town promptly at four. Sonja is there to greet me and leads me into the tiny office in the back of the building, where she has me fill out a bunch of paperwork, hands over my official Yo Town T-shirt, telling me she has to go, but that she's leaving me in good hands. Then she sends me back out into the shop so I can be trained.

By Blake.

"This job is pretty easy," he tells me as he has me run through a few practice transactions on the register. I pick it up pretty fast, which fills me with relief. The scariest thing to me was the cash register, but it's fairly simple.

"Then why do you hate it so much?" My Yo Town T-shirt is pale pink and Blake's is black. I notice those are the theme colors of the store. There's pink and black everywhere, including the cups people use to get their frozen yogurt.

And see, that's the easy part of this job. I don't have to dispense the yogurt. Or put on the toppings. The customers do it themselves and bring their yogurt to us, where we weigh it and collect the money. Easy peasy.

How hard can this job be?

"Because my parents make me work here." He smiles faintly, though he's not looking at me. "When you're forced to do something, you always end up hating it, you know?"

Right. For example, how I'm forced to be Tuttle's partner in English. I hate it.

Well, I'm *supposed* to hate it.

"You ended up finding a partner for the project in English, right?" I ask him.

"Oh yeah." He nods. "Celeste Marshall. I've worked with her before. She's really smart. Not that you're not smart, but Tuttle snagged you up first, so…"

His voice drifts and I slam the register's cash door shut, startling him. I hate that he brought Tuttle up, yet I also feel responsible for it. I'm the one who opened my big mouth.

"I'm sorry about that. I really wanted to be your partner," I reassure him gently.

Blake shrugs, his cheeks coloring. "It's no big deal. Next time, right?"

I hope there's a next time. I feel like I need to make it up to him.

Once we're finished with the cash register lesson—including me ringing up a real pair of customers who came into the shop—he brings me to the toppings bar. Pointing out what everything is, he explains I need to make sure to keep everything well stocked. Replenishing the toppings as often as I can is crucial to keeping the toppings bar in good shape. The more they pile on their frozen yogurt, the heavier their cup weighs, and the more we can charge them. Though summer is dwindling, which causes the frozen yogurt business to slow down— at least according to Blake.

"Hours will eventually be cut by mid next month, if not sooner," Blake explains as we walk back to the storage room. "Business drops once summer is really over, and by the end of football season, it really dies off."

"Why is that?"

"It's too cold to eat frozen yogurt," he says, his voice definitely carrying a *duh* vibe.

"You can still eat it inside," I point out. "It's never too cold to eat delicious frozen yogurt."

Blake studies me like I'm crazy. I sort of am, but frozen yogurt really *is* delicious and my stomach is growling, which is embarrassing. "If you can convince people of that and increase business during the winter months, my mom might kiss you."

I make a face. "I'm not into that sort of thing."

Blake's cheeks blaze up. His face is so red I feel instantly sorry for him. "I didn't mean it like that," he mutters.

"I know. I was just teasing." Could I be more awkward? Reaching out, I touch his arm and smile at him but he won't even look my way. The buzzer indicating someone just walked into the shop goes off and he's gone in an instant, not looking back at me once as he scurries out of there.

Guess he was just saved by the bell.

Smoothing a hand over my hair, I walk back out into the front of the store, my mouth dropping open when I see who's standing in front of the frozen yogurt machines, contemplating the flavors.

"Oh. Hey," Emily Griffith says distractedly, barely glancing in my direction.

White-hot rage rises inside of me as I walk over to join Blake behind the counter. I want to sock her in the mouth. Punch her in the stomach. Slap her face as hard as I can. And I'm not one prone to violence, but this chick makes my blood boil.

Worse? She doesn't even realize it.

"You don't have salted caramel anymore?" Em whines at Blake.

"We'll get it back soon," Blake reassures her with a friendly smile.

All she does is make a face as she shoves her cup under the nozzle and adds birthday cake flavored frozen yogurt to it. I watch as she examines the toppings bar, then dumps chocolate chips, M&Ms and chocolate sprinkles on top of her yogurt before bringing it to the counter.

Blake never moves away from the cash register, and I scowl at him. "Let me ring her up," I say.

"I've got it." He never takes his eyes away from Em as she stands in front of us looking positively bored. She even yawns. Doesn't bother covering her mouth either.

Again, I want to punch her. And I promise I'm not a violent person.

"I need the practice on the register." I hip-check him and bump him out of the way, flashing an extra big smile at Em. My mom always said to kill them with kindness, so I'm going for that approach. Besides, she has no idea what she did to Tuttle and me.

Or does she?

"Will that be all?" I ask Em with a sickeningly sweet voice.

"Looks like it, don't you think?" she says sarcastically.

Gritting my teeth, I set her yogurt cup on the scale, stick an orange spoon in it since orange is my least favorite of the plastic spoon colors available, and I punch in the price. She hands me a five and I hand back her change, telling her to have a nice day.

For the first time since she walked in here, she actually meets my gaze and recognition dawns, the dollar bill and loose change spilling from her hand and landing on the counter. "Amanda Winters."

"Emily Griffith," I return.

"So. How's Tuttle?" She smirks.

"I wouldn't know, considering I really don't talk to him," I say coolly, lying through my still gritted teeth.

"Funny, I heard you two were sort of an item. But maybe that was only in your imagination?" She raises her brows.

I imagine leaping over the counter and taking her down to the ground. Wrapping my fingers around her neck and choking her out, Blake cheering me on. I glance over at him, see the lust and adoration in his gaze as he stares at Em, and I know he's a lost cause.

"Funny, I heard you were passed around the locker room after the last home game. But maybe that was the truth?" I raise my brows just like she did.

The flicker of hurt on her face, in her eyes, is there and then gone in a flash. She swipes her yogurt from the counter and stomps out of Yo Town, leaving her change behind on the counter.

"Put it in the tip jar," Blake suggests, completely unfazed. Did he not just hear the awful things we said to each other?

A heavy sigh escapes me. I should've never said that to Em. It was mean and ugly and I sort of lost myself in the moment. Now I feel guilty as crap. "Go ahead. Do you mind if I take a break?"

"Sure. You get fifteen minutes."

That's just enough time to drown my sorrows in a giant cup of watermelon sorbet.

chapter five

Livvy jumps into my car the next morning, fully decked out in a PINK sweatshirt with matching leggings, her makeup perfect and her long, dark red hair pulled back into a high ponytail. She looks great.

"I thought it was pajama day," I say once she shuts the door and drops her backpack at her feet. Every day has a theme for homecoming week and I decided to have some spirit. Who wants to turn down the chance to wear pajamas all day?

"It is." She grins. "I wear this to sleep all the time."

"You do not." Her outfit looks expensive and brand new. I'm lucky to snag a PINK shirt at a thrift shop, though there was that one time last Christmas when my grandma scored me one of those special holiday only T-shirts Victoria's Secret puts out that's more on the cheap side.

"I do! Well, maybe not this exact outfit." Her grin fades as she takes me in. "You look..."

"Comfortable?" I offer hopefully. I'm wearing my favorite plaid flannel pajama bottoms I bought at our local Rite Aid because they're in our school's colors and a dark gray hoodie that's covering an old T-shirt my brother gave me after he cleaned out his closet before he left for college. It's soft and cozy, just like the hoodie, and I wear them all the time.

"Definitely comfortable." Livvy flashes me a bright smile. "You look cute. I like the braids."

I put my hair in two French braids because it was still wet from my shower and I didn't feel like blow-drying it. "Thanks." I chew on my lip, yesterday's moment with Em still weighing heavy on my mind.

"How was work?" Livvy asks as I pull my car onto the street and head for school.

Taking a deep breath, I tell her everything. How awkward Blake and I were working together, how Em came into the store and I said awful things to her. When I finish, Livvy looks…

Impressed?

"I can't believe you said that to her!" Liv shakes her head, but she's smiling. "She sort of deserved it."

"I've never heard that rumor, though," I stress. "I made it up. Just to hurt her."

Liv shrugs. "It might be true. You never know."

I'm sort of incredulous. This is her former best friend—and it wasn't that long ago that they were actual best friends. Sort of like me and Tara, though our falling out happened even before Em's and Livvy's. I haven't talked to Tara in what feels like forever, and sometimes I still miss her. And that's part of the reason I'm dealing with all this guilt over what I said to Em yesterday.

"I should've never said such awful things to her, Liv. I don't care what she's done or how she's hurt you or even me. And I said it in front of Blake. I don't really know him, and I definitely don't trust him. What if he tells a friend what happened, and then the friend tells someone else, and then it spreads like wildfire all over campus?" My worst nightmare, knowing I was the instigator of a horrible, untrue rumor.

"That won't happen." Livvy waves a hand, dismissing my concern. "There are so many rumors swirling around Em right now anyway, it's just another one to add to the list."

I pull the car over on the side of the road, put it in park and turn to stare at my new friend. We might've known each other for years, but these last few weeks are the first time we've spent any amount of time together. I'm unsure if I can trust her either. "I don't know if you've always been like this, but no wonder you and Em aren't friends anymore. It's like you don't even care about her."

Livvy's expression turns hard and her eyes narrow. "I did. I *do* care about her. There's just…so much that's happened between us. I don't know if I can ever forgive her."

"She probably feels the same way."

Liv's jaw drops. "What do you mean? *She's* the one who had sex with Dustin."

"And you're the one who keeps fooling around with Dustin on the side," I point out. "Even a few nights ago you did, Liv. Since when is it okay to toy with his heart?"

"*Toy* with his *heart*? Are you serious right now? I think you've read too many romance novels."

I blink at her words. That was sort of rude. "Don't forget Ryan in all of this. You've been dishonest with him too."

"I overreacted to that stupid picture Em posted, you know this!" The words explode out of Livvy like she's been holding them in for years. "I know it was wrong, what I did with Dustin. What do you want me to do? Tell Ryan?" She stares off into the distance, crossing her arms, and she's blinking rapidly. Like she's trying to fight off tears.

"Maybe you should be honest with him," I start, but she turns to glare at me, her eyes shiny and her lips tight.

"You don't get it. You don't know what it's like, dealing with toxic relationships," she practically snarls.

"Ha! Are you kidding me right now? I caught my best friend with my boyfriend and they were actually having sex. Naked, penis-in-vagina sex. I saw it with my own two eyes, Olivia! I know exactly what it's like! I'm way too familiar with it," I say bitterly.

"My situation is different," she says, but I shake my head and she goes silent.

"Not really. All three of you have this messed up friendship. You do realize that, right? Sneaking around behind each other's backs, messing around with each other. You were never honest with Dustin or Em and they weren't honest with you either." I hesitate, then decide to go for it. "From the way I see it, you're all equally guilty."

Now Livvy won't even look at me. "Shouldn't we get to school before the first bell rings?"

Sighing loudly, I put the Toyota in drive and pull back onto the road. We remain silent the rest of the car ride and when we arrive at school a few minutes later, Livvy climbs out of my car without a backward glance, slamming the door so hard the entire car rattles.

Great. Now I've pissed off the only friend I have left. But I had to say it. Had to point out that what she'd done with Dustin was just as bad as what Em did with Dustin. They're all guilty, especially Dustin, yet the girls are so mad at each other. Why didn't they see the part he played in this?

Contemplating the entire situation was better than focusing on my own problems, so I wallowed in the Livvy/Dustin/Em/Ryan love triangle/square as I walked through the parking lot, weaving through the cars, ignoring everyone I passed by. Not that they paid me any attention. Though I swear I hear a low whistle and when I glance over my shoulder, I see Tuttle following a considerable distance behind me.

Ugh. I glare at him, wishing I had laser eyes—a wish my younger brother Trent makes on an almost daily basis—before I turn and practically run into the senior building.

I dash into the first girls' bathroom I see to hide from Tuttle and compose myself. Of course, there's Brianne Brown and Em staring at their reflections in the hazy mirror, both of them glossing up their lips so thick I wrinkle my nose, imagining how sticky that must feel.

"Oh look, here's Little Miss Perfect," Em says, turning to face me wearing a smirk. "Where's your best buddy?"

"You mean *your* best buddy?" I say pointedly.

Brianne sends me a withering look in the mirror's reflection. "Give it a rest, flute player." Her face brightens. "Hey, does that give you an advantage with blowjobs, sucking on a flute all those years?"

Both girls laugh and I go to the empty sink next to them to wash my now shaky hands. Man, I hate drama. I'm the least confrontational person on the planet, yet I keep running finding myself mired in it. "For your information, I didn't play a flute, I played the clarinet."

They're still giggling and rolling their eyes. "There's a difference?" Em asks innocently.

I should be the bigger person and do what I've wanted since our run in. "Hey Em, I wanted to apologize for what I said to you yesterday."

Em's mouth pops open into this almost comical O shape. I turn off the faucet and dry my hands, waiting for her to say something, but she remains quiet for so long, Brianne nudges her in the side with her elbow.

"What the hell are you talking about anyway?" Brianne asks me.

"That's between Em and I," I say solemnly.

Brianne rolls her eyes, but Em watches me carefully, like she's waiting for me to give her the punch line.

"You actually mean it, don't you," Em finally says.

I nod and stand a little straighter. "I'm owning my shit. And that was a shitty thing I said to you yesterday."

"It was."

"And I totally made it up."

"I figured."

Now I'm quiet, waiting for her to apologize for that stupid picture she posted, but instead she hooks her arm through Brianne's and leads her out of the bathroom without saying a word. I deflate the second the door swings shut, bracing my hands on the edge of the sink and staring at my reflection.

That was…hard. I don't like confrontation. But I apologized and I didn't melt while doing it either. I'm going to be okay.

Maybe, eventually, we'll all be okay.

I'M HIDING OUT in the back of the library during lunch, munching on baby carrots dipped in ranch while reading my American Government and Institutions notes in prep for the quiz later this afternoon when I suddenly feel someone standing beside my table, looking right at me.

Glancing up, I fully expect to find Livvy there, contrite and full of apologies, but it's not Livvy.

It's Em.

"Hey," she says, her voice soft. She tucks a chin-length strand of highlighted golden blonde hair behind her ear and looks around before her gaze meets mine once more. "Um, can I sit down?"

I shrug and she pulls the empty chair next to mine out, plopping her skinny butt on it. I continue eating my carrots, pointing at the open snack bag as an invitation and she takes one, dips it into the tiny plastic cup full of ranch dressing and pops it into her mouth, chewing loudly.

Something you can't avoid when you eat baby carrots. They have major crunch.

"Ms. Donahue is going to be pissed if she catches you eating in her library," Em says once she swallows.

Ms. Donahue has run the school library probably longer than all of us have been alive. She's terrifying. "I'm not scared."

"Rebel," she says, nudging my shoulder with hers.

Blowing out a loud breath, I turn to look at her. "What's up?" There's no reason for her to sit by me in the library. I don't know if I've ever seen Emily Griffith in the school library even once.

"I wanted to thank you, for the apology," she whispers, glancing around as if she wants to make sure no one is near. "That, uh—meant a lot to me."

"I felt awful all last night, thinking about what I said to you," I admit.

Em raises her eyebrows in real surprise. How I can tell, I'm not sure, but I can. "Really?"

I nod my answer.

"Well, I guess I appreciate you feeling bad?"

"I'm not normally a mean girl," I tell her. "Seriously. This is so not my style. I'm quiet. No one pays attention to me at school. Not usually."

"Right. But maybe you have a secret. That maybe under the good girl exterior is a bad girl on the side who goes by the street name Stella in the House?"

I burst out laughing, clamping a hand over my mouth when I hear Ms. Donahue reprimand me with a low, "Quiet!"

The front desk is nowhere near where we're sitting, but Ms. Donahue has no qualms in silencing people wherever they're at.

"Stella in the House?" I ask Em, still wanting to laugh, but Ms. Donahue will probably kick me out.

Em shrugs. "I thought it sounded good."

"You are so weird."

"So are you. Hiding out in here when you could be hanging out in the quad with Jordan Tuttle." She sighs and shakes her head.

Why oh why does everyone mention his name to me? We're nothing. "He doesn't want me hanging out in the quad with him."

"You sure about that? He's always looking around like he lost something. I'm starting to believe he's always looking for you," Em says.

My heart trips over itself at her words then I tell myself to get over it. "Give me a break."

"I'm totally serious." She looks totally serious too.

"Well, he's not interested in me like that." I look away, wishing I wasn't interested in him like that either.

"His loss." She grabs another baby carrot and pops it into her mouth, crunching loudly. "Nominations are announced today in fifth period," she says once she swallows.

Great. That's right after lunch, and Tuttle's in that class with me. Is he going to be in a celebratory mode once he hears he's been nominated?

Because he so has. It doesn't matter how much he denies it'll happen, it's happening.

"Think you'll get nominated?" she asks.

"*Me?*" I actually scoff. "No freaking way. That's for the popular girls." I pause, studying her. "You might get nominated."

"Yeah, right. For biggest school slut? Definitely." Em laughs, but there's no humor in the sound. "Hey, I need to go. But can you, um, tell Livvy hi from me? And that I miss her?"

Aw. This makes me feel bad, especially after all the horrible things Livvy said about Em.

"Sure." Depends on if she's still talking to me or not, considering I probably made her super pissed with our earlier conversation.

"You're lucky," Em says, her gaze becoming unfocused. Distant. As if she can see something I can't. "You still have Livvy. Hopefully she doesn't burn you too hard."

Her cryptic message makes me want to ask Em lots of questions. Questions she might not want to answer.

"Okay, gotta go." Em takes yet another baby carrot before she turns and starts to walk away. "See ya later, Stella!" she yells, making Ms. Donahue offer up an almost desperate "shush" in answer.

I say nothing. Decide it's best to savor the moment rather than pick it apart and end up driving myself crazy with all the *what ifs* spiraling through my head.

chapter six

I walk into English like I'm about to face a firing squad. Slow and reluctant and ready to duck and run at the first opportunity. The relief that hits me when I realize Tuttle isn't in the classroom almost makes me sag to the floor, I'm so grateful. I fall into my chair, drop my backpack at my feet and smile at Mrs. Meyer when she makes her appearance at the front of the class.

The next fifty minutes should pass fairly easy without Tuttle around to distract me. When the bell rings, Mrs. Meyer immediately starts talking about our group projects.

"Okay, guys, this is going to be so much fun! Here's what we're going to do. I want each of you to create diary entries in the voice of famous literature characters," she explains. "These characters need to have an established relationship. Whether it's mother and son, close friends, bitter enemies, or even *lovers*."

And with that last word, all the boys go, "Ooooh."

They're so mature.

"I want you to really get into the feelings these characters are experiencing. Their deepest, darkest thoughts and secrets, I want to see it all on the page. I don't want to influence your choices, but I'd love to see a variety of relationships portrayed." Mrs. Meyer starts passing out a sheet of paper to each of us. "This is a list of famous literary characters for inspiration. You can choose someone from the list, or you can come up with your own. I just need to approve each couple first before you can proceed with the project."

Great. My partner isn't even here. How are we going to choose our characters? Maybe I could do it on my own and not even give Tuttle the choice. He'd deserve it for not showing up today.

I glance over the list, smiling when I see Moby Dick and Captain Ahab.

"Do you seriously want us to write diary entries in the point of view of a whale?" someone asks incredulously.

Mrs. Meyer laughs. "I thought it might be interesting."

My gaze snags on one particular couple and I bite my lower lip, contemplating the idea.

Romeo and Juliet.

Star-crossed lovers at their finest. A tale of passion and sadness and lust and loyalty and, overall, young, tragic love. That could be... exciting. But would it be smart to work on a romantic project with Tuttle? Or would that only end up driving me crazy?

The classroom door suddenly opens, and I know it's him. I can literally feel his eyes on me, seeking me out.

"Ah, Mr. Tuttle. So glad you decided to join us today," Mrs. Meyer says, not a hint of sarcasm in her voice. "Please sit down."

I want to look back at him. I want to ask him where he's been.

But I can't. I don't have the right. Plus, I don't want to give him the satisfaction. Instead I stare straight ahead, trying my best to calm my nerves because I know what's coming next.

"All right everyone, get together with your partner and discuss who you want as your couple. You'll need to run your choice by me before you can start, so make sure you let me know who you're going to use. No one can have the same couple, so the results will be varied." She rubs her hands together, looking pleased. "This is going to be so much fun! I can't wait!"

Within minutes everyone's rearranged themselves and we're all sitting with our group partners, including Tuttle and me. He settles into the empty desk next to mine, his gaze sweeping over me, taking in every detail, and I practically squirm in my seat, the longer he studies me.

"Cute outfit," he finally drawls, his eyes gleaming with appreciation.

"Are you just saying that?" I don't look cute. I look sloppy and comfortable. The longer the day goes, the more comfortable I look too. I'm kind of a wreck, but I don't care. "I know I look like I just rolled out of bed."

"Well, you just kicked my imagination into overdrive."

"Stop." I shove at his rock hard shoulder, but it's like trying to move a brick wall.

"You really wear all that to bed?"

It's the way he says the word bed that reminds me of the night at Ryan's house. Just last weekend we spent the night together. Jordan and I in a giant yet cozy bed, our bodies wrapped all around each other, my head nestled against his broad shoulder. We talked a little. Kissed a little. Touched a little. And then we eventually fell asleep. We really didn't do much at all, but somehow it had become one of the most intimate moments of my life.

And then it was ruined by that photo and my insecurities—insecurities that I'm thinking are actually valid.

"Minus the hoodie, but yeah." My voice is husky and I clear my throat. Wishing I could clear out this awkward moment between us.

"Don't you get hot?" His fingers trail over my thigh, smoothing over the thin flannel fabric of my sleep pants, and I jerk my leg away from his hand. It was as if he touched my bare skin. "I sleep in boxers. Gets too hot, wearing clothes."

"Jordan." My voice is firm, my gaze direct. I will not think of him wearing a pair of black boxer briefs—my imagination goes to that image because I know for a fact he wears black boxer briefs—and nothing else. I can't. "Why are we talking about what we wear to bed?"

"You're the one who started it, wearing your pajamas to school." He's wearing jeans and a T-shirt. He's not one to participate in school activities. "Remember a few nights ago when we slept togeth—"

I slap my hand over his mouth to shut him up and I swear I can feel him smile behind the wall of my fingers. Worse, his teeth graze my skin—lightly yet with just enough force that I feel it pulsate all the way through me. I immediately drop my hand from his face as if I were burned.

"You need to stop," I tell him quietly. I'm tempted to beg him to stop but that might be overkill. "And we need to pick out our couple for the English project."

He frowns. "What are you talking about?"

I explain the project details to him and hand over the list. He scans it thoughtfully, and I remain quiet. Impassive. I don't want him to think I'm excited about any one choice. I want him to make with his own decision.

"You want to work on one of these in particular?" he asks, lifting his gaze to mine.

My breath catches at the gleam in his pretty blue eyes. He has such long, thick lashes. It's kind of ridiculous. "Not sure yet." I hesitate. "Do you?"

"Mmm." He glances over the list again. "Is she serious with the Moby Dick thing?"

I nod, barely able to keep a straight face. "You can take on Ahab and I'll take on Moby Dick."

"No." His voice is firm, but his eyes are sparkling with amusement when they meet mine. "I'm thinking something a little more complex than that."

"How much more complex do you need to get? There's a whale and a man in a power struggle. I would say that's a little odd."

"True." He taps a pencil against his slightly pursed lips, his gaze still trained on the paper. This gives me time to look at him, and look I do. My eyes are like greedy little addicts as they trail over him, lingering on his dark hair, that firm, sexy line of his jaw I might've kissed once or twice in the not so distant past. His thick brows are slightly furrowed and he's squinting a little bit as he keeps skimming that list. Yet this all works for him.

Or maybe I'm just unnaturally fascinated and can't stop looking at him ever.

"I want to do Romeo and Juliet," he finally says, lifting his gaze to mine. He waits, ready for me to challenge him, and I wonder at his choice and his motives behind it.

I wonder if he chose them for the same reason I did.

Lifting my chin, I say, "I think that's a good idea."

Surprise crosses his face, but then it's gone. "I'll be Juliet."

"No, you won't." I nudge him with my elbow and he tugs on one of my braids. I sort of melt inside. "We need to run this by Mrs. Meyer. Make sure no one else has chosen them." My arm shoots up into the air and Mrs. Meyer is standing by our desks within a minute.

"What's going on? You know who you want to do your project on?" she asks pleasantly, her gaze drifting between the two of us.

"We'd like to choose Romeo and Juliet as our literary couple," I tell her, and she smiles in response, looking pleased.

"I think that's an excellent choice, especially considering my sneaking suspicion that you, Jordan Tuttle, are a closet romantic."

His cheeks actually turn the faintest shade of red. It's fascinating. Did Mrs. Meyer just embarrass him?

"Bring out the best in each other with these diary entries." Mrs. Meyer turns to me. "Share them with each other as you work on the project. Maybe even have your characters respond to each other, as if you're having a written conversation. What do you think?"

"Sounds good," Tuttle says with ease.

"Okay," I add weakly.

Great. Our assignment just turned into the two of us basically writing love letters to each other.

"Ready to be my Juliet?" he asks the moment Mrs. Meyer walks away from us. He leans across his desk, his fingers going to the end of my braid again. They brush against my chest and I feel that touch through my hoodie, my T-shirt, all the way down to my skin.

And it burns. Tingles. Makes me want more.

"Stop pulling on my braid," I tell him, ignoring his question. I don't want to be his Juliet. I don't want to be his anything.

Liar.

"What? Am I bothering you?" He tugs again, gently this time, before letting my braid go. He trails a finger along my plaited hair. "I think you look cute."

I say nothing. I can't. It feels like my vocal cords are paralyzed.

"Your hair is so soft," he murmurs. "Does it get wavy when you wear your hair in braids all day?"

I give the barest nod in answer.

"Maybe someday you'll let me undo them for you." His intense stare makes my mouth go dry and I part my lips, ready to come up with some lame answer. But then the bell rings, and I grab my backpack and bolt out of the room before I say something stupid.

AFTER SCHOOL I head toward the senior parking lot when I sense someone falling into step beside me.

Livvy.

"Where've you been all day?" she asks nonchalantly, like we didn't have a big blow up this morning.

"I could ask you the same question," I say coolly. Best to confront the issue and get it over with. "I thought you were mad at me."

She stops me with a light hand on my forearm and we turn to face each other, people rushing past us to get to their cars and make their escape. "I thought you were mad at me too! You were just so…awful this morning."

"Honest," I correct her. "I was honest. And sometimes we don't want to hear the truth." I can so relate to this statement. The truth can hurt. "Once you bailed, I figured you were ignoring me."

"I—wasn't. I was spending time with Ryan, which you have to admit, you pushed me to do." She studies me, nibbling on her lower lip. "Want to come with me and watch them practice?"

Yes. The word hovers on the tip of my tongue, but I swallow it down. Going to see Tuttle for the pure joy of watching him play football is not allowed anymore.

"I can't," I tell her, looking away, hating that I have to deny myself this tiny pleasure. What would it matter if he saw me watching him? It's no big deal, right? I'm being ridiculous. If I want to watch our football team practice, I should be able to. He's not the only boy on the team.

But he's the only boy I'm interested in on the team. I can't deny it, even though I'm trying my hardest.

"Oh, do you have to go to work?" Livvy offers up a weak smile. "I'm so happy for you, that you got the job, but I hate how it's going to tie up your schedule."

"I don't work today," I start, and Livvy squeals, launching into this weird little dance before she loops her arm through mine.

"Well then, let's go watch them practice together! It'll be fun. Like old times."

Old times? That was only a few weeks ago. Back when I went to watch them practice almost every day after school, claiming I missed being with the band, which was a half-truth.

More like I wanted to watch Tuttle without judgment. He's such a great player and his body is…a work of masculine art.

God. I sound so cheesy in my head.

It wasn't just watching him play, though. It was being a part of his life. Seeing him, remembering all the moments we shared, reliving them. He'd become such a huge part of my life in a short amount of time, and I didn't know what to do about it. He's overwhelming in both the best and most awful ways imaginable.

I try to cut him off, push him out of my life, yet he figures out how to worm his way back in every single time. It's so annoying. And exhilarating. I want him close. I want him gone. I want to touch him. I want to shove him away.

Clearly I'm confused.

"I shouldn't," I protest, but Livvy drags me forward, surprisingly strong. I didn't know she had it in her.

"Come on. Please?" She bats her eyelashes at me, and I laugh.

And I also give in. Because I'm weak and I want to see if Tuttle will wear that cropped jersey the boys like to put on when they practice on a warm day, his perfect, flat belly on display. Sometimes, at the end of practice, when it's so hot and he's worked so hard, there's a light sheen of sweat on his skin that—oh my God—makes me want to rub myself all over his damp, warm body.

Yes, clearly I've turned into a cat in heat.

I try my best to push all thoughts of a sweaty Tuttle out of my head and focus on the other reason I'm hanging out with Livvy and watching the team practice. I can use this time to talk to Livvy about Em. Those girls have too much history between them for their friendship to fall apart so easily—and over a *boy*.

"What do you think of the homecoming nominations?" Livvy asks as we walk toward the football field.

"Not surprising." The announcement had come the period after English, and I was glad I wasn't with Tuttle, having to hear them say his name over the speaker. I bet he smirked and acted like it was no big deal while the rest of the class erupted in cheers. That's how it always is with Tuttle.

"My win prediction is Tuttle and Lauren Mancini. Or—" Livvy's nose wrinkles. "Or maybe even Brianne Brown. Ew."

"Dustin's date?" Oh, I'm mean, but I had to say it. She needs to remember Dustin's already moved on and she supposedly has too.

"They've been hanging out together a lot this week. I see them everywhere," Livvy says almost bitterly.

"At least he's leaving you alone, right?" It's so much easier to focus on her issues with Dustin rather than think about Tuttle being homecoming king and Lauren Mancini possibly as his queen. Ugh. They're my prediction to win too, though I have to admit it. Those two are a perfect match.

Me and Tuttle? We are most definitely not.

Once we're settled on the bleachers, the mid-afternoon sun shining down upon us and warming my skin since I finally took the hoodie off, I turn to Livvy and spill about my interactions with Emily.

"Wait a minute. You apologized to her?" Livvy shakes her head. "Why?"

"Because what I said to her was wrong. It bothered me all night. I had to tell her I was sorry."

"You're too nice." She's still shaking her head.

And maybe you're not nice enough, I almost tell her, but I don't. That's opening up a whole new bag of trouble. "Don't you miss your best friend? She misses you. She wanted me to tell you hi. From her."

Livvy sighs, her gaze glued to the field. The boys are running through drills and I'm struggling not to seek out Tuttle. But of course I do. He's like a magnet and I'm steel and I'll be forever drawn to him.

What a depressing thought.

"I do miss her," she finally admits, turning to look at me. "But after everything that's happened, how can we get our friendship back?"

"It's not like it's gone forever," I say gently. "You still talk to Dustin and he's betrayed you just as much as Em has. Maybe even more so."

Oh yes, I dared to go there. Livvy's eyes flare and I see the anger.

Is it anger at me for reminding her of Dustin's part in all of this? She shouldn't forget. Forgiving him is somehow easy, but forgiving Em isn't?

"I've known him longer," she murmurs. "It's harder to let him go."

Because she wants him, though she'd never admit it to me. She wants both boys, but that would never work. I'm not going to say that to her. She needs to figure it out on her own.

"It should be hard to let Em go, too, Liv. I think she's suffering without your friendship." Something tells me she's been suffering for a while, and it has nothing to do with Livvy or Ryan or Dustin.

"I'm suffering too. We're all suffering."

"Then be the bigger person and make it better. Reach out to your friend. Tell her you miss her. Try your best to forgive her."

"It's not that easy." Livvy frowns and I don't think I've ever seen her look sadder. All the anger is gone. She just looks…defeated. "I'm scared," she whispers. "Em knows all of my strengths and weaknesses. She knows how to hurt me with a look, a few chosen words, a deliberate move. And since I've come back home from my dad's, she's hurt me over and over, and she doesn't seem to care. I don't know if I can trust her again."

"Then take it slow." I nudge her side with my own. "Ease into it. But don't just shut her out. I think she's hurting more than she'll ever admit."

"Don't forget how she tried to sabotage our relationships, Amanda. That photo she posted on Instagram was aimed at us. She's jealous." Liv shakes her head. "And she ratted me out to my mom about Ryan's party. You might've not got in trouble, but I was grounded for a week! That's all Em's fault."

"Maybe if you guys can talk it out, it won't happen again," I suggest, trying to sound positive. Don't know how long I can maintain it, though.

"Please," Livvy mutters, shaking her head.

She's quiet for a while and so I remain quiet too. I watch the boys play, the constant whistle blowing from Coach Halsey making me wince. He's running them especially hard this week, what with this Friday's homecoming game. And there's nothing worse than losing that game. You not only disappoint the entire school, you let down the alumni as well.

Tuttle's on fire, though. He throws the ball with expert precision, a spiral in the sky, I can almost hear the *whoosh* as it flies through the air. I have to admit Ryan catches just about every one of those passes and does his damnedest to run it into the end zone. He's a great player. Together they seem almost unstoppable.

"Okay, I'll try to talk to Em," Livvy finally says minutes later, a long sigh escaping her. "I'm probably making a huge mistake, but I'll reach out to her for you, okay?"

"Good." I smile and nod, feeling like I actually accomplished something. But Livvy's giving me a weird look, and my smile instantly fades. "What's wrong?"

"I don't know why you're trying to heal my friendship with Em or whatever. The two of us became friends because I'm not really hanging out with her anymore."

"Can't we all be friends?" Nerves bubble in my stomach. I never thought of it that way. What if Em and Livvy really do reconcile and cut me out of the relationship altogether? I would have no one to blame for that happening but myself.

"I want us to," Livvy says slowly. "But sometimes...Em can be really possessive."

"Well, she's just going to have to learn how to share," I say with a faint smile.

Livvy nods, returning a similar almost-smile before she resumes staring at the field. "Oh my God, Ryan is so awesome."

"Yeah," I say distractedly. Worry nags at me for the rest of the time we sit on the bleachers, though. What if it's not that simple?

But when is any of this ever simple?

chapter seven

Friday night. I'm working. I'm not at the homecoming game. The rally right before school ended was a study in torture. All of the homecoming nominees were brought out to the center of the gymnasium and Lauren Mancini stood next to Tuttle, beaming like a beauty queen and adorable in her cheer uniform, her ponytail bobbing as she smiled and waved at everyone.

Tuttle just stood there, stoic and handsome in his jersey and jeans, his gaze scanning the crowd as if he was searching for someone before he gave up.

It's too arrogant on my part to think he was looking for me.

After a few minutes of the homecoming court nonsense, he looked ready to bail. They dragged him back out when they talked about the game and only then did his lips curve when Coach Halsey patted his back and announced, "We're going to kill them!"

The entire gym erupted in cheers and the band started to play, the sounds so loud, Livvy and I both put our hands over our ears, laughing. When my gaze returned to the center of the gym, I saw Ryan nudge Tuttle and point at Livvy and me. Tuttle's gaze met mine and he smiled, ever so faintly. It's almost a warrior's smile, one I imagine some long-ago Viking offering up right before he charged into battle and slayed everyone.

I looked away, frustrated by my wandering yet vivid imagination.

After school let out, I rushed to Yo Town, skipping the homecoming parade, the game, all of it. Livvy promised me she'd let me know what the score was in live time, and she did. She sent me Snapchat updates and the occasional photo. Including a few from halftime, when the homecoming king and queen were announced.

The photo of Tuttle and Lauren standing together with their arms looped almost made me want to vomit.

Thankfully, business is brisk tonight at Yo Town. Time passes quickly, and after a while I can hardly think about what I'm missing. All I can focus on is the shop. Blake and I are running around like crazy, trading off working behind the register so one of us can keep the store clean and maintain the toppings bar.

At one point I'm so busy ringing up customer after customer that I don't notice the big group that comes into the shop at first. It's just been one continuous group after another, you know? No big deal.

Until the hairs on the back of my neck stand on end and my skin prickles with goose bumps. Someone is watching me. It's like I can literally feel their eyes sweeping over my body. Slowly I glance up, look to my right and discover it's…

Tuttle.

And he's with a girl.

Not just any girl either.

He's with Lauren Mancini.

My heart feels like it shrivels to half its size and all the air lodges in my chest. Our gazes meet and my breath catches. He's devastatingly handsome wearing a white button down shirt with the sleeves rolled up to his elbows, black pants and a cheap-ass crown on his head.

The same cheap-ass crown he was wearing in that photo Livvy sent me. I'm half tempted to go rip it off his head, but I contain myself.

He tears his gaze away from mine when Lauren curls her arm through his, batting her eyelashes up at him as she tucks herself in close. As close as she can get without embarrassing herself and climbing him like a tree. I stare in shocked disbelief as she clings to him like they were made for each other.

And let's be real, they sort of were. They're a stunning couple, him so tall and dark and her so slight and fair and freaking beautiful. I hate her. She's wearing a gorgeous black dress that makes her boobs look amazing and she has a sparkling tiara on her head.

Lauren is the perfect queen to Tuttle's handsome king.

"Hey." Someone taps on the scale in front of me and I startle, turning to find a guy waiting for me to weigh his frozen yogurt. It's piled high in the cup and covered with every topping imaginable. So gross. "You giving it away for free tonight, or what?"

The guy starts laughing and so do his friends. I glare at him as I ring him up, trying my best not to pay attention to Tuttle.

But it's so hard. I watch as he walks down the row of machines beside Lauren—at least she's not hanging on him anymore—a patient look on his face as she whines about calories and how we don't have her favorite flavor and what sort of toppings should she dump on her frozen yogurt because oh my God—and I quote—she loves them *all*.

He never says a word. Just nods in all the right places and

occasionally looks my way. I occasionally look his way too, so our eyes meet far too much. And I sort of hate myself for it. I shouldn't look at him. I should forget all about him and focus on my job. On my life.

He's a distraction I don't need.

"Aren't you having any frozen yogurt, Jordan?" Lauren asks sweetly, her voice carrying through the shop despite the noise level. Her voice also makes me feel stabby.

Oh, and it's like a knife to the heart, how casually she calls him Jordan. I swear I see irritation flash in his blue eyes, but maybe I'm wrong. Maybe he wants her to call him Jordan because she's earned the right and I lost it. They've become close. Homecoming king and queen close—maybe even kissing close.

Maybe she's the only one who gets to call him Jordan now.

The realization makes me sick to my stomach.

"I don't want any," he starts, but Lauren practically leaps on him, she's such a rabid Yo Town fan.

"Oh, but you really, *really* should. It's so delicious and besides, you need to celebrate your team's win tonight. And your own win. *Our* win," she tells him with a dazzling smile. "Come on. Pick something out."

He glances at me and without missing a beat he asks, "What flavor do you recommend?"

My mouth drops open. Is he seriously drawing me into their conversation right now? What the hell? "Um…what flavors do you usually like?"

Tuttle shrugs those impossibly broad shoulders, his gaze never wavering from mine. It's like everything else in the room fades away, and it's just me and him. "I like lots of flavors."

"Okay," I say slowly, my brain scrambling for a better answer. "Such as?"

"I like fruit flavors, like peachy skin and cherry lips. Oh, and dark chocolate eyes." His gaze slowly sweeps over me and I've never felt so self-conscious in my life. I look like hell in my battered jeans and Yo Town T-shirt smeared with frozen yogurt and melted candy, my hair a haphazard mess despite being in a bun. All while he looks like a god. Figures. "I also like pretty girls who bust my balls and make me feel like a jackass every time I so much as look at them."

My cheeks are on fire because he is so talking about me. He's with Lauren-the-most-popular-girl-in-high-school-Mancini yet he's flirting with *me*.

"Sounds like you need to leave those types alone," I say, my voice firm. Lauren is watching us, her head swiveling from Tuttle to me and back to Tuttle again. Like we're playing some sort of game, volleying the ball back and forth to each other.

But someone calls her name, one of her friends, one of the princesses of the homecoming court, and Lauren darts off to see what she wants.

So it's just me and Tuttle.

"Maybe I don't want to leave her alone." He stops directly in front of me with only the counter separating us, and presses his hands against the counter. "Maybe I just need to work a little harder to get her to believe we're meant to be together," he murmurs in that low, rumbly voice that makes my stomach twist and turn.

Meant to be together. He shouldn't say such romantic, swoony things. He doesn't believe that, and neither do I. I'm not sure why he continues to bother with it.

"Stop," I whisper, flicking my head in Lauren's direction. I rest my palms against the counter and lean over it a little, my face practically in

Tuttle's. "Go be with your girlfriend."

"She's not my girlfriend," he whispers back, his hands coming dangerously close to mine.

"She's your queen." I snatch my hands away from the counter and point at his crown. "Congrats on winning."

His face betrays nothing and he doesn't bother acknowledging my statement. "When did you start working here?"

I lift my chin, trying for determined and cool and collected. Most likely failing miserably. "A few days ago."

"You like it?"

I shrug. "It's a job. I need the money."

Tuttle studies me closely, like he can see right through me, and I want to take my words back. Somehow, he knows I'm lying. Well, I'm not really lying, but I am sad I wasn't able to go to the game tonight. I love football. I love watching our boys play, and they've gotten so much better this year. They have a real chance to make it to the playoffs, and that's incredible.

But I won't get to experience any of it. I'll be too busy working every Friday night, making approximately fifty dollars for my time served.

"You'll be missed," he finally says, his voice still low. Intimate. Like we're sharing a deep, dark secret. "I liked seeing you in the stands at every game."

I raise a brow, in full on skepticism mode. I can't help it. He says things like that and I don't believe him. Yet some part of me deep down inside *does* believe him. It's incredibly confusing.

"You didn't even notice me."

"I always noticed you, even when you were in band." He pauses. "I've told you that before. Why don't you believe me?"

The sincerity in his tone almost makes me want to laugh. Or throw myself at him. I'm not sure which option is worse.

I brace my hands on the counter once more, mimicking his position. "I always feel like you're yanking my chain, Tuttle."

He smirks, and it's adorable. Sexy. "Right back at you, Winters." And then he does the most incredible thing. Without saying a word, without any indication of what he was about to do, he scoots his hand closer to mine, reaching out to graze the top of my hand with just his pinky finger.

I feel that touch all the way down to my toes. It's like he electrified me. Reminded me that I'm alive. And he's the only one who can make me feel like that.

The only one.

"Does it always take this long to clean up on a Friday night?" I stuff the mop into the yellow bucket and wring it out, frowning when I notice all the dark brown water floating inside. It's disgusting. The entire shop was disgusting once we cleared everyone out.

"Nah. Tonight was an exception, with the homecoming game and all. Though it's always pretty busy when there's a home game," Blake says as he finishes cleaning up the toppings station. He made a huge deal about it earlier, like his taking on that particular task was some sort of favor to me, but I don't know.

Mopping definitely sucks.

We closed over thirty minutes ago and we're still cleaning. When I finally finish mopping, I guide the bucket out through the back door, dumping the dirty water in the nearby drain. The air is cool, tinged with the faint biting hint of autumn, and my gaze snags on the black Range Rover sitting in the mostly empty lot.

No. It can't be.

But I think it…might be.

I'm incredulous. Seriously? *Really?* I'm tempted to march out to that car, knock on the window and demand that he leave, but who am I to do that? It's a public parking lot.

And maybe it isn't him. There are a lot of black Range Rovers in the world. I'm just fixated on him so I think he's everywhere. Like I'm some sort of obsessed psycho.

Pushing all thoughts of *him* out of my brain, I go back into the shop and head straight to the bathroom, taking out all of my frustration and disbelief on the toilet and sink counter. I scrub the hell out of that bathroom, and by the time I'm finished my forehead is sweaty and wayward strands of hair stick to my cheeks.

In other words, I look awful, but I don't care. My body's tired and my muscles ache. I'm ready to go straight home and collapse into bed. At least I can sleep in tomorrow. My next shift doesn't start until noon.

"You ready?" Blake asks after I put away the cleaning supplies in the small closet.

Turning, I nod. "Yeah, let's go."

I gather up my things and head outside with Blake, watching as he locks the front door before shoving the keys into his front pocket. He offers me a faint smile as we start for the parking lot. "You did good tonight, Amanda."

"Thanks." I walk right beside him, headed toward our cars, which are parked relatively close to each other far out in the lot. I see the Range Rover out of the corner of my eye, but I ignore it.

I refuse to acknowledge him. Acknowledging means I accept what he's doing, and I don't.

"You kept up and tonight was like a trial by fire. I don't think I've ever seen it that busy since we first opened," he continues.

"Guess I proved my worth then." I smile at him and he gives me that somber Blake look, with a hint of wonder in his gaze. Like he can't believe I'm walking with him.

I can feel his pain. I really can.

"Yeah, you did. I'll have to tell my mom." His cheeks go red and I almost think it's cute.

Until I remember that a certain someone is lurking in the parking lot like a stalker.

"That's my car," I tell Blake, pointing at my Toyota. Blake nods, waves goodbye and practically sprints to his older Nissan truck. He hops in it, fires up the engine and pulls out of the parking lot without any hesitation whatsoever.

"What a jackass."

Whirling around, I spot Tuttle leaning against the side of his SUV, looking as casual as he pleases with his hands shoved into the front pockets of his black pants. He's still wearing the same clothes from earlier, though he looks a little more mussed. Wrinkled. Cuter.

Argh. I hate my thoughts sometimes.

"Are you talking about yourself?" I ask with raised brows.

He inclines his head, a silent acknowledgement, I guess. "He didn't even bother waiting to see if your car started."

"It'll start," I tell him, sounding more confident than I feel. Sometimes my car *won't* start. Back when my older brother was still in high school and drove the car that eventually became mine, he'd always leave the lights on and drain the battery. I try my best to never do that, but sometimes other things happen. The car is almost as old as me. So

I can't always count on it.

"He should've waited."

I ignore his statement. This isn't about Blake ditching me. It's about Tuttle lurking in the parking lot waiting for me. "Why are you even here?"

"Thank God I am. Otherwise you could've been left stranded." Again he avoids my question. He's really good at that.

"I'm not stranded. My car will start."

"Prove it."

Heaving an exasperated sigh, I unlock my door and climb in, pushing my key into the ignition with a little more force than necessary. Whispering "sorry" under my breath—because yes, I do talk to my car sometimes, thank you very much—I turn the key and the engine starts right up.

I roll down my window and smile triumphantly, not surprised to see him approaching my car. "See? Told you so."

He looks like he's been socked in the chest as hard as possible. Weird. Did he really think my car wouldn't start? What would he do then? Gloat? "Good. Now get out of here."

My scowl feels extra scowly and I aim it right at him. "Why aren't you with your girlfriend?"

His frown is almost comical. "Who are you talking about?"

"Are you dense?" I roll my eyes, immediately feeling guilty for insulting him. "Lauren Mancini."

"There's nothing between Lauren and I."

"Right."

"I'm serious."

Roll up the window, Amanda. Put the car in drive and get the hell out of here. Now. Before you do something stupid.

But I don't. I just stare at him from where I sit, and he stares at me. He grips the top of the car, his torso filling the empty window space, and I blink up at him, hyper aware of just how close he is. How we're the only two people in this parking lot.

How it feels like we're the only two people on this entire planet.

"I wanted you there tonight," he says, his voice dangerously low. Everything about him is dangerous, even his stupid eyelashes because they're long and thick and lush and sexy, and it's just not fair that he has eyelashes like that.

"Why? So you could rub it into my face when you won homecoming king and Lauren won queen? We both know I'd never have a shot," I say bitterly. I hate that I just said that. I don't care about that stuff. I never have. Before this school year, I knew where I stood socially and I still do. Sort of. The hierarchy is pretty straightforward and I was right in the middle of it.

Now, I feel lost. Untethered. I have no group, no one to belong to. And I say silly things I don't mean.

"I like it when you're there. You're like my good luck charm." He hesitates and I wonder if I should be insulted that he called me a charm. "I play better when you're at my games."

Ugh. I shouldn't react like what he said was sweet. "You don't really believe that."

"I do."

"Well, now Lauren can be your good luck charm." The words leave a bitter taste in my mouth. "And your dance partner." Supposedly he never goes to dances. Supposedly he hosts one of his big parties after every home game. It's a tradition.

So why isn't he at his house now, having one of his blow-out bashes?

"I didn't go to that stupid dance with Lauren," he tells me. "That was never the plan."

"I don't even care what your plan is," I retort, and I mean it. Sort of. As best as I can. "Good night, Tuttle."

I'm about to roll up the window, but he just stands there, looking as if he's struggling to say something else. He looks…unsure. That's a look I've never seen him wear before.

"So that's it. You're never going to call me Jordan anymore?" he finally asks.

I glare at him. "Isn't that Lauren's privilege now?"

He takes a step back as if I slapped him and I take my opportunity, rolling up the window, putting the car into drive before I pull out of the parking lot.

My eyes stay glued to the rearview mirror the entire time. He never moves from the spot where I left him, not even a twitch or a flick of his hand.

I watch him until he finally fades into the black.

Fades into nothingness.

chapter eight

The moment I open my locker door Monday morning, the note falls out, fluttering to the floor. I dive down and grab it, holding the precisely folded square of paper clutched against my palm, the sharp edges of paper cutting into my skin.

I shove a couple of books in my locker and then glance around, making sure no one else is nearby who might want to know what the note says.

Like Livvy. She's nosy like that, but I'd be the same way if someone were leaving her mysterious notes in her locker, so who am I to judge?

Carefully I unfold the paper, letting the open locker door be my shield. It's typed out, not handwritten, like the sender wanted to be anonymous. Who could it be? God, what if it's Blake? He acts a little awestruck when he's around me, and I wonder if he has a crush.

I hope not. He's a nice guy, but the feelings aren't reciprocated.

Once I start reading the note, though, I know exactly who sent it.

The torture is slowly killing me. That I can be around her, yet not have her, is twisting me up inside. She is forbidden. Untouchable. Off limits. But she is everything to me. She is the sun and the moon and the stars—everything bright and shiny and unstoppable.

But she is also the threatening calm before the storm, the wind that howls with anger, the rain that pounds the ground. She is love and light and sweetness and darkness and anger and passion.

She is all I could ever want.

"What do you think?"

I jump about a mile at hearing Tuttle's question so close to my ear, and I turn to glare at him after slamming my locker door shut. "You wrote this?" I try to sound surprised, but I knew it was him once I started reading. The tortured Romeo to my Juliet.

He looks offended. "Of course, I wrote it. As Romeo."

"You could've sent it to me in an email." I start to walk and good Lord, he follows me. The crowd parts for us, but that's because of him. He's their god, walking among mere mortals.

"Who uses email anymore?" Says the guy who typed it out and used a printer. Talk about old-fashioned.

"Then you could've texted it to me." I hurry my steps, but that doesn't faze him. His legs are long and his strides are too, so I'm huffing and puffing trying to outpace him while he practically glides through the halls.

So frustrating.

"I thought this way was more creative." I glance over at him, and he's smirking. He's both adorable and annoying when he smirks. "Did you like it?"

I stop at the end of the hall and so does he. He stands in front of me, his body like a shield, as if he wants to protect me from everyone rushing past us. Someone jostles him as they pass by and he takes advantage, stepping closer, and I shift. Press my back against the wall while he rests his hand on the wall above my head.

To the casual observer, we look like we're a couple. Clearly together. Having an intimate conversation. But we're not.

I need to remember that.

The way he's watching me, waiting for my answer, it's as if he's seeking my approval. And I can't help but find that endearing, even though I'm still pissed about the homecoming crap, the way he lurked around the Yo Town parking lot Friday night in the guise of protecting me.

Deep down inside, I liked it. It felt like he made an undeclared choice with that gesture. He doesn't want Lauren Mancini.

He wants me.

But I'm probably reading too much into it, so I push that thought out of my head.

"When did you write it?" I ask him, tilting my head back so I can look into his eyes.

Big mistake. His gaze meets mine, and it's like he's actually touching me. I can read all of his thoughts and they're focused on me. "Last night."

"I—I like it. It's short but thoughtful and just the tiniest bit sad. I could really feel Romeo's yearning for Juliet." He stares at me, silent for so long I want to dash away. "Um, I need to get to class, so—" I try to duck under his arm.

Jordan grabs hold of me, keeping me in place. Keeping me close. His fingers gently squeeze my arm as he says, "It's your turn."

"What?"

"Now you need to write from Juliet's perspective. About her feelings toward Romeo." He raises a brow. "That's what Mrs. Meyer wanted, right?"

I nod, unable to speak. He's still holding onto me. And I don't want him to let me go. Stupid boy. Stupid hormones.

"Text me your entry tonight." His voice drops, low and sexy and crazy making. "You know where to find me."

And then he's gone.

"Thought you said there's nothing going on between you two."

I shake my head, shake myself out of my daze, and turn to find Em next to me.

"There's not." My voice is shaky. A dead giveaway that he affects me and I'm nervous that Em heard it. Saw that. She could use it against me. I don't trust her. I believe the stories Livvy tells me. I may feel sorry for Em, but I also know she's manipulative.

For all I know, she's manipulating me. I wouldn't put it past her.

"Whatever. He looked totally into you. And he's never into anyone." I start walking and she follows. "So, um, did you talk to Livvy? About me?"

I'm surprised she's asking. She's not one for forthright and truthful. "We talked about you on…Wednesday, I think it was? Maybe Thursday."

"Oh." Her face falls. "I haven't heard from her."

"Give her time. She's trying to work up the courage to reach out to you." I don't know if that's the case. It sounds bogus, especially because Livvy's been on lockdown for the last week. Her mom relented and let her go to the homecoming game, but she wouldn't let Livvy go to the dance, which crushed her.

But she got her phone back this morning and all restrictions are lifted, so hopefully she'll be in a better mood. Girl was grouchy this weekend.

"I thought she was just busy with Ryan," Em mutters under her breath. Her expression brightens when she catches me looking at her. "I went to the dance and Livvy wasn't there. Neither were you."

"I was working. Liv was grounded."

"Oh." Em's cheeks color and I hope she's remembering that she was the reason Livvy was grounded. She ratted Liv out to her mother that we were staying the night at Ryan's house the weekend of his birthday party, unsupervised. When Livvy's mom showed up to take her home, I wanted to die. All I could think about was my mom or dad finding me like that—a disheveled mess after sleeping in the same bed with Jordan and wearing only his T-shirt.

My skin warms at the memory.

"Tuttle didn't even have his homecoming after party. It was so weird." Em sends me a look. "Were you two together or what?"

"We weren't together." I shake my head. "I know nothing about a party."

"I figured you and Tuttle might've become the party," Em says, grinning. "Or had your own intimate party."

"Ha. Funny," I say with full on sarcasm as I slow to a stop in front of my homeroom door. Em stops with me. "Listen, you have a lot to make up for too, you know. You've done some shitty things, and Liv's hurt. I know she's done some awful things too, but the both of you can't go on damaging each other like this."

Em scowls, clearly irritated. "Who died and made you peacemaker?"

I roll my eyes and start to head into my class. I don't need to put up with this.

Em chases me inside, coming to a halt directly in front of Cannon Whittaker's desk. "Oh. Hey."

"Hey." He hardly looks at her. The best linebacker at our school, Cannon is a huge guy who barely fits behind the desk he's currently sitting in. He has a player reputation like all the other guys on the football team, but he's never been anything but nice to me. Not that we're in a lot of classes together or that he's ever shown any interest, but still.

"Well." Em turns, flashing me a bright, almost manic smile. Her eyes are wide and unblinking and I wonder at the quick transformation. "Thanks for the advice, Amanda. You're such a big help, as always." She wags her fingers in Cannon's direction. "Bye," she says before she runs out of my homeroom.

My gaze meets Cannon's. "Are you guys friends?"

He snorts and shakes his head. "No." His cheeks go red. So does his neck.

Hmmm.

The day drags. I blame it on being a Monday. There's a pop quiz in my government class, but I think I mostly ace it. Lunch turns into a nightmare. An unexpected heat wave has made people cranky—myself included—and all the seniors decide to grab food off campus. I planned on getting something quick at a drive thru somewhere by myself but decide I don't want to deal with the traffic jam headache.

I'm making my way out of the parking lot when Jordan Tuttle's Range Rover pulls up alongside me. The tinted window rolls down, revealing there's no one else in the car.

Just Jordan.

"Where you going?" He's wearing sunglasses, but he shoves them on top of his head so I can see those pretty eyes of his.

"Back to the quad."

He makes a face. "It's hot as hell outside. Come with me."

I shake my head. I don't want to get in his car. I'll say something dumb. Or worse, I'll do something dumb. Something I'll regret.

"Come on, Mandy. I'll buy you lunch."

My stomach growls at the word lunch, but I shake my head again.

"We can work on our project together," he suggests, like that's going to tempt me.

"I'm not going to write Juliet's diary entry in front of you," I snap, surprised he'd even suggest it.

Now he's frowning. "Get in the car." I hear the doors unlock and he studies me with that quiet yet powerful look he's perfected. The one that says, *do as I say.*

Heaving a big sigh, I round the front of the car and open the passenger side door, plopping my butt into the seat. "There." I turn to look at him after I shut the door. "Happy?"

"Very." He pulls his sunglasses back on, puts the vehicle in drive and off we go, speeding through the parking lot and pulling out through the entrance-only side and onto the street.

"Jordan!" I did not mean to say his name out loud, but jeez. He's gonna get in trouble for pulling a stunt like that.

He grins at me and presses the gas hard, speeding down the road toward the restaurants all of us students frequent during lunchtime and after school. "Loosen up, Winters. You only have one life. Learn how to live it."

My hands ball into fists in my lap. I can't believe he just said that. He's so infuriating sometimes. "Are you saying I don't know how to live my life?" He doesn't even know me. Not really. Not well enough to give me that sort of advice.

"No." He keeps his eyes trained on the road before him. "I'm just saying you shouldn't be scared. You need to learn how to take more risks."

I've taken more risks these past few months than I ever have in my entire life. "I'm a planner. There's nothing wrong with that."

Tuttle says nothing, implying there's everything wrong with that, but whatever.

"Were you really going to lunch by yourself?" I finally ask.

"I didn't want to. I was taking a risk and hoping I could find you."

I sag against my soft leather seat. He's exhausting. Now it's my turn to not have a response.

"Do you want anything in particular?"

Shaking my head, I tell him, "You decide," and he doesn't argue with me. He pulls into In-N-Out, goes straight to the drive thru and lets me make my own order at the speaker.

"You mind eating in the car?" he asks after we finish ordering.

"Not if you don't. Though I can't guarantee I won't spill anything."

He smiles, and it's breathtaking. He just doesn't do it enough, I swear. "I'm not scared."

I bet he's not.

Jordan pays and grabs our food, handing me the bags and my drink. I take a sip and set it in the drink holder in the center console, quiet as he pulls out of the parking lot and starts driving farther away from school. I don't know where he's taking us, and I don't want to ask. I also don't want to freak out, but the farther we get, the longer it'll take for us to return to campus. And I don't want to be late to fifth period.

Finally, he pulls into a parking lot of a small neighborhood park. It's been around for a while, you can tell by all the tall trees and the worn out playground, but it's quiet and mostly empty. He parks the car in the shade and shuts off the engine, the sound of the satellite radio playing softly in the background.

I divvy out the food, giving him his burger and fries, trying to keep myself busy. I'm nervous. My hands are shaking and my appetite left me the moment I took hold of those bags, despite the delicious smell wafting from them. With grim determination I pull out my burger and stare at it, wondering how I'm going to choke this down.

It's so frustrating, how he affects me. How I let him affect me. I shouldn't give him so much power.

"It won't bite you," he says softly, and I jerk my head toward him, the amused look on his face making me feel dumb. "I thought you were hungry."

"I told you I wasn't hungry." Well, I didn't actually say it out loud. I only shook my head.

"I heard your stomach growl."

Ugh. My cheeks grow hot. "I'm not hungry anymore," I mutter.

"Why not?" He takes a bite of his cheeseburger, and I don't know how he does it, but he makes even that sexy.

What can I say to him? Can I tell him the truth?

You make me nervous. You make me self-conscious. What if I get sauce on my chin? What if I drip ketchup on my shirt? What if I take a drink of my Coke and slurp on the straw by accident? What if you watch me eat and think it's the most disgusting thing you've ever seen in your life?

These are the silly things that go through my head in Tuttle's presence.

"Hey." My eyes snap up to meet his and I realize he's holding a fry in front of my face. "Eat this." And then he feeds it to me. I open my mouth like a baby bird and he drops the fry inside, his thumb brushing against my lower lip. His eyes smolder and he goes still as I slowly chew the fry and swallow it.

The tension grows between us, until it feels like a living, breathing thing sitting in the car with us. All over a fry. All over his thumb barely grazing my lip. He's staring at my mouth now as he sips from his drink, and of course my gaze goes to *his* lips wrapped around that straw.

All of a sudden I'm ravenous. I grab my burger and bite into it, not caring if I look like a slob or not. The burger tastes delicious and I take another bite, catching him watching me out of the corner of my eye.

"What?" I ask when he doesn't look away.

"Why do we keep doing this?"

I take a sip of my drink. "Doing what?"

"Playing this game. Pretending we hate each other when we don't."

"I don't hate you."

"I definitely don't hate you either."

"But I don't want to be with you."

He raises a brow. Remains quiet.

Ugh.

"I don't," I reiterate.

Somehow the brow rises higher. How does he do that? He said about a billion words with that one gesture.

"It won't work." I look away from him. It'll be easier to say these things if I don't have to see his gorgeous face. "You're you and I'm me and we're not a match. I'll be insecure and you'll get tired of my clingy ways and break up with me immediately. Then I'll be devastated and pissed at myself because I knew it was a bad idea, being with you."

"You're not clingy."

I whirl on him, irritated that he...actually complimented me. "How do you know?"

"I just know."

"How?" I ask again. "You don't know me. We've never really gone out. We go to a few of the same parties and always end up together, but we're never really doing anything."

"Oh, we've done a few things." His suggestive tone makes my entire body go hot. With irritation.

With...hmmm...desire? Is that the right word?

I also want to hit him. Seriously. What is up with me lately with the violent tendencies?

"Nothing serious," I mumble, keeping my head bent. I need to stick with the don't-look-at-Tuttle plan. It's easier to say things when I don't have to see him. I should've never gotten into his car.

He exhales loudly and resumes eating. I can tell because every few seconds his hand rustles around in the bag, grabbing fries. Or he takes a sip of his drink. Eventually I start eating too, and we remain quiet. It's not a comfortable silence, though. Not even close. It's tension-filled and edgy and it makes me uneasy. I can feel the irritation and frustration radiating from his body, and I decide to talk about something safe.

"I heard you played a really great game Friday."

Tuttle pauses mid-chew and then swallows before he answers. "I did all right. It was really the team. Ryan, he ran in three touchdown passes."

"He's a great player."

"He is."

"So are you." I get a shrug as an answer. "I hate that I missed the game."

"I know you love football."

"Sucks that I have to work every Friday night."

"You should tell them you're busy."

I huff out a laugh. "Yeah, that'll go over real well with my new boss. 'Sorry I can't work Friday nights. I gotta watch the football game.' She won't go for that."

He's quiet. Contemplative. "What if I could give you a valid excuse?"

"An excuse for what?"

"To come to every football game."

"How are you going to do that?"

Tuttle grins. Full on grins so broadly, I'm slightly taken aback. "Watch and see."

chapter nine

"They're in a relationship. Like boyfriend and girlfriend already. He's probably had sex with her." Livvy shudders, her gaze locked on what's unfolding on the other side of the quad during lunch. It's the day after Tuttle took me to In-N-Out and now I'm back to eating lunch at school. The temporary heat wave has passed and it actually feels like fall today.

"So?" I sound bored because I *am* bored. She needs to stop focusing her energy on Dustin and Brianne Brown and instead pay attention to Ryan. He's totally into her. Like, he acts the fool around her all the time and she thinks it's adorable.

I find him annoying, but that's me.

"He took her to the homecoming dance, they went out Saturday and Sunday. And they've spent every free moment at school together," Liv continues.

"How do you know all of this? And I thought you were *over* Dustin."

We should stop talking about him. Ryan could appear at any moment.

She rolls her eyes. "I promise, I'm trying my hardest to get over him, but it's—difficult. I still miss him. He was a daily part of my life for so long, and now he's gone. Poof. Like our friendship never existed." A pained expression crosses her face. "Gross, he just kissed her. I think I saw tongue."

Dustin and Brianne Brown were bound to happen. The girl has been working him over since the school year started. Actually, she'd been after him for years, according to Liv. Dustin had just been so wrapped up in Livvy, hoping he had a chance with her. Until he blew it. And she blew it. Oh, and Em blew it too.

Literally.

Ha ha. Bad joke.

"They wouldn't be doing the tongue tango on the quad," I reassure Liv just as Ryan sits down next to her, plopping his tray full of food on the table. He's laughing, his gaze meeting mine.

"Who's doing the tongue tango?" he asks.

"Brianne Brown and Du—"

"Hey, baby." Livvy cuts me off and flashes Ryan a seductive smile as she strokes a hand down his chest. Guess she doesn't want to look like she's spying on Dustin in front of Ryan. Smart move. "What did you get for lunch?"

He points it all out, offering her some, but she shakes her head and holds up the prepackaged salad she brought from home. I'm munching on carrot sticks again and guzzling water. Ryan is eating pizza and a hamburger and a salad, plus he has a brownie that he claims his mom made. Right before Livvy bursts into a giggle fit. I'm thinking it might be a pot brownie, but what do I know.

"Hey." I glance up at the sound of the familiar voice, the sun so bright I can't make out the face of who's standing by our table, but I recognize his shape. It's Tuttle. And he doesn't wait for an invitation, he just sits down next to me, lifting his brows as he shows me the Subway bag he's carrying. "Want to split a sandwich?"

Before I can ask him when he found the time to go to the Subway down the street, he's unwrapping the sandwich and giving me half. "What's on it?"

"Turkey with everything except tomatoes, pickles and peppers."

"Onions?" I wrinkle my nose. I don't want onion breath around him.

He nods. "Oh yeah."

"I don't know…" I start, but he silences me with a look.

"Eat it."

I dutifully pick up the sandwich, take a bite and almost moan at how good it tastes. I didn't realize how burnt out I am on baby carrots and ranch until this very moment. "Thank you," I say once I swallow.

"I have good news," he says casually, facing Ryan and Liv. Making me think the good news is for either Ryan or Liv.

"What is it?" Ryan asks.

Tuttle turns to look at me. "You're our new team water girl."

I'm packing up my carrots and ranch, and I pause, meeting Tuttle's gaze. "Are you talking about me?"

He nods. Takes another bite of his sandwich. There's a tiny gob of mustard stuck in the corner of his mouth and I'm tempted to wipe it off with my finger.

Or my tongue.

My cheeks go hot at the mere thought.

"But I can't do it. I work on Friday nights."

He licks the mustard from his mouth and I feel a little weak at the sight of his tongue. What's up with all the tongues today? "Find someone to cover you."

"I can't do it this week." No way. "Maybe I can work next week's game."

"But we need you this week. It's an away game, and that's when we need our water girls the most."

The water girl title is so undignified. "What happened to your previous water girl?"

"Turns out she's allergic to the grass on the field and can't do it anymore. I told Coach about you and he knows how much you love the game and our team. He said he wanted no one else. Just you." The smug look of satisfaction on Tuttle's face was more than obvious.

And sort of annoying.

"You can't just volunteer me up for a job when I'm not sure if I can do it," I tell him.

"When do you next work?"

"This afternoon."

Tuttle frowns. "A closing shift?"

I bite my lip and nod. Then I open up my sandwich and pick off all the onions, one by one. I am not risking onion breath while I'm around him.

"By yourself? Or with that drippy guy?"

I'm offended on Blake's behalf. "Don't call Blake drippy." I put my sandwich back together and take a bite.

"He seems sorta drippy."

"Aw, look, Ryan. They're having a lovers' quarrel," Livvy teases as she nudges her boyfriend right before they both start cracking up.

I send them a withering stare before I resume my conversation with Tuttle. "Don't be so mean. Just because he's not some big, sexy jock like you."

Oh, the look he sends me is priceless. "You think I'm a big, sexy jock?"

"You *know* you're a big, sexy jock. Everyone thinks so."

"I only care what you think," he says as he leans in close, his voice low. Too low. Sexy low.

There he goes again, saying dangerous things. "You shouldn't."

"Too late." He resumes eating like the conversation is over.

I push his shoulder out of irritation, and because I want to touch him. Shoving him when you're me is pointless considering he's a solid wall of muscle. "I can't ask my boss for every Friday off. I just started there."

"Just through the football season, Amanda." Oh. He said my name. He doesn't say it very often, but it sounds nice falling from his lips. His perfectly kissable lips. "Maybe until mid November, but that's it. Then you can work every Friday night for the rest of your life if you want to."

I'm tempted. I think he knows it too because I see the light catch in his eyes and the warm way he studies me is enough to make me want to squirm.

"Just ask," he says, his voice soft. He sends a quick glance in Ryan and Livvy's direction, but they're too wrapped up in each other to pay attention to us. "The worst she can say is no."

"I'll ask," I say, my voice as soft as his.

"Promise?"

I nod. "I'll let you know what she says."

We both eat for a while before he asks another question. "You're really closing by yourself tonight?"

"Yeah. It's my first time." I swallow past the sudden nervousness that swamps me. "Blake said I could call him if I need help."

"Please." Tuttle scoffs. "Like that guy can help you."

"I mean, with like the register or whatever. The money I have to put in the safe in the back before I leave. There's this whole closing up procedure I have to follow and I don't want to mess it up."

Jordan studies me, the concern in his eyes obvious. "I don't like the idea of you being alone there at night."

"I'm a big girl." I smile but it feels fake, so I let it fade. "I'll be fine."

"Uh huh." He reaches out and brushes the corner of my lips with his thumb. "Mustard," he tells me.

Just before he sticks his thumb in his mouth and licks it off.

Tuesday night at Yo Town is pretty boring. The shop is located in a busy shopping center, but once it hits about eight o'clock, business dies. The last hour would've dragged if I hadn't prepped for closing during that time. I'm confident closing will be a breeze, but I can't help but feel a little nervous after Tuttle showed so much concern about my being alone.

If he never would've acted like that, I'd be fine. He put too many dark thoughts in my head.

He's pretty good at that.

My phone buzzes in the back pocket of my jeans and I pull it out to find a text from Blake.

You doing okay? Have any questions?

I text him back.

I'm fine. Last hour has been dead but that gave me time to clean up

a lot.

That's what I usually do too. Call me if you need anything.

Will do! ☺

I put my phone away and start to cover the toppings that can stay out overnight. I'll put the ones that need to be refrigerated in the back after I lock the front door. I check the clock. 8:47. Thirteen minutes 'til closing time.

I've got my back toward the door when I hear the buzzer indicating someone entering the building. I whirl around, a strangled sound leaving me when I see who's standing there.

Tuttle. Of course.

"Why are you here?" I ask once I find my voice.

"Couldn't stop thinking about you alone. Thought I'd come be with you. Make sure you're okay." He approaches the counter, walking with that unmistakable Tuttle swagger. He looks windblown—his hair is ruffled and his cheeks are red. A storm is coming in, nothing serious, but enough to drop the temps and kick up a gusty wind. He's wearing a school hoodie and dark gray sweatpants. I have never in my life thought sweatpants were sexy before.

At this very moment, they are the sexiest things I've ever seen.

"Oh." I stand up a little bit straighter. "I can handle it."

"I know you can. I just don't like thinking about you here. All by yourself. Anyone can see that you're alone." He waves at the giant windows that line the front of the store, then turns to meet my gaze. "The parking lot isn't safe either. Who knows who's out there?"

I fight the shiver that wants to take over me at his words. Talk about putting fear in me. "I'm parked pretty close."

"Not close enough," he retorts.

"Tuttle..." My voice drifts and the glare he sends me cuts like a knife.

"Don't call me that," he snaps.

I take a step back at the anger in his voice. "Sorry. I didn't mean to offend you."

He comes around the counter until he's standing right in front of me. Blocking everything out so all I can see is him. "I told you before— call me by my first name."

"Okay." I nod, trying to ignore my racing heart at his nearness. He's moody tonight. A little restless. I wonder why? "Jordan."

The tension eases out of him and he relaxes. "You've got the braids in again." He reaches out and touches one, tugs on the end like he's six and a pain in my butt. "You look cute."

He always tells me I look cute. I want him to think I'm beautiful. Gorgeous. Stunning. All those pretty words boys say to girls. Boyfriends say to girlfriends.

Oh my God, now I'm the one whose acting like she's six.

"Thanks." I glance around, trying to look anywhere but at him. Why, I don't know. It's like all the awkwardness of this entire situation has just hit me full force and I feel silly. Lacking. Which is dumb. He's never done or said anything to make me feel less than in comparison to him.

But he doesn't have to. He's just…him. And I'm only me.

"Amanda." I look him in the eyes when he says my name. "Do you need my help or anything?"

"Can you sit out here while I do some stuff in the back?"

"Yeah." He reaches out and brushes stray strands of hair away from my forehead, his fingers skimming my skin, making my blood hum. "Can I buy some yogurt first?"

I burst out laughing. "Absolutely."

Once I ring him up, I start putting away the toppings in the refrigerator, then I make sure the bathroom is clean. I wipe down the yogurt machines, run a quick broom over the floor since I already mopped, then turn off the "open" light and lock the door.

"It's only 8:59," Tuttle reminds me. He's sitting at one of the tiny tables, eating his frozen yogurt like he has all the time in the world as he checks his phone. I'm instantly curious. Who texts him? Snapchats him? He has an Instagram profile but barely uses it, though he has tons of followers, including myself.

"I'm a minute early. So what?" I smile at him and he doesn't return it, which makes me a little sad.

"You talk to your boss?"

I frown. "What do you mean?"

"About Fridays."

"Oh!" I brighten. How could I forget? I was so worried about closing I guess I shoved it out of my mind. "I did talk to her. She said that was fine, mentioned that she could cover this Friday's shift if I was needed that badly, which I assured her I was. I made it sound like I tried to line up the water girl job before I started at Yo Town and she was totally cool with it."

"So you're our new water girl."

I nod, pleased with the happy expression on his face. "Thank you for arranging this for me."

"I'm glad." He offers up a smile. "Really glad you'll be at all the games, Mandy."

"Me too," I murmur.

"You work on Juliet's diary entry yet?"

I frown at his change of subject. "Um, not yet."

He sends me a look, one I can't decipher. "Better get to it."

"I'll work on it tonight."

"You'll text it to me?"

"Sure." I don't know if I want to do that. Talk about taking a chance. What if he shares the entry with his friends? That would be humiliating. He'll probably make it sound like I wrote that to him, not Juliet to Romeo.

Yeah. I am so not sending him the entry via text. Forget that.

I slip behind the counter and work on closing out the cash register. Once I'm done, I go to the back and stash the money in the safe, then lock it and the office as well. Turning off all the lights, I come out into the store to find Jordan leaning against the counter and typing on his phone, a scowl on his face as he stares at the screen.

"All done," I tell him weakly. Why does he look so mad? What's going on? Who's he talking to? I kinda lift up on tiptoe to see his phone screen and I can tell he's texting.

But with who?

"Ready to go?" He clicks his phone screen off and shoves it in the front pocket of his sweats, waiting for me.

"Yeah. Let's go out the front door." He heads toward it and I shut off the rest of the lights, then follow him, walking through the door he holds open for me. I pull the door shut and lock it with the set of keys Sonja left with me earlier this afternoon, then shove them into my front pocket. "I did it."

"Yeah, you did." He glances around before he takes my arm and leads me out into the parking lot and toward my car. I hurry to keep up with him, shivering when the cold wind hits me. I'm only in my Yo Town T-shirt and jeans. I didn't bring a sweater because I came straight from school and earlier in the day it had been warm.

"Your teeth are chattering," he says when we reach my car. "Here."

I watch in mute fascination when he tugs his hoodie off, his T-shirt catching on it for a brief moment and riding up, revealing his perfect, flat stomach.

Oh God. I feel faint. I've touched that stomach before. Not enough times, though. I'd give anything to touch him again. Totally dumb, but true.

Next thing I know, he's tugging the hoodie over my head and I shove my arms into the sleeves, smiling when the hoodie hits me at about mid thigh. It's warm from his body heat and smells like soap and spice and Jordan Tuttle. Which means it smells freaking amazing.

"That better?" He tucks the sweatshirt around my neck, his fingers brushing against my sensitive skin, and a soft gasp escapes me, making him frown. "Mandy? You all right?"

I finally do it. I give in. I throw myself at him, wrapping my arms around his waist, soaking up his solid warmth, the shape of him, the thin fabric of his T-shirt, the thump, thump, thump of his heartbeat against my ear. Oh God, I could hold onto him forever like this. And when he puts his arms around me, pulling me even closer, I snuggle in and close my eyes.

"Thank you," I whisper, my throat scratchy. Raw. "For everything." I need him to know how much I appreciate what he's doing for me. How he's watching out for me. Protecting me.

It's sweet. Thoughtful.

"You're welcome." He presses his lips to my hair and I clutch him tighter. I want more. More of Jordan's lips on my skin, on my lips. But I don't get it. And I don't ask for it. I'm too scared.

Apparently so is he, because eventually he lets go of me and I let go of him with a bashful smile. "I'll see you at school tomorrow?"

"Yeah. I'll wait until the car starts, okay?"

"Okay." I unlock my car and climb in, then start the engine, sending him a thumbs-up. He nods and then goes to his car, which is parked near mine, and when I pull out of the parking lot a few minutes later, he follows me.

All the way home.

chapter ten

When there are away games, the school doesn't hold rallies. If that was the case, we'd be having rallies every Friday and nothing would ever get done. Not that anything much happens on a Friday at our high school. Though drama always seems to break out on a Friday.

Or a Monday, or a Tuesday. Pretty much any day that ends in "y."

I've been on edge all day, worrying about how I'm supposed to get to the game tonight. I don't want to drive, not in my crap car, considering we're playing a town over forty miles away. Plus, I don't want to spend the money on gas. I'm trying to save every dime I'm making right now to put away toward college.

So when I spot Coach Halsey hovering by the quad near the end of lunch, I approach him with all the courage I can muster.

Why am I such a coward sometimes? God, I hate it. I need to get a backbone, damn it.

"Hey Coach."

He smiles when he sees it's me. "Amanda Winters. Very excited about having you as our new water girl." We've talked about it briefly, but he's been busy and so I'm a little freaked I might not be the best water girl in the world. But if he has faith in me, I need to have faith in myself.

"Thanks again for the chance. I really do appreciate it." I pause. Lick my lips. Fight the nerves. "Um, what time do I have to be at the game tonight?"

"Bus leaves at four, JV game starts at five."

I frown. "Wait a minute. You want me to ride the team bus?"

His frown matches mine. "You *are* on the team now, correct?"

"Um, I guess so…"

"The team rides together for away games on the bus. The cheerleaders go too." Great. Lauren Mancini will be there. Can't wait. "The bus leaves promptly at four."

"Okay. Cool."

"Don't be late. You don't want the bus to leave you behind." He smiles and starts to walk away. "See you tonight, Miss Winters," he calls over his shoulder.

"Why is he seeing *you* tonight?"

I turn at the snide tone, surprised to find Lauren Mancini standing in front of me, looking perfect in her cheer uniform. The sleeveless top shows off her perfect toned and tanned arms, and it fits her tight across the chest so her boobs look amazing. The skirt is short, revealing her long, thin legs. She has curves, unlike me, and a beautiful face, beautiful hair…beautiful everything.

She knows it too.

"Um, I'm the new water girl for the JV and varsity football teams,"

I tell her.

Lauren sneers, but she still manages to look pretty. "Really? Are you so desperate to get Tuttle's attention you'll do anything, even hand him over a water bottle during the game?"

Ouch. "I'm not trying to get Tuttle's attention." *I've already got it.*

"Oh, really? Could've fooled me." She crosses her arms in front of her chest, plumping up her stupid perfect boobs, and I try not to glance down at my own imperfect, very flat chest.

"I don't want to fight with you, Lauren," I say wearily, just before I turn and start to walk away.

But she follows after me, so close I can practically feel her breathing down my neck. "You're not his type, so stop chasing after him. You look desperate. And pitiful."

I hear a few snickers, and I realize I'm not only being followed by the captain of the cheer squad—there are other cheerleaders trailing after her. Like I'm being chased by Lauren and her cheer posse.

Best not to acknowledge them.

"I'm serious, Amanda." Lauren grabs hold of my arm and stops me from entering the building. I turn to face her, jerking out of her hold when I find myself surrounded by a group of five cheerleaders, including Lauren. "Give up on Jordan Tuttle. He's *mine.*"

"I don't see your name stamped on his ass." I stand up straight and shake my hair back, trying for the you-don't-scare-me look, but I'm not sure if it's working.

Lauren's mouth pops open as the other girls titter nervously. The glare she sends them shuts them up before she turns it on me. "You should watch what you say. Your words might get you in trouble."

"Oh my God, Lauren. Stop being such a bitch and leave her alone." Em magically appears by my side like my long-lost guardian angel. "Go on, find someone else to terrorize." She waves her hands at the girls, like they're annoying bugs she swats away.

Lauren sends me one last long look before she turns and leaves, her little posse following her. The moment they're out of earshot, Em turns to me and rolls her eyes. "You sounded like you were holding your own, but she's a total bully. I had to step in."

"Thank you." I offer up a shaky smile. "Seriously. She was sort of freaking me out."

"Don't let her bother you. She's just jealous because Tuttle pays attention to you and not her," Em says.

"You really think she's jealous of me?" I'm incredulous. Both at the idea of Lauren Mancini being envious of me, and that Em actually helped me out instead of making the situation worse.

Em laughs and shakes her head. "*Duh.* Of course, she's jealous of you. You have what she wants—Jordan Tuttle."

"I don't really have him," I mumble, dropping my head so I can stare at my feet. It's true. I don't *have him* have him, but I guess I sort of do? He has been paying attention to me a lot lately. Even after I pushed him away. Even after I hurt his feelings and told him I didn't want to be with him because I didn't believe he could be faithful.

Which was…stupid. I don't know him, not really. But I never claimed to be smart when it comes to relationships. My experience is limited. The only real boyfriend I ever had was Thad, and look where that ended up.

"Please. He's totally into you." Em leans in close, her mouth at my ear. "He's watching you right now. In fact—oh shit—he's headed this way."

I glance up to see Tuttle walking toward us, his expression grim. My heart starts to thump wildly and I take a deep breath, remind myself to calm down.

"Hey," he says to Em before his gaze settles on me. "What did Lauren want from you?"

"Nothing." I smile, trying to communicate with Em with just my eyes. I can see she wants to say something. Tell Tuttle the truth. But I don't want her to. I don't need to burden him with my so-called troubles. I can handle Lauren Mancini on my own.

"Really?" He sounds doubtful. "She can be kind of a—"

"Bitch?" Em supplies helpfully, a giant smile on her face. "So accurate."

"Em. Stop." I don't know why I'm scolding her. Do I really want to defend Lauren Mancini? I don't think so. I decide to change tactics. "Excited for tonight's game?" I ask Jordan.

He shrugs. "The team we're playing is number one in the league right now."

"Oh." Yikes. That might prove to be a challenge.

"You guys will do great," Em says cheerfully.

"Yeah," Jordan says, returning his attention to me. Not that it's ever really left. He won't stop looking at me and I'm suddenly self-conscious. I run a hand over my hair, touch the corner of my mouth in case there's a crumb lingering. Nothing. I drag my finger under one eye, then the other, picking up bits of stray mascara, and I wish I could slick on some lip-gloss. Anything to look prettier. "You look good."

I blink up at him. "What?"

"You're fidgeting. Stop worrying." He reaches out and slides his fingers through my hair. Gently touches the corner of my mouth. Glides his index finger under my left eye, his gaze locked with mine. "You're perfect," he murmurs as he trails his finger along my cheek.

I'm also breathless. How does he do that?

Em clearing her throat breaks me free of the trance Jordan just lulled me into. "Guys, I feel like I'm interrupting something, so I'm out. Good luck on tonight's game, Tuttle. I'm sure you'll kill 'em." She flees before we can say anything else.

"You're friends with her?" he asks once Em's gone.

"Sort of." I don't know how to explain my relationship with Em, so I don't.

"Her and Livvy were best friends."

"I know. But now they're having…trouble." I wrinkle my nose. No need to go into the details. I think Jordan knows a few of them anyway.

"And you're wanting to help them out?" He whistles low. "You're a good friend."

I laugh softly. "Probably too good of a friend. I've let too many people take advantage of me."

"Like who?"

"Like Tara." When he frowns I remind him, "My former best friend. The one who was…"

"Screwing your boyfriend at my house? Yeah. She sucks."

"So does he."

"Nah, he's just an idiot."

"What do you mean?"

"Letting a girl like you go? He didn't know how good he had it." He tilts his head to the side, contemplating me while I digest what he just said. Yet again, he renders me silent. "You never did send me your diary entry."

"For Juliet?" I wrote it late last night, when I couldn't sleep. Might've poured my heart into it too, reliving the hug in the parking lot moment over and over, like I'm twelve.

"Yeah. Where is it?"

"I'll show you in class."

"I want to see it now."

"No, in class." He grabs my waist, holding me in place, and I look up at him, surprised to see the amusement in his eyes. "What are you doing?"

"Looking for any excuse to touch you?" He raises his brows and I blush. My cheeks go warm and he squeezes me, his thumbs sneaking under the hem of my T-shirt to touch my bare skin. "For once, you're not fighting me."

"Jordan." My voice is a warning, but I don't want him to stop. "Public displays of affection are strictly prohibited on campus grounds."

I sound like I'm reciting from the school code handbook.

"Not like I'm trying to kiss you." His gaze drops to my lips, and it actually feels like he did just kiss me. "I'll save that for later."

Um. "What are you talking about?"

"You'll see." The bell rings and he curves one arm around my waist, guiding me so I'm walking beside him and into the building. "Need to go to your locker?"

I nod, dumbfounded that we're walking down the hall and Jordan has his arm around me. Like we're a bona fide couple. Meaning I'm having a surreal moment. He doesn't do this sort of thing. He never has. So I don't get why all of a sudden he's choosing me.

Jordan stops directly in front of my locker and leans against the one next to mine, waiting for me as I fumble with the lock. It takes me three tries before I can get it open, and once I do, he's right there, offering to hold my backpack, asking if I have everything I need before he shuts the locker door for me.

"You need to go to yours?" I ask as he slings my backpack over his shoulder. I walk beside him, trying my best to ignore the stares, the whispers that grow into low murmurs, a few snippets of conversation caught as we pass people by.

"Who is she?"

"Why is Tuttle walking with her?"

"Are they—*together?*"

But the worst moment is when I glance up to find Lauren Mancini headed straight for us, the scowl on her face right out of my nightmares. She looks furious, her eyes going from Jordan to me back to Jordan again. I watch as she switches it on, that beaming, perky cheerleader smile aimed right at him.

"Jordan! Ready for tonight's game?" She stops directly in front of him but he dodges her, grabbing my hand and pulling me along with him.

"Yeah," he says, not even looking in her direction. He laces our fingers together, giving mine a squeeze, and I just want to die on the spot.

Somehow I keep moving, keep walking straight like a normal person, though deep inside I'm warm and fuzzy and tempted to launch myself at him.

"I'll see you tonight!" Lauren shrieks from behind us, but he doesn't even give her a second glance. Instead he looks at me with an intimate smile, like we share this big secret.

It's my most favorite Jordan Tuttle smile ever.

By the time we walk into the classroom, the bell is ringing. I let go of his hand and scramble for my seat. Jordan ambles over to his like he has all the time in the world, and I turn around to watch him, letting all of my inhibitions go. Not caring what anyone else thinks.

We just walked down the hall together. First with his arm around me, then holding hands. I can look at him all I want.

"Let's not waste any time," Mrs. Meyer says after she takes attendance. "Get with your group partner and work on your projects, please. You should at least have one diary entry each, maybe even two."

I immediately feel behind. Panicked. The guy who sits next to me moves out of his desk to go join his partner and Jordan is there, easing into the desk and scooting it toward me. We're so close our arms practically touch.

"You look freaked out."

Leaning in closer, I whisper, "Did you hear Mrs. Meyer? She said we should have at least *two* entries done *each*. We only have one."

He's so close I might be able to count every single eyelash that lines his eyes. There is the faintest bit of stubble on his cheeks and I want to touch it.

"Maybe I've already finished my two entries," he murmurs, his eyes sparkling.

I suck in a breath. "You have not."

"I have." He flicks his chin in my direction. "Let me read your first entry."

Nerves assail me and I swallow hard. I don't want him to read it right in front of me. But how else can this go down?

"Um…" My voice trails off.

"Hand it over." Ugh. He can be so bossy sometimes.

I grab my backpack and unzip it, randomly digging around even though I know exactly where the paper is. Jordan leans back in his desk with a bored expression on his face, like he knows I'm trying to fake him out, and I give up. I reach for the thin folder, pull the sheet of paper out of it, and hand it over, just like he asked.

Then I lay my head down on the desk and wait quietly for the humiliation to be over.

chapter eleven

Tuttle

Amanda hands me the fluttery piece of paper and I realize her hands are shaking. She's nervous, those big brown eyes staring at me, her teeth sinking into her plump bottom lip. I want to lean in and suck on that lip so damn bad it's killing me.

Killing. Me.

She lays her head on top of the desk and buries her face against her arm while I start to read her Juliet diary entry.

It is so very difficult, to want what you cannot have. To love who you fear you've already lost. They say we're too young to know what real love is. They say we're foolish and reckless and stupid, that we can't make our own choices. We don't make a proper match, they remind us. We're too different.

But when he looks at me, I don't feel foolish or reckless or stupid. I feel beautiful. Special. Loved.

So loved.

We are not so different after all. When we are together, we are one and the same. We are like a puzzle, each of us made up of so many varied pieces. And those pieces only make sense when we come together.

They say we can't make our own choices, but they're wrong.

I choose him.

I stare at the paper for so long the words start to blur together. It doesn't feel like she's talking about Juliet and her feelings for Romeo. It feels like Mandy is talking about her feelings for me. She's my missing puzzle pieces. She's the only one I need.

"You hate it."

Her flat voice makes me jerk my head up to find she's watching me, her eyes full of worry. She'd be a terrible poker player. She wears her every emotion on her face, with her body language, even the tone of her voice.

"I definitely don't hate it." I glance over the words again, sticking on one sentence.

I choose him.

Does she choose me? Most of the time she acts like she's running away from me.

"Do you think the puzzle analogy is bad? I don't know if they had puzzles during Shakespeare's time, so maybe it's inaccurate. Maybe I should ask Mrs. Meyer." Amanda raises her hand into the air.

I immediately pull it down, my fingers circling around her wrist. I can feel her pulse and it seems a little fast. Did I do that to her? I smooth my thumb along the inside of her wrist to calm her down. "Don't ask her. Not right now."

She frowns. "Why not?"

"I don't want her to interrupt us." I gently squeeze her wrist before letting her go.

"Oh." She visibly swallows. "By the way, I, um, didn't mean anything by those love references. Just to let you know."

"I understand." I pause. "You were just—getting into character."

"Right." She nods. Flips her hair behind her shoulder, reaches up to twist the tiny pearl earring in her ear. She fidgets when she's nervous. I've noticed that about her.

I've noticed lots of things about her.

I let my gaze roam over her face, drinking in every tiny detail. Her pretty dark brown eyes and smooth cheeks and perfect, sexy lips. I'm kissing her tonight. I don't care what happens or how she acts toward me, it's been too long and nothing is going to stop me.

I'm kissing her. And I'm going to kiss her for a long time. Until we're both out of breath and our mouths are sore and she's probably late for her curfew but she doesn't care. I won't care either.

Yeah. That is definitely going to happen.

"Where's your next diary entry?" she asks, her sweet voice knocking me out of my thoughts.

"You wanna read it?"

She rolls her eyes, a big smile on her face. "Yes, I do."

I make a production out of pulling it out of my backpack, then glance over it real quick, frowning when I realize just how...needy this thing sounds. I wrote it last night, thinking about that hug in the parking lot. I sort of poured all of my own feelings into Romeo's diary entry and now I'm having second thoughts about her reading it.

"You can't back out now." She tries to snatch the paper out of my hands, but I lift it up, away from her grasping fingers. "Hey! That's not fair. I let you read mine."

"After I already let you read mine," I remind her.

"That you shoved into my locker like some sort of love note." She blushes. I love that I can make her do that. If she'd give me half a chance, I can do a lot of things to her that would make her blush. And I'd get to see if that same pretty shade of pink blooms all over her body.

"Maybe it *was* a love note," I say as I set the paper on my desk face down. Her blush deepens. "To Juliet from Romeo."

"Whatever." She shoves me and I grab her hand, linking our fingers together. I rub my thumb against her fingers, her soft, soft skin. Her nails are painted a pale pink and cut short. She wears a ring on the index finger of her right hand and I touch it. Trace it. It's a braided silver ring, thin and delicate, old and worn.

"Where'd you get this?" If she says that dick ex-boyfriend gave it to her, I will rip it off her finger and crush it.

"It was my grandma's." She meets my gaze and smiles, but it's sad. "We were really close. She died when I was thirteen."

"I'm sorry." I have no idea what that's like, losing someone I love. I honestly feel like I've never really loved…

Anyone.

"She gave this to me right before she died of cancer. Said her dad gave it to her when she was little. My mom tried to take it and put it away for safe keeping after Grandma passed, but I told her no. Grandma wanted me to have it." She studies the ring and I touch it again, tracing it all the way around her finger.

"A family heirloom," I tell her.

Amanda nods but doesn't say anything. If she cries, I'm gonna lose it.

"How'd you get this scar?" I touch a jagged one across the top of her hand, between her thumb and index finger.

"My cat Stubbs. He was super feisty when he was a kitten." The sadness is gone, replaced with a faint smile.

"Did it hurt?"

"Not really."

I hate the thought of her in pain. Which means—holy shit—I've got it bad for this girl.

Really bad.

"How's it coming, kids?"

Amanda jumps in her seat and rips her hand from mine, looking up at Mrs. Meyer. She watches us with full on amusement in her face, like she knows exactly what we've been up to. "We're sharing our entries with each other," Amanda says. "Well, I did. Jordan hasn't yet."

Mrs. Meyer looks at me. "And why is that, Mr. Tuttle?"

She is the only teacher who adds the mister to the front of my last name. Everyone else just calls me Tuttle. No one ever calls me Jordan.

Except for Amanda. Oh, and Lauren Mancini when she thinks she can get something out of me.

"I'm still working on mine. Amanda's is so good, I want to make sure my next one is too," I say smoothly.

Amanda glares. Mrs. Meyer smiles. "Well, that sounds like a compliment. Don't you agree, Amanda?"

She mumbles, "I guess," and then Mrs. Meyer is gone, moving on to the next group project.

"She saw us holding hands," Amanda says.

"So?"

"I'm surprised we didn't get in trouble."

"Mrs. Meyer doesn't care. Besides, we can tell her we're getting into our parts." I reach for her hand again, but she snatches it away. "You're going to deprive me?"

"Stop." She sends me a look. "You aren't going to let me read it?"

"I'll let you read when I have something to read from you," I remind her. "Sounds like a fair deal, right?"

"I guess."

"Hey." I slip my fingers beneath her chin and tilt her face up. I could kiss her right now. We are in perfect position. But I'm not going to let it happen in the middle of Honors English. "You'll sit with me on the bus?"

She frowns. "Tonight? To the game?"

I nod, releasing my hold on her chin. "I want to sit with you."

"What about your friends?"

None of those guys are my friends. Not really. Ryan is the closest thing to it, and I cultivate that friendship out of needing his trust on the field. "They can live without me."

"Jordan." She rests her hand on my forearm. "You're their quarterback. Their leader. You can't ditch them. You need to spend time with them and get them pumped up, so you'll get pumped up."

Amanda has a valid point. "I'll sit with you on the ride back home then."

She nods. "Okay."

No other girl would've suggested what she just did. They all want a piece of me. And don't want to share with anyone else. I'm willing to give my all to this girl, yet she wants to make sure I'm taking care of everyone else in my life.

She's unreal.

And soon she's going to be all mine.

chapter twelve

Amanda

I've been on the football field plenty of times in my life, but always as a band member. Always as one of the girls in her scratchy polyester blend uniform, trying her best to run as fast as possible while playing the clarinet. Working hard to keep up with the coordinated moves and praying my too large hat doesn't fall off my head and trip the person running behind me.

But tonight, I'm on the sidelines, keeping my boys hydrated. Running around with the other water girl as we try to keep up with the boys as they come off the field. We help tape them up too, Coach Halsey barking at us when a player needs help. Most of the boys try to refuse us but Kyla, the other water girl, is a force to be reckoned with. She won't take no for an answer.

"Don't let those boys boss you around," she told me as we sat on the bench in between the JV and varsity game, trying to rest up. "If Coach says they need to be taped up, do it. If we need to spray their knuckles with Neosporin or whatever, do that too. Don't let them whine at you and tell you they're fine." The look she sent me made me laugh a little. "They're usually not."

Our little conversation was interrupted by the reappearance of Coach Halsey, who clapped his hands together and demanded we get ready for the boys to come out onto the field. I watched in awe as they jogged out, the visitor section filled with parents and fans from our school cheering loudly. It was exciting. Exhilarating. I've never experienced anything like it before.

I wish I could've discovered this water girl job a lot sooner.

Livvy came to the game. She got a ride with one of the other football player's girlfriend and they're both up in the visitor stands, their boyfriends' jersey numbers written on their cheeks in blue and white face paint. They yell and scream and Livvy goes especially crazy when Ryan scores a touchdown, and it's super hard for me to keep my crap together.

I'm envious of their jumping around. I want to be able to jump around for my favorite player too. But I can barely talk to him, let alone act like a crazed fan. Jordan is kept busy the entire game, going over plays, in the huddle with his team, playing out on the field, sitting on the bench, or taking one of the many water bottles I hand him. He always gives me a nod of acknowledgement, but I know he's so incredibly focused on the game, he's barely registering it's me. Just a few minutes ago he was shaking off Coach Halsey when he suggested they put in the backup guy for a little bit, just to give Jordan a rest.

"Fuck that, Halsey," I heard Tuttle mutter, and I know he meant business. So did the coach, considering he didn't reprimand him for foul language. Jordan is so edgy, so freaking intense while playing football. It's kind of scary.

It's also really sexy.

So I remain cool. Calm. And busy. Incredibly busy because I sort of know what I'm doing, but then again I don't. Kyla is the calm in the storm and I hope after a few games I'm like her, efficient and organized. I'm almost thankful when Cannon Whittaker sits with me for a few minutes right before halftime while I tape up both of his hands. He's shredded his knuckles and while it looks painful, he keeps brushing me off like it's no big deal.

But I persist and he eventually lets me tape him, all the while giving me some tips and asking a few personal questions—though nothing *too* personal. He may act like a total dog with the girls, but he's actually kind of sweet. And he's also very passionate about football.

And Jordan? He acts like his normal untouchable self. He paces the sidelines, growls at the defense. Oh, and he also growls at his offensive line too, because he's an equal opportunity growler. He tosses water bottles and slaps guys on the back or the butt and he never, ever wants anyone to step in for him when it's his turn out on the field.

You'd think the coach would get this by now.

I don't bother trying to talk to him because that wall is up so high, there's no way I'm penetrating it. Not right now. The score has remained close through all three quarters. Now we're in the fourth and final quarter and I'm nervous as crap, bouncing my leg so hard I'm making the entire bench vibrate.

The cheerleaders start up a chant about holding that line and I hate to tell them, but they're off—we're currently playing offense. They probably wouldn't appreciate my correction.

It's hard not to cover my eyes while watching Jordan play. Not that he's awful—he's the farthest thing from it. It's more that I'm totally nervous. He throws the ball and I'm terrified someone from the opposing team will intercept it. Or one of our players will drop it. We need this last touchdown. It will most likely ensure our win.

But the home team's crowd is roaring loudly, trying to distract us. They don't want their team to lose. Though guess what?

We don't want *our* team to lose either.

I perch on the edge of the bench as Jordan drives the ball down the field. Coach Halsey is eerily calm as he watches, his expression blank, his gaze never leaving that field. I nibble on my thumb, fighting the nerves that threaten to overload me. Kyla's pacing, looking at a loss, but that's because no one wants to be hydrated right now. Everyone's too tense.

When Ryan catches the pass and runs it into the end zone, I leap from the bench, bouncing up and down, screaming at the top of my lungs. I can hear everyone in the visitor stands behind me yelling and cheering. The cheerleaders are squealing and chanting Ryan's name.

Jordan runs up to Ryan and they high five, then Jordan slaps his hand against the back of Ryan's helmet and pulls him in close, knocking their helmets together. I can tell he's saying something, but what? I wish I knew.

The kicker comes out and they line up to go for that point, and of course they get it. The lead is solid and with what time remains on the clock, the game is essentially over. Our boys won.

I hand out water as the boys pass by and a few of them take the bottles, squirting the water all over their heads after they take the helmets off. They're in good spirits and I congratulate them all, laughing when they say something funny. They've been nice to me, every one of them, and even Ryan comes up to me and tells me, "Good job," before he slaps me on the back and jogs off.

When I see Jordan approach, I busy myself with cleaning up the portable water station, stashing the empty water bottles in their carriers, doing what Kyla tells me to. I feel him drawing closer, but I won't look up. Not yet. My entire body prickles with awareness and I go completely still.

"So, what did you think?"

Glancing up, I meet his gaze. He's a sweaty, dirty mess. He's clutching his helmet in one hand and his hair is standing up on end. The black lines under his eyes are smudged and there's a giant grass stain streaked across his chest from when he got tackled earlier. He'd fallen hard and I'd leapt to my feet when it first happened, my heart racing so fast I thought it would gallop right out of my chest.

"You played great," I tell him, offering him a tiny smile. "Congratulations on the win."

He grabs my hand and pulls me closer, his gaze unwavering. "I played for you." His voice is achingly sincere, and I swallow past the sudden lump in my throat.

"Jordan…"

He cuts off my protest with a kiss. It's soft and sweet and so fast, I almost think it didn't happen, but the satisfied gleam in his eyes tells me it did. "You need to wear my number next time."

"Huh?" I'm in a daze over his lips connecting with mine. We've kissed plenty of times in the past, but it's been a while. And his lips have always had a way of rendering me senseless.

He points to the number eight on his chest. "I can give you an old jersey if you want."

"I'm supposed to wear this." I point at the navy blue polo that Kyla gave me to wear. She has on a matching one.

"I want to see my number on you." The possessive gleam in his eyes sort of turns me on.

"But—" Without warning he tugs me in close, his mouth at my ear, his breath so hot I shiver.

"Stop pretending this isn't happening, Amanda. I'm tired of fighting it." He kisses my ear, the sensitive spot just behind it, and I sag against him.

He's right. I'm tired of fighting it.

I'm ready to give in.

THE BUS RIDE to the game had been loud and chaotic. The cheerleaders were obnoxious, squealing and yelling and shooting lusty glances in the players' directions. Coach Halsey kept trying to give the boys "let's get pumped up" speeches, and they worked. They sounded like roaring beasts ready to unleash and conquer by the time we pulled into the opposing school's parking lot. I even had the fleeting thought that I needed to bring my ear buds next week so I could avoid the noise and listen to music.

The ride home is completely different. It's quiet and dark in the bus. Most everyone is worn out and there's not much talking. I do see a lot of faces illuminated by the glow of their phones.

I sit with Jordan, his legs spread wide in that way boys like to sit, taking up all the space, but with him, I don't mind. His knee is pressed against mine and he has his arm slung over my shoulders casually, his big hand lightly gripping my upper arm. I feel...owned. He's declaring to everyone on this bus that he wants to be with me, and I bask in his attention.

"Yo, Tuttle." It's Ryan.

Jordan leans his head against the wall of the bus for a moment, closing his eyes. "What?" He sounds irritated.

"You having a party at your house?"

Oh. Is he? I can't remember the last time he had one. It's been a few weeks. I turn to watch him, noting how thick his eyelashes are when his eyes are closed. He is too pretty for words. I can't help the little sigh that escapes me.

He cracks his eyes open. "You don't want me to have them over, do you." It's a statement, not a question.

I want him all to myself, but I can't say that out loud. Can I? "Only if you want to."

"No party tonight," he calls out, and they answer him with groans and protests. But he ignores them. He just focuses on me, pulling me in closer so I'm snug against him. His lips press against my forehead and I close my eyes, sitting with him, soaking him up. His scent, his warmth, his strength.

"Are you sure?" I finally ask, my voice soft and only for him.

"I want to be alone with you."

My heart drops, then picks up speed again. We've been alone plenty of times, but usually with other people in the house. Namely Livvy, who I could always text and say, *get me out of here*, and she would rescue me every single time.

I pull away from him so I can look into his eyes. "Are your parents home?"

He makes a face. "When are they ever home?"

Never. I know they're busy and they work a lot, but they're never around for their son. Ever. "I don't know…"

"I'll have you home by your curfew," he murmurs. "Promise. Just say yes."

"Yes," I tell him, and his eyes light up, though he doesn't smile.

He kisses me gently on the lips instead. So gentle, my entire body tingles in anticipation. I know what that mouth can do. I know what his hands can do as well. Not that we've taken it too terribly far, but we've done a few things. I've let him touch me in certain places. But I'd always push him off if we got too carried away, scared he'd use me and leave me.

Like he does to all the other girls.

The rest of the ride home we're quiet, and I get lost in my thoughts. I'm excited and scared for what might happen next. Will he take me to his room? Or will we watch TV? A movie? Maybe hang out outside? The Tuttle backyard is amazing. I don't know what we'll do, but I will soon find out.

Once we arrive on campus, we unload in the school parking lot, Jordan taking my hand the moment we're off the bus.

"I have to drop off my equipment in the locker room before I leave." He glances around the lot. "Where's your car?"

"My dad brought me. My brother had to borrow my car tonight. He's home for the weekend." I'm terrified he'll try and take it back with him to college and then I'll be out of a car for good. I can't afford for that to happen. I need the car to get to my job. I can't rely on the kindness of strangers to always give me a ride.

"Is he going to pick you up?" Jordan frowns.

"No, I texted him and let him know I had a ride." I smile and poke him in the ribs. "That would be you."

He grabs my hand and brings it to his mouth, kissing the back of it. "Stay here. I'll be right back." He leaves before I can say anything else.

I lean against a nearby ledge and check my phone, though I don't have any text messages. There are a few random Snapchats, including one from Livvy that's part of her story. A photo of her kissing Ryan's cheek out on the football field right after the game, it's captioned "my boo," accompanied by a bunch of heart-eyes emojis. It makes me happy to see her acknowledging Ryan and not stressing over Dustin.

"You really think he likes her?"

I lift my head when I hear the question, though I don't see anyone else around.

"Of course not. It's just a phase. Like she's worthy of Tuttle. Have you ever really looked at her? She's so plain and boring."

"They looked pretty cozy on the bus. He had his arm around her. I saw him kiss her too."

"Please. I don't know why he's doing this. Maybe he's slumming it? Oh!" Lauren Mancini and her gang suddenly appear, Brianne Brown one of them. The shocked look on Lauren's face is totally fake. She knew I was close by. She made sure to say all of those mean things on purpose.

And I can't deny hearing them talk about me cut like a knife.

I cross my arms and glare at her, but otherwise don't say a word.

"Oops. Guess you overheard us, huh?" Lauren giggles, and so do the rest of her friends.

I remain quiet. What can I say? They'll tear me apart no matter what. I can't win with this group.

"What, can't bother to defend yourself since deep down inside, you know we're speaking the truth?" Lauren's perfectly arched brows rise. "Whatever you're doing with Jordan Tuttle, it's going to end badly. For you."

She's right. I'm sure she's right. It's why I avoided him in the first place. Why I pushed him away when he tried to take it further. Here I go again, allowing him to get closer, yet I still don't know much about him. He's so secretive. Not much of a talker. I think I want to know more, but do I really?

Why should I bother if all it's going to get me is grief and heartache?

A car pulls up and Livvy leaps out of the passenger side, running toward me with a big smile on her face. She skids to a stop when she spots Lauren and the rest of her gang and the smile fades.

"Am I interrupting something?" she asks.

"Nothing important." Lauren beams. "Gearing up to give Ryan an extra good blowjob for winning tonight, huh? I'm sure that's his favorite way to see you—on your knees." They all start cracking up.

Livvy glares, her eyes lingering on Brianne Brown. Of course. "At least I have a gorgeous boyfriend who wants me to suck his dick, unlike you," she says to Lauren. The sharp gasps that ring through the air make Liv laugh. She takes my hand. "Come on, Amanda. Let's ditch these bitches."

I let Livvy pull me away from Lauren and her mean girls, but I start dragging my feet when she doesn't stop. "I can't leave. I promised Jordan."

"Are you two getting together tonight?" Livvy sucks in a surprised breath. "How exciting! Are you gonna hang out? Go to dinner or something?"

"We're going back to his place," I mumble.

Livvy's face falls. "Oh. Don't tell me you're going to watch a *movie*."

I frown. "Why do you ask?" He hasn't mentioned exactly what we'll be doing, and I hadn't thought to question him.

"It's just that…" Her voice drifts and she clears her throat. "I'm going to be honest with you, Amanda. And I'm not saying this to be mean like Lauren, but I want you to know the truth."

"The truth about what? Come on, Liv. You're scaring me."

"Okay." She takes a deep breath, like she needs to prepare herself. "Whenever Tuttle takes a girl into the theater room at his house, that's basically code for, 'Give me a blowjob now.' That's all he ever wants from girls. Blowjobs. That's it. He's a total BJ whore." Livvy's expression is full of sympathy. "You don't think that's all he wants from you, do you?"

"I don't know. I didn't think so." But what do I know? Look what happened with Thad. I didn't give it up to him quick enough, and he screwed my old best friend instead.

Maybe I'm too much of a prude. Maybe guys give up so easily on me because I don't put out. Maybe that's what I need to do—put out for Jordan Tuttle. Get on my knees and...

I wince. I have no idea how to do something like that. I'd probably make a fool of myself and do something wrong. And then Tuttle wouldn't like me anymore. It would be over. He probably prefers a girl with experience, and I am not that girl.

Dumped because I can't give a blowjob. Or even a hand job. That would be awful. Humiliating.

"Don't do anything you're not ready to do," Livvy says firmly. "I'm serious. Don't let him pressure you."

Turning away from her, I blow out a harsh breath. "What's it like anyway?"

"What's what like?"

I turn back around to face her. "Giving a blowjob. Or a hand job—like, what does it feel like, touching his..."

Livvy looks like she wants to smile, but she's doing her best to keep a straight face. "Touching his—penis?"

"Well, yeah." We both dissolve into giggles. I'm not used to saying the word penis. I'm guessing she's not big on it either.

"I don't know if I can have this conversation right now," Livvy finally says once she's composed herself. "I need to have, like, three drinks in and be at a party. We can't talk about dicks here in front of the school."

"Who's talking about dicks now?" Ryan rushes up behind Livvy and wraps his arms around her, lifting her up off her feet and twirling her around. Livvy squeals and struggles against his hold, but I can tell she's loving every minute.

I guess there goes our dick talk.

"You are," Livvy says in between peals of laughter as he swings her around. "Now put me down!"

He does as she says, but not before he lays one on her. The kiss is long and tongue-filled. I know this because I see actual tongue.

Ew.

I avert my eyes, feeling like an intruder. When Ryan finally breaks the kiss, Livvy is wobbly on her feet and she shoots me a lopsided smile. "Um, we'll have to talk some other time."

"I'm holding you to it," I tell her, pointing a finger in her direction.

She laughs and stumbles into Ryan, who tugs her close. "We'll wait with you until Tuttle comes out," he says to me.

My chest goes warm. How sweet. "Thanks, Ryan."

"No prob." He shrugs. "Tuttle said I couldn't leave you, so..."

So he didn't do it out of the kindness of his heart. Figures. "I'll be all right alone."

"No way." Ryan shakes his head. "If Tuttle knew I left you alone, he'd kill me."

I doubt that, but whatever.

Within minutes Jordan approaches and the four of us chitchat until he takes my hand and asks me, "Are you ready?"

I nod, pressing my lips together. "Yeah."

"We should double date sometime," Livvy says, like she's trying to gauge what Tuttle's intentions are.

"We should," he agrees, though his expression is reluctant. He lets go of my hand, and I immediately miss his touch.

"Us girls will have to plan something soon." She grins at him before pulling me into a tight hug. "Remember what I said," she whispers into my ear. "Don't do anything you don't want to do. If he's a good guy, he won't pressure you."

"Okay. Thanks for the advice," I whisper back. I squeeze her and she squeezes me in return. "Have fun tonight," I say as we pull away from each other.

"Mama's not home until late, so we have the house to ourselves," Liv says with a big grin. "She went to a concert with her gross boyfriend."

"Fitch?" I've met him. He's sort of a creeper.

Liv shudders when I say his name. "Please. Don't ruin my good mood."

We say our goodbyes and I turn to look at Jordan, see the impatience written all over his face.

"Come on." Jordan takes my hand once more and leads me toward his Range Rover. He opens the passenger side door for me and I climb inside, breathing deep the leather scent that lingers once he closes the door. My heart thumps wildly and I rest a hand over my chest, telling myself I need to get a grip.

I'm in control of my destiny. What I say, goes. I know he won't push me to do anything I don't want to do.

But what if I get caught up in the moment and want to do... everything?

Guess I'll figure it out as we go.

chapter thirteen

We walk inside the quiet, dark house and the second the door is shut, Jordan gathers me in his arms and pushes me up against the wall just before he kisses me. I open my mouth in shocked surprise and his tongue is there, sweeping inside my mouth, circling my tongue, making me gasp. I clutch at him, my arms going around his neck, my hands sliding into his thick, soft hair.

He presses into me and I can feel his hard, hot body. When we've kissed before, it's always been different. Lighter. More explorative. This is nothing like that. It's urgent and edgy and full of passion. I break away from the kiss first so I can catch my breath, and he dives for my neck, his damp mouth blazing a trail of hot kisses along my throat.

"I've been dying to kiss you like that for hours," he murmurs against my skin. "Days. Weeks."

I squirm from the sensation of his breath on my skin. "You're tickling me."

"Mmm, not the reaction I had in mind." He cups my face and tilts my head back so our gazes meet. "I liked having you on the sidelines."

I smile tremulously, my nerves coming at me full force.

"Why were you talking to Whittaker?"

It takes me a moment to figure out who he's talking about. "You mean Cannon? I was taping his knuckles."

"Hopefully that's all you were doing." His eyes narrow and I swear his nostrils just flared.

"Wait a minute." I think about tugging out of his grip, but it's nice having his hands cup my cheeks like this. The way he absently rubs my skin with his thumbs feels amazing. "Are you—*jealous* of Cannon Whittaker? Because he talked to me?"

He says nothing. Just keeps watching me with those narrowed eyes and the still flaring nostrils, his breathing a little heavier than normal.

"Jordan." I stare into his eyes. He needs to know I'm serious. I may be setting myself up for a torturous heartbreak, but he needs to know how I feel. "I don't notice anyone else. Just you."

The faintest smile curls his lips and he kisses me. This time it's softer, a little more controlled, and I fall into the kiss, twirling my tongue around his, savoring the taste of him, the feel of his hands cradling my face.

"I need to take a shower," he says once he breaks away from my lips. He presses his forehead against mine. "Wanna join me?"

I freeze. My body screams *yes!* But my mind says *absolutely not.* The struggle is real. "Um..."

"I was kidding." He kisses the tip of my nose. "But you should come upstairs and wait in my room for me."

So I do. It's sort of weird and awkward sitting on his bed and looking around his room, because I've never waited for a boy while he takes a shower—in that huge, gorgeous bathroom, I might add. All I can think about as I hear the water running is of Jordan. Naked. With hot, steamy water pouring down his body, making his skin all slick and shiny. I'd help him soap up. I'd wash his hair. I'd rinse him off. I'd grab his…

The water shuts off, and I leap to my feet and wander aimlessly around the gigantic room. I stop at his dresser and study the few photos that are on display. One is of him and other football players, I'm guessing from last year? They're all smiling except for Tuttle. His expression is serious.

Always so serious.

The other photo is old. I think it might be him as a little boy with his parents, and maybe that's his sister? He looks like he's barely two, dressed in a miniature suit that matches the man's. The girl I assume is his sister is your typical sullen teenager forced to pose. The parents look stern-faced and solemn. No one looks happy.

It makes me sad.

The door opens and I whirl around like I just got caught stealing his underwear. He stands in the open doorway, steam billowing out of the bathroom, his hair wet and slicked back from his face, and clad in only a towel.

Only. A. Towel.

I clutch the edge of the dresser, praying I don't go down in a heap of melted bones. The towel is white and thick and hangs dangerously low on his hips. One wrong move and that sucker will fall right off.

"Snooping?" He magically produces another towel out of thin air and dries his hair with it, his biceps bulging. He has really nice arms.

He has really nice everything.

"No." *Sort of.* "Just looking at the photos on your dresser."

His expression turns grim and he drops the towel he held in his hands on the floor before he makes his approach. "Which one?"

"Both of them." I point. Hold my breath when he comes to stand directly beside me. He is naked. *Naked* under that towel. And he smells amazing. All clean and fresh and delicious.

"That's my parents." He picks up the photo of the stone-faced family. I wonder why he'd keep such a depressing photo of them in his room, but maybe he doesn't even notice it anymore. "And my sister."

"I figured."

"I was two. Already a non-believer in the fairytale." He sets the photo back down and then opens one of the drawers, pulling out a pair of neatly folded gray boxer briefs. "Do you mind?"

"Do I mind what?" I back away from him slowly.

"If I get dressed?" He waves the underwear in my direction and I want to die. "Turn around if you can't handle it. I'm about to drop the towel."

"Jordan!" I spin away from him just as I hear the towel hit the floor with a wet plop. I keep my back to him. Hear the rustling of clothing being pulled on, the sound of another drawer being opened and closed. My mind is running in circles, imagining all the things I'm missing because of my prudish ways.

"It's safe to look now," he drawls, and I turn around slowly, relief and disappointment hitting me when I see he's clothed.

But not *fully* clothed. He's wearing a pair of black sweatpants and that's it. They're slightly fitted, and they cling to his thighs, ride perilously low on his hips. I swear his chest is still damp and his stomach is utterly lickable and…

Oh my God, my thoughts are all over the place.

"What time do you have to be home?" he asks, his extra low voice knocking me out of my thoughts.

"Midnight."

He glances at the clock on the bedside table. "Little less than two hours then."

"And it takes at least fifteen, twenty minutes to get to my house from yours," I remind him.

"So we have about ninety minutes."

I nod. Wondering what he's going to suggest we do.

"You should take off your sweater." My shocked gaze meets his. "Aren't you hot?"

It *is* a little warm in here. I shrug out of my oversized cardigan and leave it on top of his dresser. "Do you want to watch a movie or something?"

I cringe the moment the words leave my mouth. I didn't mean to sound like every other girl he's been with. Or maybe he's the one who suggests they watch a movie. I don't know how this works. I feel so... stupid.

Inept.

"I'd rather just get into bed with you and hang out." I must look totally freaked out, so he feels the need to clarify. "I just want to relax, Amanda. I'm beat after tonight's game. Figured we could talk or whatever."

It's the *or whatever* that has me curious. But at least he didn't suggest the theater room. "That's fine," I say with a shrug, like I'm cool. Like I've done this a million times.

"Mandy." His voice is soft, barely above a whisper. "We've done this before. A few times. Remember?"

He's right. We really have done this sort of thing before. It's just that tonight, it feels like there are all of these expectations riding on me. Though I'm just putting unnecessary pressure on myself, which is dumb.

I watch as he goes to his bed and pulls the comforter and sheets back, then plumps up the pillows. We may have cuddled together on a bed before, but never under the covers. That somehow feels more intimate.

"Come here." He pats the empty spot, then looks up at me.

I go to him, take his offered hand, and let him pull me down so I'm sitting in his lap. "You look scared," he whispers, tucking a lock of hair behind my ear, his fingers lingering on my skin.

"This feels different with you tonight." I rest my head in that spot between his neck and shoulder. I breathe in his scent and close my eyes, savoring the quiet, the stillness, his steady breathing the only sound.

"I don't want you scared of me."

"I was more scared you'd suggest we go watch a movie in that fancy theater of yours," I admit, feeling bolder now that I'm not looking directly in his eyes.

He sighs. "The number of blowjobs I've received in that theater room is vastly exaggerated."

I sit straight up, startled he'd even mention it. "But it *is* true. That you get—serviced in the theater room?"

Jordan looks away, and has the decency to appear faintly embarrassed. "I can't lie and say I've been a saint, Mandy. I've done stuff with a few girls. But not as many as the rumors say I have. My actual number is surprisingly low."

He wouldn't lie to me, would he? Or is he trying to save my delicate feelings? "I really don't want to talk actual numbers."

"We don't have to. None of those other girls matter anyway." He gathers me in his arms and stands, making me squeal and cling to him.

Gently he sets me down on the bed, then climbs in beside me, pulling the sheet and comforter up so we're facing each other, covered to our chins.

I start to giggle. I can't help it. He looks so cute with the covers pulled up, his hair still damp, his eyes sleepy and that tiny smile curving his lips.

"What's so funny?"

"You." I slap my hand over my mouth to contain the giggles. I'm tired too. "You look cute."

"Cute?" He yawns, quickly covers his mouth. "Really?"

"Really." I reach for his wrist and slowly move his hand away from his face. "You're adorable."

Jordan grimaces. "You make me sound like a baby."

"You are definitely not a baby." I shift closer, my hand skimming his stomach before I wrap my arm around his waist. "You have too many muscles."

He pulls me in until our legs are tangled and my head is resting on his chest. "You're wearing too much clothing," he murmurs against my hair.

I go still. "What do you want me to do? Strip?"

Next thing I know I'm flat on my back and he's hovering above me, his hand at the front of my jeans, his fingers toying with the button. "I could take these off for you."

"I don't know…" Nerves make my stomach clench and I tell myself he'll only take it as far as I'll let him. And it isn't very comfortable, lying in bed with him wearing my jeans.

"Only if you want," he whispers against my lips just before he kisses me. "I don't want to make you nervous."

He touches my stomach, brushes his knuckles across my skin,

and I suck in a soft breath, closing my eyes. It feels so good. His hand pauses over the front of my jeans again and I open my eyes to find him watching me carefully. I give a little nod, my silent permission for him to continue, and he undoes the snap. Slowly pulls down the zipper, his fingers spreading open the denim and exposing my panties.

"I want to see you," he whispers, and I close my eyes again, turning my head so I can bury my face into the pillow. "Come on, Mandy. Don't be shy."

I shift so I'm facing him once more and thrust out my arm, pushing the covers off the both of us. He immediately looks down, his gaze locked on my spread open jeans and the front of my gray-and-burgundy striped panties. He almost reverently traces the waistband of my underwear, his fingers barely touching my skin, and I hold my breath, waiting for his fingers to dive beneath the thin fabric.

But he doesn't do that. Instead he grabs hold of my jeans and starts to tug them down, pulling them to about mid-thigh before I take over and shimmy them down my legs, kicking them off and onto the floor. He shoves the covers back even farther, until they're bunched behind me and we're both completely exposed.

"You have the longest legs." He caresses the outside of my thigh.

"I hated them when I was twelve. I looked ridiculous." I was taller than most of the boys in seventh grade, even Tuttle, until about midway through. He shot up, way past me, but his height did me no favors. I was still one of the tallest people in class, and my long legs just made me look gawky and weird.

"You were cute." He smiles. "Adorable."

"Stop." I shove at his bare chest, letting my fingers explore all of that exposed skin. His shoulders and pecs, the spot in between them where the faintest bit of dark hair grows. His ridged stomach and the mysterious trail of dark hair that leads from the bottom of his navel and into his sweatpants. I still want to follow that trail with my tongue.

I don't know if I'll ever have the nerve to do it.

"You should take off your pants," I suggest, and he shakes his head, the smirk on his face warning me he's going to say something wicked.

"Take off your shirt and then I'll take off my pants," he murmurs.

Before I lose my nerve I sit up and whip off my shirt, then grab the covers and pull them over me. My least favorite body part is my boobs. I'm flat chested. I mostly wear a padded B cup when really I'm more of an A cup, though tonight's bra choice is new and chosen just for Jordan. Unfortunately, I just…never got boobs. My mom isn't gifted in the chest department either, so I was doomed.

And boys like Tuttle like boobs. The bigger the better. He may approve of my long legs, but he'll be disappointed in my chest.

"Why you gotta go and cover yourself up?" He reaches for the comforter but I clutch it tighter, keeping it close. "Let me see."

I shake my head. "No way."

"You're being ridiculous."

"I don't want to see the disappointment on your face." When he frowns, I explain, "My boobs are really, really small."

"I don't care, Amanda. I don't like you for your boobs." He grins, and the sight of that smile steals my breath. All my brain cells too. "I like you for your legs."

I nudge his shin with my foot. "Jerk."

"Come on." His smile fades and his expression turns sincere. "Let me look at you."

"Fine." I let him tug the comforter away from me and I close my eyes. I can feel his gaze on me, drinking me in, and he's so quiet for so long I start to freak out. "Is it so bad that you'll never be able to speak again?"

He chuckles. And when he touches my chest, his fingers tracing the edge of my burgundy lace bra, I nearly jump out of my skin. "You're beautiful."

The words I've longed to hear. I open my eyes and then he's there, kissing me, devouring me. His hands are on my breasts, his thumbs brushing back and forth across the lace and driving me crazy. I pull him in closer and pour all of my feelings for him into that one kiss. I need him to know how much I like him. How much I've been holding back.

"Your skin is so soft." His fingers fumble over the front clasp of my sheer lace bra—well, they call it a bralette because there's nothing to it—and then it springs open. He pulls away so he can look down at my chest, carefully pushing away the thin lace so he can really see me.

I sling my arm over my eyes so I can't see his reaction.

"So pretty," he murmurs as he touches me. "God, Amanda, I've dreamed of this."

"You have?" I drop my arm away from my eyes so I can look at him.

He nods, but he's too busy concentrating on my chest. "Endless dreams. Always like this. With us in my bed and you letting me touch you."

"I…" I hesitate. Decide to go for it. "I want to touch you too."

He pulls away from me and kicks off his sweatpants, until he's almost as naked as I am. I'm only in my panties. He's just in his boxer briefs. I can feel him straining against the front and it seems…big. Extra large.

I don't think I can deal with that tonight.

And then we're kissing. It's so much easier when we're kissing.

When we're so wrapped up in each other, it feels natural to touch and explore and test barriers. He seems to have none, but I have a few. I'm scared and excited and want more, yet I don't.

It's confusing, the rush of emotions that fill me.

I end the kiss and my lips travel the length of his neck, nibbling on his skin and making him actually growl. I touch his stomach, tease the waistband of his boxer briefs, briefly skim my fingers along the front of them, and I feel his full body shudder to the very depths of my soul.

He doesn't push. He doesn't say a word. Just lets me touch him and he touches me, and when he kisses my neck, my collarbone, then moves his way down to my chest, I throw my head back against the pillow, moaning so loudly I put my hand over my mouth.

We keep this up for a while. Until I'm lost in his touch and his lips. Until I'm anxious and needy and straining toward something I can't quite find. Jordan slips his knee between my legs and I press closer, a sharp inhale leaving me when he bumps a particular spot.

I want more of that.

It's like he knows and he keeps pressing his knee against me, his mouth fused with mine. The kiss turns sloppy and unpracticed and out of control and I love it. He's losing control with me. And I can't help the thrill that comes with the realization. I grind against his knee, not caring what he thinks or how I might look or what I might say. I lose all of my insecurities at that very moment when his touch, his mouth, his freaking knee sends me flying right off that ledge.

And straight into bliss.

chapter fourteen

"Amanda. Are you even listening to me?"

I glance up to find Mom watching me with a concerned expression on her face. "You were talking to me?" I ask weakly. My thoughts are filled with Jordan and what we did last night. That one particular moment was a first for me, and it had been perfect. Thad definitely never made me feel like that either.

I'm glad it happened with Jordan Tuttle.

Jordan drove me home and thoroughly kissed me in the Range Rover before he said good night. I stumbled up the walkway and barged into the house, thankful my parents weren't up to see me.

My little brother Trent snickers before shoving an overflowing spoonful of Lucky Charms into his mouth. "She's been talking to you for the past five minutes, dingus."

"Don't call your sister a dingus," Mom says irritably as Trent cracks himself up. He's twelve and a complete nuisance.

"What did you say?" I ask, ignoring Trent, who's still muttering the word *dingus* under his breath.

"I wanted to make sure you're going to take the SAT next Saturday." She catches my eye roll and scowls. "You should. It wouldn't hurt to try and up your score."

"My score is a 1300." They changed the scoring of the SATs this past year and a 1300 is solid.

"Yes, but you could do better. You need as much advantage as you can get, since you dropped out of band."

The disappointment still rings in her voice. My parents are never going to let that go.

"I'm on the yearbook staff." Though all I do is help with page layout so far, which is fun. It'll look good on college applications. Oh, and now I can add water girl too, which shows I'm responsible. Right?

I hope so.

"And that's great, it really is," Mom says as she sits across from me. "But is it enough?"

"I'm out." Trent grabs his bowl and leaves it in the sink before he exits the kitchen.

"That boy," Mom mutters under her breath, shaking her head, her gaze shrewd when it lands on me. "So. Where were you last night?"

Her quick change of subject has me floundering. "Uh, at the football game?"

"The game doesn't last until midnight, Amanda. What did you do *after* the game?"

Got naked with Jordan Tuttle?

I can't tell her that. Can you imagine?

"I hung out with Livvy." Sort of the truth. Not really.

"Oh, that's nice." Mom pauses. "What's going on with Tara? You're never together anymore. I miss having her around the house."

Mom has no idea that Thad and Tara cheated on me with each other. I never told her. I couldn't. I was too humiliated. I just said I broke up with Thad and had a falling out with Tara. She never put two and two together.

"That friendship is over and done with," I say firmly.

She sighs and shakes her head. "After all those years and all that history between the two of you. Please don't tell me it was all over a boy, Amanda. I've often wondered if it was because of Thad."

"Actually Mom, it *was* because of Thad. I caught them together. *Together* together," I emphasize.

She frowns. "Kissing?"

"Worse." I decide to go for it. "They were naked together. As in, having sex."

"What?" Her mouth drops open. "And you caught them like that? Where?" She sounds positively scandalized.

"At—at Jordan Tuttle's house." Any excuse to mention him, huh? "He goes to my school."

"They were having sex at another student's house? Who is this Jordan Tuttle?"

Hopefully he's my boyfriend. I know for sure he's the boy who took my bra off last night. The boy I was wrapped around like a pretzel only a few hours ago. The boy who is slowly but surely stealing my heart and making it his.

"He's a good guy, Mom. I promise. He's, like, the most popular boy in school," I tell her.

"And they're usually the ones who cause the most trouble, especially if other kids are having *sex* at his house. Where are his parents anyway?" She sounds absolutely disgusted.

I have opened the most giant can of worms in the universe. Mom and Dad are pretty strict. They are firm believers in no sex before marriage and they would flip out if they knew I went to parties and drank on occasion.

The thing is, I never went to parties and definitely didn't drink ever the first three years of my high school life. Tara and I were pretty much scared of everything. We weren't part of the popular kids' social circle, so I don't know exactly how this happened but...

I've done a one-eighty compared to last year's version of Amanda Winters. A different set of friends, a different extracurricular activity, and I sort of have a boyfriend. My parents would hardly believe it.

And if they knew I was with Jordan last night all by myself, pretty much naked in his bed with his hands all over me? Forget it. I'd be grounded for life.

"I'll take the SAT again next Saturday," I tell her, desperate to change the subject. "Maybe I can up my score."

"Oh, I think that's a really smart idea." The relief on her face is evident. "Your father feels the same way. We know you can do it, honey."

"Thanks." The overachiever in me knows I should study all week and prepare. But that sounds so boring. I'd rather spend my time with Jordan, if he wants to spend time with me. I work this afternoon from noon to six but don't work Sunday. Maybe we could get together then...

"I have something else I want to talk to you about," Mom says.

Oh. She sounds serious. "What's up?"

"Your brother needs to take your car back to school with him." She holds up a hand when I open my mouth, ready to protest. "I know you need that car to get to work, but he needs it more to get to his new job, sweetheart. I hope you understand."

I don't. Yeah, I so don't. "How am I supposed to get to *my* job? The job you made me get in the first place?"

"We did not make you get that job."

"You so did! You told me I didn't have a choice. That you didn't have enough money to pay for my college education so I better start saving my money." I stand, my blood boiling. "Now I'm going to have to quit!"

"You will not quit," she says, calming studying me. "We'll figure out a way to get you there. You can ask your friends. I'm sure they'll help you."

"Not like I have a ton of friends to ask, Mom."

Ugh. My older brother is the biggest pain in the ass ever. He always gets what he wants, no matter what. Our parents always give in.

"Tell George thanks a lot for ruining my life," I toss out as I stalk out of the kitchen.

"Quit being so dramatic," Mom yells after me, but I ignore her.

Instead I go to my room and slam the door, falling onto the bed with a huff. It's barely nine o'clock. I could go back to bed and sleep until eleven. Then take a shower, get ready and go to Yo Town—

I frown. If I even have a car to drive to Yo Town. I'm sure George is already gone, headed back to college with the car, firmly believing it was always his so he deserves it.

Whatever.

My phone dings from my bedside table and I grab it, melting when I see who the text is from.

Jordan.

I can't stop thinking about you.

My smile can't be contained as I read his text over and over. How should I respond? I need to say something cute. Something flirty. But my mind is drawing a total blank.

I can't stop thinking about you either.

Not incredibly original, but it's true.

He immediately starts to text me back. I see the gray bubble and wait, sliding under the covers and rolling on my side, my gaze never leaving my phone screen as I wait for his response.

You work today?

Nibbling on my lip, I answer.

From noon to six.

What are you doing after?

Hanging out with you? ☺

He doesn't respond right away and I wonder if I screwed up. Ugh. I'm still not confident with this dating thing, especially the dating Jordan thing.

A few minutes later he finally responds.

Want to go out to dinner?

I am giddy with excitement. It's like a real date. I have to contain myself not to answer with a thousand exclamation points. I go for calm and collected instead.

That sounds good.

My phone buzzes with a text from Livvy as I wait for Jordan's response.

Tell me you were with Tuttle last night after the game.

I smile.

I was with Tuttle last night after the game.

Yay!!!!!!! OMG!!!! What happened?????? I want deets!!!!

There's nothing much to tell.

Meaning there is no way I'm telling her what happened between us last night. Forget that.

You're being a tease. Are you two getting together tonight too?

I think so.

Let's double date! I bet Ryan would be up for it. I can ask him.

I don't know...

We're doing it. Let's go to dinner together or something. It'll be fun!

Huh. Will he think it's fun, to hang out with Liv and Ryan tonight instead of just the two of us? I don't know.

I need to ask him first.

I already asked Ryan and he's totally up for it.

Man, she's fast.

Chewing on my lower lip, I go to text Jordan.

Want to go to dinner with Ryan and Livvy?

No. I'd rather be alone with you.

We can't always be alone, Jordan.

Why not? That's the way I like you. R&L will be a distraction.

I want to be alone with you.

I'm seriously blushing right now, and no one's around to see it, so this is stupid.

What if I got hungry?

I'd always feed you.

Thirsty?

I'd bring you whatever you want to drink.

You're being silly.

The phone rings, startling me. It's Jordan.

"Why are you calling?"

"I needed to hear your voice."

Everything inside of me goes warm at his admission. "You really don't want to go out with Ryan and Livvy tonight, huh."

He sighs, the sound rough and slightly disappointed. "Can't we do that next weekend?"

"Come on, Jordan. What's the big deal?"

He's quiet for a moment and I worry I might've made him mad. My phone is dinging in my ear with new text alerts and I know they're all from Livvy, but I can't answer her.

"I'd rather go out with them another time," he says quietly "I just—I want to get to know you better, Amanda. I want to spend time with just you and no one else."

"Okay." My heart is turning to mush. How can I make him go on a double date when all he wants is to spend time with me?

I can't.

"What time are you done with work again?"

"Not until six." Realization dawns. "I don't even have a ride to work."

"I'll take you."

"What? No, you don't have to do that." Panic makes my heart race.

"I want to. I'll pick you up at your house."

"Jordan…"

"What?"

"My parents don't know we're—seeing each other."

"Okay."

"So they'll be here."

"Do you not want me to meet them?"

I don't know how I feel about that. Mom freaked out when I mentioned Jordan and the party and all that craziness. Then he's the boy who comes to pick me up to take me to work? Talk about awkward.

"They sort of freak out when I date guys." That's not too far from the truth. They weren't thrilled when I started dating Thad. But I'm seventeen—I can't live like a nun my entire life.

"I'll probably scare the hell out of them," he says with a warm chuckle.

"You probably would," I agree.

"How about I just pick you up? You can call me a friend," he suggests.

"You are my friend."

"Really?" His voice deepens. "Is that all you think of me?"

"Oh, you're definitely more than a friend," I tease.

I hope he feels the same way.

chapter fifteen

"Whose car is that sitting out in front of our house?" Mom asks as she ducks and peers through the living room window.

I glance outside. Jordan's black Range Rover is sitting there, idling by the curb. Within seconds of spotting him, my phone buzzes with a text.

I'm here. You ready?

"It's my friend. He's giving me a ride to work," I say nervously as I type out my reply.

Give me a minute. I'll meet you out there.

Mom, of course, picks up on my nerves. She studies me carefully, so carefully she freaks me out and I drop my phone on the hardwood floor with a loud clatter. "A *male* friend?"

I nod, scooping up my phone and checking it for damage.

Thankfully, there isn't any. "He's in a few of my classes. We're working on a project together. For English. It's focused on great literary couples."

Hitting her with boring stuff proves to be the distraction she needs. "English, hmmm? That's nice, dear. His car looks very expensive."

"I guess it is?" I know it is, but playing dumb sometimes works too.

"Very nice of him to drive you to work. I knew you could round some friends to help you." And with that, she drifts out of the living room and heads to the kitchen. I nearly sag with relief.

But I don't have time to sag or be relieved. Or be annoyed she basically said, "I told you so," without saying those words at all. I can't worry about that. Instead, I gotta go to work.

Grabbing the backpack I use for overnight stays—I packed clothes to change into after work—I sling it over my shoulder, calling out a, "Bye Mom, see you later!" before I slam the front door and dart down the walkway toward Jordan's car.

"Where do you think you're going, young lady?"

I skid to a stop and turn to see my dad approaching. He's dressed in ratty, faded black cargo pants and a white T-shirt that's seen better days. He's been working in the yard all morning and he's filthy. But he loves it. He's why our yard looks so good.

"Um, work?"

"He's taking you?" Dad flicks his chin at the Range Rover.

I nod and smile at him. "Yeah. He's just a friend." I hate that I'm downplaying what Jordan means to me, but I can't make a big deal about him. Not right now. Mom would start questioning me and it would end up being a huge mess.

"Some friend. Must be loaded."

"I guess so." Okay, this conversation is awkward. Why are my parents so focused on his car?

"What's his name?"

I sigh. "Do you want to meet him, Dad?"

He grins. "Yes, Amanda. I'd love to."

Trying my best to shoot meaningful looks in Jordan's direction, I lead my dad to the driver's side of the car. I thought Jordan would roll down the window to talk to us, but instead he opens his door and hops out, his expression earnest, maybe even a little nervous.

It's so…cute.

I smile at him and turn to look at my dad. "Dad, this is Jordan Tuttle. Jordan, this is my dad, Rick.

"Hello, Mr. Winters." Jordan holds out his hand and Dad shakes it. "Great to meet you."

"Nice to meet you too, son. Your family is a part of Tuttle International?"

Jordan's jaw goes tight and his eyes turn cold. "Yes," he bites out.

But Dad doesn't even notice. "How exactly do you know my daughter?"

"Uh." Jordan sticks his hands in the front pockets of his jeans, clearly uncomfortable. "We've gone to school together since kindergarten."

"Really?" Dad sounds surprised. "She's never mentioned you before."

This is true. There's no point in talking about Jordan Tuttle to my parents, when I never had a chance with him. Now, though, there's a chance. And I guess I should've been talking about him.

"Jordan's always been in my honors classes, Dad," I interject. "He's also our varsity team's quarterback."

Dad's eyebrows rise. "Impressive. I've heard about you."

"Hope it was all good," Jordan jokes. And he never jokes.

My dad says nothing. I decide to speak up and end this conversation.

I turn to face Jordan.

"We gotta get going. I need to be at work in less than fifteen minutes."

"Then let's go," Jordan murmurs, his eyes never leaving mine.

"So," my dad says, and I wince, waiting for the bomb to drop. I can tell just by the way he's taking. "Are you two dating, or what?"

Oh, God. I just want to evaporate into thin air at Dad's question. He's so nosy. But then Jordan says the craziest thing.

"We are, sir." He flashes me a sweet smile.

"Why haven't we met you until now?" Dad's demeanor changes in an instant. He's standing up straighter, his gaze questioning as he checks Jordan out like he's some sort of criminal.

"We've only just started dating." Jordan's gaze locks with mine, his mouth curved in this intimate smile that makes me tingle. "But I really like her. A lot."

"Good," Dad says gruffly, nodding. "Treat her with respect and we shouldn't have a problem. Am I making myself clear?"

"Dad." I'm whining, but I don't care. This conversation has made a mortifying turn. "I gotta go or I'll be late." I shift closer to my father and kiss him on the cheek. "I'll see you later tonight, okay?"

"Have a good afternoon, Amanda." He smiles but then turns his icy gaze on Tuttle. "Nice meeting you, Jordan."

"Nice meeting you, too, Mr. Winters. Bye."

I walk over to the passenger side of the Range Rover and Jordan keeps pace, opening the car door for me. I climb inside and he shuts the door, rounds the front of the car and then he's sitting behind the steering wheel, starting the car and smiling at me like we're in on a private joke together.

"What's so funny?" I mutter. That conversation had been all sorts of awkward.

"Your dad seems—nice."

"He can be very nice." I pause. "But also very protective."

Jordan pulls onto the road. "I can tell. I'd be protective of you if you were my daughter too, I guess. Wouldn't want some sleazebag kid who drives a Range Rover and plays football trying to feel up my daughter."

"Jordan." He described my father to perfection. I'm sure that's exactly what Dad's thinking. "When you put it like that…"

"Yeah, I know. I sound like an asshole." He glances over at me. "But it's probably the truth, right? That's what your dad's thinking?"

I nod. "Maybe?"

"I've never met a girl's dad before," he says conversationally, though I notice how he's gripping the steering wheel extra tight. Did that encounter make him nervous?

"You haven't?"

He shakes his head. "Always figured it was pointless. Would put too many ideas in a girl's head."

"What sort of ideas?"

"That I was serious about her." He won't look in my direction and I wonder why.

"Are you saying that you're—serious about me?" My heart starts pounding and I swear my palms are sweating. Why does that question and his answer freak me out so much?

He gives me a trademark Tuttle smirk. "What do you think?"

That is not a real answer. I'm about to question him further, but I decide against it and clamp my mouth shut.

Maybe I don't want to know the answer to that particular question.

Maybe it's best I leave well enough alone.

We get to Yo Town less than ten minutes later and I'm about to hop out of the car when Jordan grabs my hand and stops me from leaving. "What?" I ask when I see the expectant look on his face.

"You want me to pick you up at six, right?" He slowly slides his palm against mine, interlocking our fingers, his thumb rubbing my hand. A jolt of electricity shoots up my arm at the intimate touch.

"Please. If you don't mind." I smile at him, but he acts like he's not going to let me go any time soon. "I need to get inside, Jordan. I'm going to be late."

He tugs on my hand and pulls me closer. Then he kisses me, a soft yet lingering kiss, the both of us leaning over the center console. It's sweet and romantic, and I tell myself I shouldn't read too much into it.

But I do. I can't help it.

"I definitely don't mind," he murmurs against my lips. "See ya later."

He gives me one last kiss and I almost fall out of the Range Rover when I climb out of it seconds later, I'm so dazzled by his talented lips. I practically float into Yo Town, like a girl with a major crush on the hottest boy in school.

That description isn't too far off the mark.

chapter sixteen

"**M**y parents want you to come over for dinner," I tell Jordan over the phone, then mentally brace myself in anticipation of his answer. I tried to talk them out of it, but when I walked through the door last night at exactly 11:59 p.m., I found my parents sitting in the living room waiting up for me.

"Were you with that boy?" Mom asked. "The one with the Range Rover?"

"His name is Jordan Tuttle, sweetheart," Dad told her.

"Oh." Mom's face fell and I knew she remembered what I told her. "That boy who has the sex parties?"

And that comment blows up the entire conversation—to the point where I felt like I was being questioned by the cops.

"Are you two serious?"

"Are you boyfriend and girlfriend?"

"How long has this been going on?"

"Have you met his parents?"

"Been to his house?"

"Why didn't you tell us about him before?"

"Are you in love with him?"

"Is he in love with you?"

"He is worth a lot of money, Amanda. More money than we could ever make in our lives."

They hit me with one question after another, until I wanted to run screaming from the house. Then Mom said I had to invite him over for dinner. "So. We can get to know him better."

Uh huh. They wanted to drill him like they drilled me last night.

"When?" he finally asks, knocking me from my thoughts.

"Um, tonight?" My voice squeaks and I clear my throat, hoping he doesn't catch on to my nervousness.

"You sound worried."

So much for that.

"I'm not worried," I reassure him. "It's just that…I'm pretty sure you're not going to say yes."

"What makes you think so?"

"You just told me you didn't like to meet parents because it gives the girls false hope," I remind him.

"Well, I happen to like you, Amanda. There's a difference." He hesitates before he adds, "A big difference."

He says a few choice words and I want to melt into a puddle. "Will you come over for dinner, then?"

"Do you want me to?"

I sigh. "We should get this over with if you want to continue dating me."

"Is that what you're calling it? What we're doing?"

"Dating?" Did I use the wrong word? Are we just an endless string of hook ups to him? I hope not. God, I really, really hope not, because I feel like a fool if that's the case. A total and complete fool—

"Yeah." His voice deepens. "We are."

"Is that okay?" I ask carefully.

"What do you think?"

"I asked first."

"Well, when it comes to answering, I'm going with ladies first." I can hear the amusement in his tone and it makes me laugh.

"Whatever." I hesitate. "Let's say it together. At the same time."

"What exactly are we saying?"

"You can say we're dating, we're hooking up or..." My mind searches for another word for what we're doing. "Or we're boyfriend and girlfriend."

"So serious," he murmurs.

"Stop. Okay." I exhale loudly. "On the count of three."

"I never said I was down for this."

"Come on, Jordan," I plead, laying it on thick. "Just go along with me. Please?"

"Let's do it." He pauses. "One."

My stomach twists and I take a deep breath.

"Two."

What am I going to say? What should I say?

"Three," Jordan says, pauses, then blurts out, "Girlfriend."

Right when I blurt out, "Dating."

We both go silent.

"Did you just call me your girlfriend?" I'm incredulous.

"Did you just say we're only dating?"

"Well..." My voice drifts. "I didn't want to push."

We're quiet for a moment before he finally speaks again.

"Are you scared of me, Mandy?"

"It's too early in the morning to have this serious of a conversation," I tell him, trying to make a joke out of it. Even though it really is too early to have a serious conversation. It's barely ten on a Sunday.

"Are you?"

I sigh. "No." *Ha.* "Maybe." *Be honest.* "Okay, yes. Just a little, though."

It's his turn to sigh. "I don't want to scare you."

"You don't. Not really."

"I'm coming for dinner tonight," he says firmly, like he just made up his mind right then. "What time should I be there?"

"Oh, uh, we usually eat Sunday dinner around six."

"Do I need to bring anything? Dress a certain way?"

"Just bring yourself. And dress how you usually dress to—school."

"You want me to wear sweats and an old hoodie?" Now he's the one who's teasing.

"You don't always dress like that."

"When it gets colder in the mornings I do."

"Dress nice," I tell him. "But not too nice."

"I can probably manage that."

"You should probably come around five-thirty."

"This is an event, huh."

"It's a nice way for us to be together and talk about stuff. Otherwise, we rarely all sit down to eat dinner together."

"I hope they don't hate me," he says, sounding the tiniest bit nervous.

I hope they don't either."

I'M TRYING TO decide between a dress or a sweater and jeans combo when my little brother knocks on my door.

"Your boyfriend is here," Trent sing-songs.

My stomach plummets and I check my phone. It's not even five-thirty. He's early.

"Aren't you gonna come kiss him hello?" Trent asks when I don't answer.

"Go away!" I shout at the door like I'm twelve. Screw the dress. I don't have time to primp. Instead I slip on my favorite jeans, the ones that make my butt look curvy, and then I pull on my new sweater. It's cream-colored, made out of a thin material, and it splits in the back, exposing my lower back.

Hmmm. I should probably wear a tank with it. Mom will probably throw a fit. Ask me to change.

After putting on a white tank, I go to the full length mirror hanging on the back of my closet door and check myself out. I look good. I'm having a good hair day and I'm wearing a good bra. I look almost as good as Miss Perfect, AKA Lauren Mancini.

Seriously, I need to stop comparing myself to Lauren Mancini.

"Amanda! Your guest is here!"

Ugh, my mom could shout down the rooftop, she yells so loud. "Coming!" I yell back, tucking my hair behind my ears. Yeah, that doesn't look good, so I untuck it, spritz on some body spray and then calmly walk out to greet Jordan.

I stop in my tracks when I spot him in the living room. He's talking with my dad as they stand in front of the TV, most likely about football.

Jordan's wearing dark rinse jeans, a blue plaid shirt and black Vans, and ohmigod, he looks adorable. Like, I want to run and tackle him adorable, but I'm guessing my parents won't appreciate that.

So I calm myself, take a deep breath and make my presence known. "Jordan, hi."

He turns his appreciative gaze on me, and those beautiful eyes somehow warm even more when he takes me in. "Hey. Amanda. You look…pretty." I wonder if he's almost afraid to give me a compliment in front of my dad.

"Thanks. You look good too." I go toward him and give him a hug, feel his lips briefly press against my forehead. He wraps his arms around my waist and his hand presses flat against my bare lower back. I wonder if that surprised him. "I'm glad you made it," I murmur against his chest before I pull away.

Dad clears his throat and I glance his way, not missing the amused look on his face. "Glad you could join us, Amanda."

I make a face at him and look around the room. "Where's Mom?"

"In the kitchen finding a vase for the flowers Jordan brought her," Dad says.

I turn to look at Jordan. "You brought my mom flowers?"

He shrugs, looking embarrassed. I notice he's wearing a white T-shirt beneath the plaid shirt, and that just makes him look even cuter. "My mom always taught me you should bring your host a gift. Sorry I didn't get you anything, Mr. Winters."

"Making my wife happy is gift enough," Dad assures him.

I'm still stuck on the casual way Jordan mentioned his mom. He never talks about his parents. Ever. It's like they don't even exist, though I know they do, because otherwise he wouldn't exist. But still. He does not bring them up in normal conversation.

Until now.

"The flowers look lovely on the table, Jordan." Mom joins us in the living room, her smile brittle, her gaze sweeping over me before she returns her attention to him. "Thank you again."

"You're welcome." He smiles sheepishly and I feel suddenly awkward. Something's up with Mom. She's probably remembering all those things I told her about Jordan and is now seeing how he measures up. I don't want her judging him for what happened with Thad and Tara having sex at his house. That was completely out of his control.

Of course, the Thad and Tara incident only confirms her suspicions everything that happens at his house is out of control. Meaning, he can't win this argument.

Dad offers Jordan a seat and we all sit down in the living room, making small talk, mostly about football. Dad's bombarding him with all sorts of questions and I'm listening closely, curious to hear how Jordan answers about where he wants to go to college.

Not that I want to follow him to his college of choice or anything. That would be ridiculous. He's so smart, and talented on the football field. Plus he's rich, so he could go to whatever college he wants. I fight the jealousy that wants to sweep over me. I wish I had it that easy. His life seems like a piece of cake. Yeah, he might have crappy parents, but he has all the money he could ever want, and his crappy parents let him do whatever he wants.

He's lucky.

"He is the boy who had that party, right?" Mom asks me, her voice low, just for me to hear.

"Mom." I send her a look. "He couldn't stop that from happening. Don't blame him for it."

"I just wonder what sort of parties he has if things like that happen.

You shouldn't go to parties like that. They're demeaning. What if—"
Mom lowers her voice to almost a whisper. "—what if something like
that happened to you? Against your will?"

I roll my eyes. "He's very protective of me, Mother. Jordan would
never let something like that happen."

Mom checks him out before she returns her attention to me. "He's
very good looking."

I feel my cheeks go hot. "I know."

"He seems popular too."

"He is."

She studies me carefully. "I'm not trying to be rude, dear. But what
exactly does he see in you?"

My mouth drops open. I'm at a complete loss for words. Parents
are supposed to be your backup, right? The people who think you're
perfect no matter what, no matter if you screw up on a regular basis,
they're there to pick you up when you're about to fall.

I feel like my mom just kicked me in the stomach and stole my
breath with just a few words.

"I think your daughter is smart," Jordan says, and I whip my head
in his direction, my eyes going wide. Crap, he heard what my mom
said. "And she's kind. She makes me laugh, and not many people can
do that."

My heart aches a little at that statement.

"She's beautiful." His voice, his gaze is solemn as he watches me.
"And she's fun. Her smile brightens my day."

I unleash a big one at him and he smiles in return. "And I just really
care about your daughter. A lot." His gaze never leaves mine with that
last statement.

Again, I want to throw myself at him and kiss him senseless. But I remain where I'm sitting, hoping he can see all the affection shining in my eyes directed straight at him.

Does he see it? Does he know how fast I'm falling for him? The more days that go by, the less anxious I feel when I'm with him. I was always waiting for that bomb to drop. Always waiting for the punch line, when Jordan—or someone else—would yell out, SURPRISE! Joke's on you.

I don't think that's going to happen anymore. I really believe that Jordan is into me.

"Aw." Mom looks ready to cry when her gaze meets mine. "That is the sweetest thing I've ever heard."

And that, folks, is how Jordan Tuttle wins over my parents.

chapter seventeen

Tuttle

I feel like I'm in a freaking dream. At the very least, I'm sitting on the set of a TV sitcom, appearing on some over the top show about a sweet family who loves each other so much they gather around the dinner table every Sunday night to break bread.

This shit is usually something I mock. Who does this? Definitely not me. I don't remember the last time I ate a meal with my parents, especially at our house. We just don't give a damn anymore.

But as I sit in the small dining room just off the kitchen in the Winters' house, I feel…warm. Cozy. Like I belong here.

Though really? I don't.

The dad is nice. Likes to talk football, and I'll always talk football. Our conversation is easy and it's a relief because Amanda's father is interested. Genuinely interested in my opinion, in what I tell him, and he doesn't criticize. My father only wants to tell me what I do wrong when I play. Or he'll remind me what I need to keep doing in order to move on to the college of my dreams.

More like the college of his dreams.

I have no real dreams. I just go through the motions. I have all the right traits to get what I want and I use them when I need to, but I don't give a piece of myself to anyone. Not a soul.

My gaze drifts to the girl sitting across from me. The one who's scowling at her little brother after he teases her about her hair or what she ate or maybe there's something in her teeth. I didn't catch what it was. I do know this—even when she's irritated, she's gorgeous. Her hair, her face, those eyes, her mouth…all of her is perfection.

I'd give her every piece of me. All she has to do is say the word and I'm hers.

Crazy, right? I don't do this. And if I think about it too much, I'll panic and back away from her. Because that's what I do. Commitment is a dirty word in my vocabulary. I never wanted it before. Yet I want it with Amanda.

Proving the point that you always want what you can't have. More like what I don't deserve.

And I don't deserve her. She's too good for me.

She snaps at her brother, Trent, and her mom scolds them both, but gently. Everything is gentle in this house. No one yells, no one snaps, no one drinks, no one accuses anyone of any wrongdoing. It's actually a pretty pleasant atmosphere, despite Amanda's mom dissing her earlier, which had been weird.

I honestly didn't think this life could exist. I'm wondering now if they're on their best behavior and the minute I'm gone and the curtain drops, they'll all go back to their mean selves.

"Do you want something more to eat?" the mother asks me, a

concerned look on her face. I could tell she didn't like me at first. She was sizing me up, examining me closely. I can't blame her. She should kick me out and tell me to stay the hell away from her daughter. After what Amanda and I did...

Yeah. We didn't take it too far last night. But I did have my hands up Amanda's shirt when we made out in the back seat of my Rover. I tried to take her back to my house, but she wouldn't do it. So we parked. Like we didn't have a choice.

That's okay, though. I'll do whatever it takes to make her happy. See her smile. Kiss her lips. Touch her body—

"Jordan?" the mother asks me again, and I snap out of my dirty thoughts, smiling at her.

"No thanks." She made a pot roast and potatoes and vegetables that she cooked all in one pot—along with the roast. I've never had anything like it before and it was good. "I'm stuffed."

"Not too stuffed that you'll have to turn away dessert, I hope."

I'm intrigued. "Dessert?"

Mrs. Winters smiles. "Homemade cheesecake."

"It is the best cheesecake you'll ever have," Mr. Winters adds.

"It's really good," Amanda says with a shy smile.

My whole body goes tight at seeing that smile. She makes me fucking crazy with her sweet smiles and bashful ways tonight. I can't wait to get her alone and kiss her until she's begging me to touch her. She did that last night. Begged. Whispered in my ear, pleading with me to put my hands on her. Slip my fingers under her shirt and touch her. Just a little bit, though. Never too much, yet I push every time we're together. Push a little harder. Push a little more.

"Amanda, will you help me clear the table?" Mrs. Winters says as she starts to stand.

But I stand instead, my gaze locked on Amanda's. "I'll help her clean up, Mrs. Winters."

"Oh, but you're our guest—"

"I insist," I say firmly, softening my tone with a smile aimed right at Amanda's mom.

She smiles back, looking pleased. "Well then. If you insist…"

Amanda doesn't say a word. Just sends me a cute little smirk as she starts to help me clear the table. I follow her cues since I've never cleaned up a table before in my entire life, and we walk into the kitchen, setting the dishes on the counter next to the sink.

"You're going to help me wash them too?" She flashes a smile at me over her shoulder.

"Whatever you need," I say easily, fighting the urge to grab her and push her hair away from her nape so I can kiss her neck. My gaze drops to all the exposed skin of her lower back and my fingers literally itch to touch her.

The moment she sets her dishes on the counter, I'm on her. I rest my hands on her back, sliding them to her waist, and I grip her there, standing directly behind her, my nose buried in her fragrant hair.

"Jordan…"

"Give me a minute," I murmur. "I need to touch you."

She goes still. I swear she's not even breathing. But then I reach up and brush her hair away from her nape, just like I envisioned and she gasps softly. Her thick, dark hair drapes over her shoulder, exposing her neck, and I lean in, pressing my mouth just below her ear.

A shuddery breath leaves her and she melts into me, turning her head more to the right. "You should stop," she says shakily. "What if my parents catch us?"

"One more kiss." I slide my hands along her waist, kissing her neck, her ear, tasting her skin.

"Okay." She sounds breathless. "But hurry."

I kiss her cheek and whisper in her ear, "You wore this sweater to drive me crazy, didn't you?"

"I almost wore a dress."

"A dress?" I think of all the things I could do to Amanda if she wore a dress. "I like easy access."

"Stop." She pulls out of my grip and turns to face me with a stern look on her face. "Now you're trying to drive me crazy."

I grin. I can't help myself. That's what she does to me. She makes me smile too much. Like I have a problem or something. "We should go clear the rest of the table."

She sends me a look. One that tells me she's going to ask a question. "I was wondering. Have you ever helped clear a table before, Jordan?"

I slowly shake my head.

Her eyes fill with surprise, but she recovers quickly. "What about washing dishes? Have you ever done that?"

Again, another slow shake of my head.

"Seriously?" Her voice squeaks. "Well, I'm going to teach you."

I frown. "What about the cheesecake?"

Amanda laughs and it's the best sound. I don't need alcohol or weed or whatever when I have her around to fill me up with her laughter. "We'll finish gathering the dirty dishes and then we'll have cheesecake. After cheesecake, we'll wash the dishes. Deal?"

I pull her into my arms and give her a quick kiss, wishing I could give her more. "Deal."

chapter eighteen

Amanda

"He came over to your house for dinner?" Livvy sounds shocked. Not that I can blame her.

I'm still fairly shocked too. I'd been so nervous yesterday, but the moment Jordan showed up with flowers for my mom and I saw how naturally he talked to my dad like they were old friends, I couldn't believe how easy the night became.

Jordan enjoyed the meal—Mom was super nervous about that— he laughed when my brother told him stupid jokes and he gave Dad the scoop about the football team and what their chances are to go all the way to the state championship.

I loved watching them talk about football. I got my love for the game from Dad, who has been a Raiders fanatic forever. They're not the best team, but Dad doesn't care. He's loyal to a fault, and while George never showed much interest in football and Trent gave up playing league football last year, I'm the one who'll sit with Dad and watch the games. Listen to him rattle off stats and explain what's happening and why certain players make certain plays.

"You two are getting serious," Livvy says, pulling me out of my thoughts.

We're hanging out in her mom's car in the senior lot before the first bell rings. It's drizzling outside and windy. We don't want to get out of the car and Liv has texted Ryan multiple times, asking if he'd meet us with an umbrella in the next five minutes.

So far, no response.

"I guess so." I don't want to say anything more for fear I might jinx myself—and us. And when I say us, I mean me and Jordan.

"What did your parents think? About Tuttle?"

"They liked him a lot. He brought my mom flowers." A beautiful arrangement of fall flowers, including sunflowers, which are my favorite. I was jealous of that stupid bouquet too. He hasn't brought me flowers, yet he gave some to my mom?

Life isn't fair sometimes.

"Wow, slick. He's good with parents then. No surprise." Livvy whistles, making me laugh. "I'm serious! The most Ryan has brought my mom is trouble." We start laughing even more.

"Your mom doesn't like Ryan?" I already know the answer. Liv's mom wasn't thrilled she spent the night at Ryan's house for his birthday party, so he has a mark against him. And that's a pretty big mark.

"She's getting better. Fitch seems to like him." Liv makes a face. Fitch is the guy her mom is dating. Liv hates him, says he gives her the creeps. I've been around him a couple of times, and I have to agree.

"Did Ryan ever get back to you about the umbrella or whatever?" I glance out the window. The rain is now coming down hard, and the parking lot always fills up with major puddles when a good rain comes through. I'm going to get soaked and look terrible for the entire day if I have to walk outside even a few feet without an umbrella. And the main building is more than a few feet away from my car.

Grabbing my phone, I send off a quick text to Jordan.

Rescue me from the rain and I'll be yours forever.

I get an immediate reply.

Was that a line from a Juliet entry or what? Very poetic. ☺

He actually sent me a smiley face.

No. I'm being serious. Rescue us from Liv's mom's car. It's raining so hard and I don't want to walk in it. Neither does Liv. We're in a newer silver Accord.

You want me to come to your rescue.

Yes.

And you'll be mine forever if I do.

I chew on my thumbnail before I answer him.

Yes.

So I can do whatever I want to you and you have to agree.

My skin goes warm. What kind of question is that?

Depends on what you're talking about.

You won't be disappointed. Promise.

Within seconds I hear tires screeching and there's Jordan parking right alongside Livvy's car.

Get your stuff and get in my car. Tell Livvy to stay put.

"Jordan is giving us a ride to the front building," I say to Livvy.

She turns to look at me with a frown. "What are you talking about?"

"He's right there." I indicate his parked car with a wave of my hand. "I'm going to jump in his car but stay put. He'll drive around to your side of the car in a minute."

I grab my backpack and bail out of the car, hopping into the passenger side of the Range Rover within seconds and only the tiniest bit damp. He smiles at me, leans over to give me a little kiss, then throws the car into drive and wheels it around to the driver's side of Liv's mom's car. Livvy goes through the same process, and after she climbs into the Rover, Jordan takes her keys and hits the remote to lock it before rolling up his window.

"You're my hero!" Liv says from the backseat of the car. She reaches forward and gives Jordan a playful shove on the shoulder. "Better than Ryan. He hasn't even bothered to text me back."

"You're welcome," Jordan says with a hint of sarcasm, which makes me smile. He returns the gesture with one of those secretive smiles only for me, the ones that say, *I've had you nearly naked in my bed and I'm going to do it again.*

A shiver moves through me at the possibility.

He drives the Range Rover to the front of the main building and Liv hops out the moment he puts the car in park, not even bothering to look back or ask me to come with her. We watch her go and then I turn to look at Jordan, ready to offer him a thank you.

But he's watching me with the most intense look in his gaze. All thoughts, all words, disappear in an instant.

"I did what you asked of me," he says softly. "I came to your rescue and now you're mine." He pauses. "Forever."

Oh. That's right. I forgot I said that. Sort of.

"I was just kidding."

"I take all requests from you seriously." He waves a hand toward the building before us. "Like rescuing you from the rain."

"I still need to go back out in it to get in the building." I glance behind me, checking out the backseat. This of course, reminds me that a few nights ago, I'd been rolling around in that very backseat and it had been awesome.

"Want my hoodie?" He starts to take his off and I grab his arm to prevent him from taking it any further.

"No, stop. It's okay. I have my own." I'm dressed pretty sloppily today, with the weather spurring my choices. I have on a school hoodie, leggings and a pair of shiny black designer rain boots I found on clearance at the Nordstrom Rack this past spring. I put zero effort into my outfit, yet here I sit with Jordan in his fancy car and he's wearing fancy clothes and fancy cologne he most likely bought at a high-end department store. A place I probably can't even afford to walk into, let alone actually buy something.

Uh oh. I'm having one of those moments where I feel inferior yet again.

"Thank you for rescuing me," I murmur.

"You're welcome. I'll expect full reimbursement this afternoon. After practice."

"What are you talking about?"

He smiles and kisses me again, his lips lingering, his voice so deep, so low, I swear it vibrates within my soul. "You'll see."

HE TAKES ME to his house after practice. I text my mom saying I won't be home for dinner, that I have to work on my English project with

Jordan. When she asks where we're working on it, I make up a lie and tell her we're going to the school library, then to a mutual friend's house, implying a bunch of us are working on this project together.

There's no working on the project. The project is long forgotten. He's keyed up after a particularly intense football practice played out in the rain. I hung out with Kyla while he took a shower, and when he came to get me after he was finished, I lost all train of thought at first sight of him. He glowered, his muscular body practically vibrating with frustration.

There were no friendly greetings, no acknowledgement of Kyla. He just looked at me and said, "Let's go."

Now we're hanging out in the kitchen and he's given me a Coke to drink. He has a beer. Odd choice for a Monday afternoon, but I don't question him. He seems tense. Annoyed. And I don't know why. He won't talk to me.

"Are you okay?" I finally ask.

"Tough practice today." He looks away, staring out the giant window that sits above the sink. "Really, it was the talk afterward that was tough."

"Why?"

His gaze meets mine. "We were talking about our futures."

"Do you not have a plan?" I figured he would. We're all supposed to have one. My plan includes taking the SAT this upcoming Saturday. I should study for it.

I will later.

He shrugs. "I have a plan. My father's plan."

I frown. "Is it what you want to do though?"

"I've never really thought about it." I catch a flicker of emotion in his eyes that tells me he's...holding back.

I set my drink on the marble counter and approach him. "What does your dad want you to do?"

"Go to the same college he went to."

"And where's that?"

"University of Oregon."

"He's a Duck?"

Jordan cracks a smile, but his eyes are still dark. Full of anger. "Yeah."

"And you don't want to be a Duck."

Another shrug, but no words are said. They don't need to be said.

He doesn't want to go there. He's only going along with that plan to please his father.

An ache tugs at my heart and I set my hands on his chest. "What do you want to do, Jordan?"

"Stay here in California. Go to UC Berkeley or USC." He blows out a harsh breath. "They both have excellent football teams. Excellent academics. But my father doesn't believe they're good enough in his eyes. He wants me to follow in his footsteps. He doesn't care what I think or what I want."

I can't help but wonder if his father doesn't think Jordan is good enough either.

"I don't want to talk about this." His voice is hard, as is the look on his face. He wraps his arms around my waist and pulls me in closer to him. "Let's do something else."

"Like what?" I ask, but he doesn't answer me with words.

He kisses me instead.

It's an aggressive kiss. Hungry. Possessive. No gentle brushing of lips, no tender explorations. He's consuming me, his tongue thrusting into my mouth, his hands gripping my hips. I let him, because it feels good. The kiss is raw and full of untethered emotion and that's what I want from him.

I want Jordan to lose control.

Out of nowhere he lifts me up and sets me on the kitchen counter, the marble cold beneath my butt. He pushes my legs open and steps in between them, devouring my mouth once more, his hands slipping under my hoodie, the hem of my T-shirt, to touch bare skin. His hands are big and warm, and they slide over my stomach, shift up to touch my bra, and then he's breaking the kiss to pull off my hoodie.

He's so frantic, it feels like he's trying to pull off my head.

"Jordan." I want him to slow down, but it's like he can't. "Hey." I touch his cheek and he lifts his gaze to mine. "Are you okay?"

"I don't want to talk," he murmurs. "Please."

"All ri—"

He cuts off my words with his lips and I lose myself in his kiss. He seems almost desperate, like he's trying to chase after something he can never catch, and I try to calm him down. Soothe him. I run my hands over his shoulders, down his chest. I try to slow the tempo of the kiss.

But he won't have it. He just keeps pushing, becoming bolder. I'm not scared—he doesn't scare me, I know he would never hurt me. I *am* confused, though. And worried. This has nothing to do with me.

He's upset about something else. Something he's not really telling me.

"Really, Jordan? In my kitchen? You could at least take her to the theater room."

An unfamiliar female voice makes me jerk away from him. He doesn't move, though. Just stands there right next to me, his hands still on my hips, his entire demeanor changing in an instant.

A woman stands in the doorway of the kitchen. She's elegantly dressed in a pale gray sweater and black pants. Her blonde hair is swept back into a ponytail and giant diamonds dot each ear.

"What are you doing here?" Jordan snaps.

The woman enters the kitchen, not ruffled by Jordan's hostile tone in the least. "I came home early."

He mutters a curse under his breath and lifts me off the kitchen counter, setting me on my feet. "We'll leave then."

"Don't go on my account." The brittle smile the woman offers me looks downright painful. Like she'd rather be anywhere else than dealing with me. "Are you Jordan's friend?"

She has to be his mother. I see a familiarity in her features, a fleeting expression that reminds me of Jordan, but otherwise I wouldn't say he got his looks from his mother. He must resemble his father.

She's a beautiful woman, though. Her skin is smooth and not a wrinkle in sight. Her lips are full and shiny with nude gloss. Was she a teen mom or what?

"This is Amanda," Jordan says gruffly.

Her smile fades. "I've heard about you."

What? "Um, hi." I run a hand over my hair, wishing yet not wishing I had a mirror to check myself out. I look like absolute hell. On Monday mornings I lack motivation to put together a cute outfit, and with this morning's rain, I really took the slacker's route. She must think I'm an absolute bum, especially compared to how well put together she is.

"We're in English together," he tells his mother. "We've been working on a project."

"Some project." Amusement tinges her voice and I feel my cheeks burn with embarrassment. "You should take her to the library then. You two can work on your *project* there."

There's a library in this house? I had no idea. How many rooms do they have anyway?

Jordan's hand is still on my waist but I slide out of his grip. I grab my hoodie from the floor where he dropped it only minutes ago. "It was nice meeting you," I tell his mother.

"Likewise." Her mouth twists into what I think is a smile, but looks more like a grimace.

He doesn't say a word. Just tugs on my hand and leads me out of the kitchen. We walk right past her, but he doesn't acknowledge her. She just watches us coolly, her expression betraying no emotion.

I've seen that look before. She reminds me of Jordan.

We end up in his room, not the library. He shuts and locks the door, leaning against it while watching me go to the mirror that sits over his dresser.

"I look terrible," I moan as I stare at my reflection. My mascara is smudged under my eyes. I'm wearing an old T-shirt I never planned on anyone seeing and my legs look like black legging-covered sticks.

He walks over so he's standing directly behind me, our gazes meeting in the mirror. "I think you look beautiful."

My heart leaps at the compliment, but he must be blinded by our earlier kisses. "Your mom must think I'm a scrub."

He chuckles, then leans in and nuzzles my neck. "I don't care what she thinks about you."

"Well, I do. I want to make a good first impression, like you did with my parents." I elbow him in the ribs and he lifts his head, glaring at me, though there's no real anger there. "You didn't even tell me her name."

"It's Celeste." He resumes kissing my neck, his lips lingering. "Celeste Tuttle the ice queen."

His tone and his words make me sad. "You don't get along with her."

"She's rarely home, and when she is, she's either drinking or high on pills," he explains with a weary sigh. "She needs them to cope."

"Cope with what?"

"Life." He lightly bites my neck, making me shiver. "I don't want to talk about all this shit, Mandy. I've had a bad day."

He wraps his arms around my waist and I rest my hands on top of his. "You never really want to talk to about anything."

"Because there's nothing really good in my life that I ever want to talk about," he says, his voice soft, his gaze locked with mine in the mirror. "The only thing that's good in my life right now is you."

"Oh, Jordan." He's breaking my heart. I don't know what else to say to him, don't know how to make him feel better.

"It's true," he whispers against my cheek just before he kisses it. "How I feel about you scares the hell out of me."

His confession should make me feel good. I know it should.

But it doesn't.

chapter nineteen

The rest of the week buzzes by. I studied for the SAT when I could and didn't even go out with Jordan Friday night because of it. Mom wouldn't let me, claiming I needed to work on my future.

When I went and took the test, there were so many other people there, including Em and Livvy and Ryan and Cannon Whittaker and Brianne Brown and Dustin, too. No Jordan, though. He told me his score was good enough—no surprise—and he even applied early at a few colleges.

I totally bombed the SAT. My mom is going to be so disappointed.

I worked from three to seven at Yo Town, and Livvy agreed to pick me up. She's helping me get ready for our double date tonight with her and Ryan. Somehow I convinced Jordan we should go out with them tonight and he reluctantly agreed. We stopped by my house and grabbed a few things before we went back to hers, where I took a quick shower and then Livvy did my hair and makeup.

I'm both excited and nervous about tonight. I like having Jordan all to myself, but I don't like how he isolates himself all the time. His explanation makes perfect sense—everyone wants a piece of him and he doesn't have enough pieces to give. I get it.

Sort of.

"It looks so pretty curled," Livvy says as she lightly sprays the ends of my hair with hairspray. "You should curl it more often."

"Takes too much time." I'm sitting on a stool in the bathroom with my back to the mirror because Livvy doesn't want me to see myself until she's finished. I've never let a friend give me a makeover before and I can tell she loves every minute of it.

Me? I'm apprehensive about the date. Jordan texted me earlier about what time he made the reservation for and where—some fancy place I could never afford. I told him I'd meet him at the restaurant and he seemed okay with it. But it's kind of weird how I'm hitching a ride with Ryan and Livvy.

When she starts layering on the makeup, I tell her not to put on too much. "I don't want to look totally different."

"I'll just emphasize what you have." She grabs hold of my chin and contemplates my face like a doctor. "You have really good skin and your eyes are beautiful."

I roll those supposed beautiful eyes. "They're brown and boring."

"No, they're not! They're so dark. Full of mysterious depths." Livvy giggles. "And you have great eyebrows. Can I pluck them?" She whips out a pair of tweezers and I dodge them when she waves them close to my face.

"Why? I thought they were great!"

"You need to clean them up a little bit." When I shake my head, she mock pouts. "Come on, please? What I plan on doing will really make them pop."

I glance at my phone to check the time. "It's getting late."

"Stop worrying. Just let me work my magic." She grabs hold of my shoulders and gives me a little shake. "Trust me."

My nod is reluctant and she gets to work, plucking my eyebrows with those tweezers like she's wielding some sort of torturous device. I keep jerking every time she pulls out a tiny hair and she practically stabs me with the tweezers at least three times.

"Keep still!" she reprimands like she's my mom. "And never forget these words—beauty is pain."

"What?" That sounds crazy.

"I'm serious. My mom used to always say that to me. Beauty is pain, pain is beauty, it's all the same. To look good, we have to make sacrifices. And sometimes, those sacrifices hurt." Livvy smiles mysteriously. "It's a small price to look your absolute best, but trust me, it's worth it."

"You keep telling me to trust you, but all you're doing is hurting me," I point out, hoping she'll see the logic and stop with the tweezing already.

Liv rolls her eyes. "You are such a baby."

Once she's done with my hair and makeup, she grabs the dress she picked out for me to wear and I tug it on, nearly jumping out of my skin when she yells at me to watch out for my hair. It's this cute black-and-white striped T-shirt dress I bought on a whim last spring when I found it on a clearance rack. I've never worn it, though. Dresses, skirts—they're not my thing. I feel weird in them and a lot of the time they show too much leg because they're always too short on me.

"He is going to *die* when he sees you," Livvy breathes as she stares at me.

I tug at the fabric of the dress. "It's too clingy."

"It's perfect. You're so thin you can carry it off." She shakes her head, but she's beaming. "You look *so* amazing!"

"Oh my gosh, stop. You're gushing." I whirl around, my eyes widening when I catch myself in the mirror.

Livvy's right. I do look pretty damn amazing, if I do say so myself. My hair has these sexy "beach waves," as Livvy calls them, loose and touchable despite all the hairspray she used. My makeup is subtle, not too overdone, though my eyes are intensely dark. I like them. I'll never be able to duplicate this look on my own, but I don't care.

For one night, I'll feel like a princess.

"What do you think?" Livvy practically squeals when I remain too quiet for too long. "Do you like it?"

"I like it." I turn to smile at her. "I really do. Thank you."

"So. Excited!" She tugs me into a hug then pushes me away, frowning. "Don't want to mess up your hair."

"When is Ryan getting here?" I ask nervously. Now I wish Jordan were picking me up. I'm both scared and excited to see his reaction to my new look. Will he like it? Or will he think I'm trying to be something I'm not? What about the dress? I take a step away from the mirror, trying to catch my legs in the reflection. They look like long, pale sticks, almost too skinny.

Ugh, I need to stop being so critical of myself.

"He'll be here in about fifteen minutes," Livvy reassures me.

I can't stop staring at my reflection in the mirror. And the longer I look, the more nervous I get. Jordan might not like the new me. Or he might like it, I don't know.

I hate feeling so unsure.

"What shoes are you going to wear?" Livvy asks.

"I brought some flat sandals."

"You don't think you should wear heels?"

"I'd probably twist my ankle if I wore them."

"But men love high heels! It makes them think about sex." When I send her an incredulous look, she explains further. "I saw it in a movie once."

"Just because you saw it in a movie doesn't mean it happens for real," I tell her. "I hope men aren't that shallow." And while I wouldn't mind looking sexy for Jordan, I don't want his mind to automatically go to sex when he sees me. Though maybe it already does, I don't know.

My cheeks go warm at the thought.

Livvy actually snorts. "Have you met the guys we spend time with? They're all shallow."

Her words fill me with sadness. Does she really believe that? I don't. Jordan definitely has substance.

"So you and Jordan are for real, huh?" Livvy asks.

I shrug, my cheeks going even hotter. "Yeah, we are. Though I don't want to push him too hard." He's the type of guy who'll run if he feels cornered, so I do my best to give him space.

"He always wants to hang out with you. I take that as a good sign. Though I understand not wanting to push too hard." Livvy smiles. "But I think you two are on the right track."

"Thanks," I murmur, feeling weird. I like talking about Jordan, but then again, I don't. She wants more details. I can see it in her eyes. Everything Jordan and I do together is so private. I don't want to share it with the rest of the world. It feels like I'm breaking some major rule if I tell Livvy what's happening between Jordan and I these last few weeks.

I want to savor the moment, keep it to myself. It's my secret with

Jordan. I'm excited to see him tonight. Will he give me one of those knowing smiles?

"What's he like?"

"What? Who?"

"Tuttle. What's he like, when it's just the two of you alone? He's always so closed off and acts like we're all bugging him most of the time. I'm guessing he's already opened up to you?"

"Sort of." I shrug, feeling inadequate. Has he really opened up to me? I don't think so. A little bit but not much. "We're taking it one day at a time."

"So no juicy details yet?" The crestfallen expression on her face tells me she was hoping for something more.

"Sorry to disappoint you," I say with a shake of my head.

Within a few minutes Ryan shows up at Livvy's house, ever the gentleman as he speaks with Fitch, Livvy's mom's boyfriend. They make idle chitchat while Livvy and I lurk in the hall, watching them.

"I don't know why he's so nice to Fitch," Livvy says irritably. "That guy is creepy."

"Is he still giving off bad vibes?" She's complained to me about him before.

"Totally. I don't get my mom's relationship with him. I really just don't get Fitch. He's odd, but I can't put my finger on exactly why," Livvy explains.

"Olivia!" Fitch yells from the living room, making both of us wince. "Your boyfriend is waiting for you!"

We both enter the living room together, Livvy going straight for Ryan while I stand there awkwardly waiting for them.

"You look amazing," Ryan whispers as he rests his hands on her hips, pulling her in for a quick kiss.

Fitch scowls. I'm guessing he doesn't like public displays of affection. His gaze slides to mine, and he smiles, though there's something almost sinister about it. I offer him a faint smile in return and he looks me up and down, like he's totally checking me out.

Ew.

"Come on, let's go. I don't want to leave Tuttle waiting at the restaurant," Livvy urges, taking Ryan's hand and leading him toward the front door. I follow after them. "Bye, Fitch," she yells as she opens the door.

"Be back by one," he tells her just as she slams the door in his face, making Ryan chuckle.

"You're so rude to him Livvy," he teases as he leads us toward his car parked in front of Liv's house.

"He's gross. Look at how he acts like he's my dad! It's ridiculous." Liv shakes her head.

"Where's your mom?" Ryan asks her as he opens both doors on the passenger side of his sleek white BMW. I climb into the back seat and he shuts the door for me, then does the same for Livvy. I smooth my hands over my dress and tug the skirt down, trying to cover my thighs. I feel totally overexposed, which is silly since I wear shorts all the time.

Livvy doesn't answer until Ryan is sitting behind the steering wheel. "She's working until nine. Some weird shift change she had. So Fitch said he'd supervise me until I left. Then he's going to go pick her up from the hospital." She mock shudders. "I wish they'd just break up already."

I remain quiet for the entire drive, listening to Ryan and Liv's conversation. They talk about football and the restaurant and Ryan tells her how hot she looks in her dress. She's wearing a light gray T-shirt dress, though hers fits a little looser.

My phone buzzes and I check it.

I'm at the restaurant. Where are you?

We're almost there.

Good.

I tuck my phone back into the small purse I brought, letting that warm, fuzzy feeling wash over me. I can feel his frustration even through those few words he texted. He likes me. He wants to be with me. I've spent a lot of time with him lately, and I even met his mom.

That has to count for something, right?

We arrive at the restaurant and Ryan turns his car keys over to the valet before walking us inside. Jordan's sitting in the lobby waiting for us and he rises to his feet when he sees me, his eyes going wide as he slowly approaches.

"You put our name in already?" Ryan asks him.

Jordan never takes his gaze away from me. "Yeah. Table will be ready in a few minutes."

And then his hands are on my waist, pulling me into him. "You look gorgeous," he whispers just before he kisses me lightly on the lips.

I'm thankful he's holding onto me. Otherwise I probably would've slipped to the floor in a boneless heap at his very public claiming of me.

"So, Tuttle. You like her makeover?" Livvy asks Jordan, amusement lacing her tone. She's loving every minute of this.

"I do," he tells her before he leans in and murmurs in my ear, "Though I think you're even more beautiful when you're wearing sweats and no makeup on."

"Stop." I lightly smack his chest, my entire body flushing hot.

"Just stating the truth." He kisses my cheek before we both turn to find Ryan and Livvy watching us with surprise etched across their faces. "What?" he asks crossly.

They both stand up straight, their expressions going neutral. "Not used to seeing you like this, bro," Ryan says.

"You pretty much hate everyone," Livvy adds.

Jordan slips his arm around my waist. "I don't hate everyone," he drawls. "I'm just picky."

What a way to put it. So is he saying that I should feel special because he picked me?

The hostess calls Jordan's name and we follow after her as she escorts us to our table. The restaurant is small and intimate, with dark walls and low lighting, candles burning on every table. Colorful fall bouquets sit next to lit votives in the center and the tables are draped in white cloth. It's all very elegant and fancy and I'm not used to this sort of place whatsoever.

Thad never took me to fancy dinners the few times we actually went out on a date. And my family doesn't come to places like this. The fanciest we get is Applebee's or Chili's. I know that sounds lame, but it's true.

I pick up my menu and flip it over. It's only printed on one side and I frown, reading over the small list of appetizers and entrees they serve.

"The chef changes the menu every few weeks, and themes it by whatever's in season," Jordan explains to me, like he can sense my confusion.

"Oh." I scan it, unease slipping through me. None of it sounds that great, though mostly that's due to me never eating this kind of food. I'm not an adventurous eater. I'm not much of an adventurous anything. Glancing around the table, I see Livvy smiling over at Ryan as he says something flirtatious. She's not worried about ordering, so I shouldn't be either.

"You want me to order for you?" Jordan offers, his voice low and only for me to hear. "What looks good to you?"

There's not one item with chicken in it, and that would've been my go-to. There's some strange ravioli thing that sounds sweet and kind of odd. There's also steak on the menu, but I'm not that crazy about red meat.

"I guess," I finally say to him with a tiny shrug, keeping my gaze fixed on the menu. I'm feeling helpless and stupid, and that is one of the worst feelings in the world.

The server appears, a guy who's not much older than we are, and his gaze fixes on Jordan like he knows exactly who he is. Which he just might. Jordan doesn't acknowledge him in a friendly manner, though. He orders a goat cheese appetizer that makes me wrinkle my nose, and the waiter jots everything down before offering a dazzling smile and saying, "Your father is dining with us tonight."

Jordan frowns at the server. "Are you talking to me?"

"Yes." He bobs his head up and down in some strange display of manic behavior. "Perhaps you would like to join him?"

"Perhaps another time," Jordan says coolly, glaring at the waiter until he finally slinks off.

"What the hell was that about?" Ryan asks once the server's out of earshot. "I don't think I've seen your dad ever."

"You haven't known him very long," Liv says just before she turns to Jordan. "Though I haven't seen your father much either, and I've known you for what feels like forever."

She's right. I've gone to school with Jordan Tuttle since the dawn of time and I've yet to see his dad materialize anywhere. Not at open houses or back to school nights. Not at evening plays or holiday programs. Not at any of his football games, not at honor roll assemblies, not at any of it.

"He's out of town a lot," Jordan says through clenched teeth. I see a tic in his firm jaw, his eyes so dark they almost look black. He's angry. I can feel the emotion radiating off of his tense body in giant waves. "Not big on family time."

I want to reach out and touch him, offer some comfort, but he looks like he might shatter if I so much as say something, let alone touch him.

The next few minutes are agony. Liv and I try to make small talk, but it's uncomfortable. Ryan has completely checked out and focuses on his phone. Jordan sits as still as a statue, only his eyes scanning the room every few minutes, like he's trying to prepare for that excruciating moment when his dad will pop out of the background and terrorize all of us.

When the waiter returns with our appetizer, Jordan places my order as well as his own, offering me a tight smile after he finishes. The moment the server dashes off, Liv is setting her napkin on the table and sending me a look.

"I need to use the ladies," she sing-songs. "Want to come with, Amanda?"

Nodding, I push out of my chair and set the cloth napkin on my chair before I follow Livvy to the back of the restaurant, where the bathrooms are. The moment we slip inside, Livvy zooms over to the giant mirror, checking her reflection before pulling a MAC Lip Glass out of her tiny purse and applying the gloss to her lips.

"Your boy got super tense," she says, her gaze meeting mine in the mirror.

I go to the spot next to her and wash my hands. "I don't know what to do about it."

"Clearly he has daddy issues." The knowing look she sends me makes my blood simmer.

I don't answer. Her comment is rude. She *totally* has daddy issues, so who is she to talk? Or judge?

Maybe going on a double date with Ryan and Livvy was a big mistake.

chapter twenty

Tuttle

I wish I had a drink. No mixed drink either. I need something strong, straight up. I don't care what kind of alcohol, I need something to take the edge off. Soften me up. Instead I'm tense as hell, clutching my water glass so tight I bet it could shatter if I squeezed just a little more tighter. Ryan is trying his best to make conversation with me, but my terse responses—or worse, lack of response—is crapping him right out. To the point he'd rather pay attention to his phone while we wait for the girls to come back from the restroom.

Talking about me, I'd bet. Wondering at my reaction. My over-the-top behavior. I can hear Livvy now, wondering why I'm so cranky. I can hear Amanda too, defending me, saying I must be upset.

She would be correct.

My father is here, in this very restaurant on a Saturday night, when he should be home with my mother. His wife. Meaning he's in town, with someone else instead of coming home—something he does a lot. I haven't seen him in weeks. And the last time we actually made real eye contact, he was on his way out of the house as I was walking in. When he caught sight of me, his eyebrows had risen and he'd appeared surprised. Like he forgot I even existed.

My biggest dream is to forget his existence, but it never works. The rat bastard always pops up in the most inconvenient places.

Like this stupid restaurant while I'm on this stupid double date, when I wish I could be at home alone with Amanda.

I think of her and she magically appears. I watch as she and Livvy make their way back to our table. Heads turn as both girls pass, and I clutch my right hand into a fist, feeling protective. Primitive. I never feel that way about anyone, least of all some girl.

But she's not just some girl. She's Amanda Winters. I've had a ridiculous crush on her for years. Not just for her beauty—and she's pretty, don't get me wrong—but it's her mind that I'm attracted to. She's smart. And funny. She makes me smile and she makes me think. She challenges me. Half the time I think she doesn't like me and that is a fucking challenge like no other. These last few weeks we've spent a lot of time together, and I am determined to make her fall in love with me.

Though what will that get us? Get her? Pain? Unhappiness? I don't believe in love, not really. So why would I torture her—and myself?

I tell myself I don't need her. But the more time we spend together, the more I'm starting to believe that's not true.

They draw closer and I watch Mandy walk, her hips swaying gently. The dress she wears clings to her like a second skin, turning her body into long lines and subtle curves. I remember the times I've touched that body. How responsive she always is. The sounds she makes.

I need to quit reminiscing or I'll be sporting a major boner soon.

But I can't stop thinking about her, about having her in my house, my room, my bed...

Makes me want to keep doing it. Keep her. Which is ridiculous. That sort of thing is what fucks up your life. Falling for someone, needing someone—you'll only end up getting hurt.

I'll be hurt. She will be too. This won't end well.

Yet I can't stop it.

She settles into the chair next to mine and I can smell her fragrance, delicate and sweet and infinitely Amanda. She smiles at me, her eyes full of fear, and I know I've acted like an asshole since I heard my father is here, but I can't help myself. I won't be able to ease the edge until I see him.

Or the edge will get sharper. More painful.

"Try the appetizer," I tell Amanda when she just keeps staring at me with those big brown eyes. She looks like she wants to either comfort me or run screaming from the building.

I'd advise her to do the latter, but I'm selfish. I want to keep her near me.

"Is it good?" She sounds, looks unsure.

I take a thin cracker from the plate and dip it into the goat cheese and jalapeno jelly mix, then hold the cracker in front of her lush mouth. "Try it."

Her lips slowly part and I feed her the cracker. She chews thoughtfully, the tension slowly leaving her expressive face just before she swallows. "That was delicious."

"Told you." I turn away from her and point at the appetizer, saying to Ryan and Livvy, "Eat up."

They do as I ask like puppets on a string. But I can tell they're enjoying the food. And they only jumped at my command because they know I'm a pissed off ball of rage.

"Jordan." Amanda's soft whisper curls through my blood, settles in my balls because as mad as I am, I still want her. "Are you all right?"

"Never better." I give her the best smile I can muster, but it's more like a baring of teeth. "Why would anything be wrong with me?"

"You can be honest with me." She rests her hand on my thigh and her touch burns in the best way possible. "If you need to talk…"

"I'm good." I settle my hand over hers and give it a squeeze, then remove mine. She frowns, like she wanted me to keep holding her hand, but I can't. Looking happy with my father nearby would be a sign of weakness. He'll see it and drive a stake right into my heart.

Or Amanda's. And I refuse to let that happen.

"Are you sure?" She moves her hand from my leg and I immediately miss her touch.

"I said I was fine." My voice is clipped and the hurt on her face is undeniable.

To anyone else—to Amanda—I look like I'm overacting. So what if my father is here tonight? Who cares?

But I care. I have my sneaking suspicions, and if he makes an appearance, if he comes out of that private back room I know he requests so he can dine in private and bring his special dinner "guests"—mistresses, sluts, whores, whatever you want to call them—I might take all of my rage out on him. Let him know exactly how I feel.

You'd think the old man would already know, but I'm not too sure about that. I think Mom has hidden my animosity toward my father for a long time as a way to—what? Protect him?

Whatever. That guy doesn't deserve *any* protection.

Minutes later our salads are brought out and I pick at mine. I quietly offer the waiter two hundred bucks to bring all of us mixed drinks, preferably heavy on the whiskey, but he wavers too long so I snatch the offer back. Screw this guy if he can't meet a simple request.

"Son. What are you doing here this evening?"

I slowly lift my head to find him standing by our table, with a hot blonde who doesn't look much older than us hanging on his arm.

Emerson Tuttle, in the flesh. An older version of me, which I hate. I look just like him. When I'm older I will be his mirror image. I will have the same dignified silver at my temples and the broad shoulders, and I will wear an expensive designer suit because I'm a Tuttle and we're expected to do no less.

"Who's your friend, Dad?" My voice is falsely cheerful and he knows it.

The smile on his face is tight, though his eyes are cold as ice. Eyes the same color as mine, though I swear his are colder.

"I could ask the same of you, Jordan."

Huh. I'm surprised he even remembers my name.

"I asked first."

"She's a co-worker," he starts but I laugh. The sound is unpleasant, harsh in the silence that has taken over our table. I quiet immediately, sending him a disbelieving look.

"Give me a break, Dad. We know what's going on here," I say bitterly.

His smile cracks. Fades into nothingness. "Don't disrespect me in public."

"Why not? You're disrespecting Mom in public right now. At least I don't put my whores on display for everyone to see."

The woman gasps, my father growls, but I don't give a shit. I'm done. I push out of the chair, toss my cloth napkin on my salad plate and glare at my father.

"Have a great evening." I pull my wallet out of my back pocket, peel off a few one hundred dollar bills and let them flutter to the table. "Sorry," I mutter to my friends at the table before I walk out of the restaurant.

I'm halfway to my car when I hear someone call my name.

Turning, I watch as Amanda comes running toward me. She stops a few feet away, like she's afraid to get too close. Her expressive face is full of concern, her eyes full of pain—for me. And that touches my heart more than I'd want to admit. "Are you okay?"

"Don't worry about me. You should go home with them," I tell her.

Her expression falls and she does nothing to cover it up. She is the most openly honest person I've ever known. "You want to be alone tonight?"

I struggle with my answer. I should be alone. I'm angry and I won't be good company. Mom is home and she'll take one look at my face and know something bad happened. Then she'll probably want to talk, while bombed out on pills, and maybe she's already a few drinks in. My life is a fucking disaster. I shouldn't let Amanda witness any of it.

I should push her away.

But I remain silent. She approaches me cautiously, like someone might approach a wild animal. No sudden movements, no words said. And then she's there, directly in front of me, so close I can feel her body heat radiating toward me. A tentative hand rests on my chest, curls into the front placket of my button front shirt, and then she's tugging me close. Resting her head on my shoulder and wrapping her arms around me.

Wrapping me up in her.

"My parents think I'm spending the night at Liv's," she says, her words like a promise.

I can keep her with me all night.

"I won't be good company," I admit, hating the shame I hear in my voice. I should have nothing to be ashamed of. Yet I am.

"I'll take care of you," she whispers against my neck. "I want to. Let me. Please."

Those are the only words I need to hear.

chapter twenty-one

Amanda

H e sneaks me into his house like we're doing something naughty, which we are, because his mother is home and he doesn't want her to know I'm here. I can hear my own mom's voice droning in my head as Jordan leads me up the back staircase, reminding me I am worth more. No boy should treat me like I'm a secret. No matter how fun or illicit it sounds, he's probably hiding me because he's ashamed.

Of me.

I don't really believe that's the case with Jordan, but either way, I don't care tonight. He's hurting and I don't like it. I want to take care of him. Make him feel better. Make him forget how angry his father just made him. Maybe, just maybe, I can get him to open up and talk to me.

He pulls me into his bedroom and shuts the door behind us, holding his finger to his lips before he starts to speak.

"I need to go downstairs and talk to her."

"Your mom?" I frown.

"Yeah. I'm sure he's already called her."

My frown deepens. "You're talking about your dad, right?" When he nods, I continue. "Really? Why would he do that?"

It doesn't make any sense. I'm not used to manipulative people tricking each other, and I feel like that's all I've been dealing with since I became friends with Livvy. Since I let Jordan Tuttle feel me up in his bedroom on a hot June night. Just after I caught my boyfriend cheating on me with my best friend.

Ugh. I'm stuck on repeat. I need to get over myself, and all the bad crap that's happened to me. If I'm going to live in this new world of mine, I need to own it. Rise above it.

"My father is doing damage control. He talks to her first and manipulates the conversation. He can say whatever he wants and she'll believe him. And I know he'll make me out to be the bad guy," Jordan explains. "I'm the one who caused a public spectacle in a full restaurant on a Saturday night, right?"

Well, he's right. Meaning his father is right, too, which I hate to think. But Jordan is the one, after all, who called the woman with his father a whore. But there was so much animosity and anger bubbling just beneath the surface when those two locked eyes at the restaurant. It had been almost unbearable. The history, the pain, is long and buried deep, and I could feel it. Seeping its way into me, into everyone. I can't judge. I don't want to judge.

I want to be here for him as bet as I can.

"Go ahead," I tell him softly. "Talk to her." I'm still not sure if he really wants me here. He doesn't even bother to kiss me before he exits his bedroom, shutting the door quietly behind him. I flop onto his neatly made bed and stare up at the dark ceiling. The starry ceiling that I remember from the summer. It's velvety black, just like a night sky and when it's powered on, tiny pinpricks of light shine among the velvet. He never turns on the lights anymore though, and I wonder why.

I wonder about a lot of things. He's quiet. Closed off, even. We talk, and just when I get him to admit a few small things, he retreats. I wish I knew more. I'm going all in with this relationship, yet he's pushing me away.

Makes me worry I'm going to get hurt, just like with Thad.

Only worse. What I felt for Thad doesn't even come close to what I feel for Jordan.

My phone buzzes and I grab it to find a text message from Livvy.

Are you okay? Ryan said he would come pick you up if you don't want to stay the night at Tuttle's or if you're uncomfortable. We're both worried about you.

Aw. Just when I think those two are completely wrapped up in each other and don't care about anyone else, they go and do something like this. I'm touched.

I'm good so far. But I hope the offer stands for the next few hours? Just in case…

You got it babe. Text anytime. xoxo

I send her some x's and o's back along with some kissy faced emojis and then start scrolling through my phone. Instagram—boring. Facebook—I don't even bother checking because, what? I'll see photos from my mom's friends and video recipes and crap? No thanks. I open up Snapchat to check out people's stories and see Brianne Brown posted endless photos of her and Dustin kissing. I swear I see shiny pink tongues in a few of the shots. Gross. Hope Liv steers clear of Snapchat tonight.

Somehow I am still following Lauren Mancini and she's following me. It was all innocent good fun when we first became friends on Snapchat. I did it because I know her brother Sam. He was in band with me and is generally a nice person—unlike his older sister. I liked seeing all of her photos. Her life seemed so glamorous and far-reaching to me. As in, I could never reach it.

The photo I see that she's included as part of her story sets my heart to pounding—and not in a good way either.

It's her and Jordan in their homecoming court regalia. Her sparkling tiara on her head, his cheap ass crown tilted to the side on his. They're dancing. Someone else took the photo and must've sent it to her. The caption on the photo is completely ridiculous.

#tbt but not Thursday so maybe just #tb? King & Queen never looked so good. #bestnighteverrrrr #homecoming #seniors #jordanandlauren

She is freaking unbelievable.

It's the Jordan and Lauren hashtag that makes me want to tear her hair out like a jealous wench. Worse, though? I have zero reason to be jealous. Who's the one spending so much time with Jordan these last few weeks? Who's the one who's lying on Jordan's bed at this very moment?

Me.

I sit up and glance around, trying to find something obvious, that will clue people into the fact that I'm in Jordan's bedroom. He doesn't have many personal items in his room. In fact, it's pretty bare and impersonal, which as always, makes me sad. The two photos on his dresser are actually lying facedown and I wonder when he did that.

It's a total invasion of privacy, but I end up wandering around his room. I peek in drawers and immediately shut them because it's wrong, what I'm doing. I enter his closet and am overwhelmed by the sheer size of it. How much clothing does a guy need? I guess Jordan Tuttle needs a lot. When I find some of his jerseys hanging on the bottom rung, I pull one off the hanger and hold it up in front of me.

It's huge.

Going on pure instinct, I kick off my sandals and then shuck off my dress, pulling the navy-and-white jersey over my head, not surprised when the hem falls to the top of my thighs. An idea is brewing in my head. A bad one, but I want to go through with it. I'm feeling vindictive and rotten and evil. What I'm doing is ridiculous, and Jordan might not like it at all.

But I don't care.

I cut through his bedroom, swipe my phone off the bed where I left it, and head into the bathroom. Standing in front of the mirror, I run my fingers through my hair until it's a tousled and possibly sexy mess, and then I pose, snapping a photo with the camera.

Looking at the photo, I realize it's not good enough. The message isn't quite clear.

So I take a few more, then turn around so my back is to the camera. *Tuttle* is emblazoned across my shoulders, the number eight covering almost my entire back. Tuttle's number. I'm looking over my shoulder, see that my butt is almost showing, and I realize right then, *this* is the photo I need to capture.

I open up Snapchat and take at least twenty selfies, deleting every single one of them until I finally settle on the one that works the best.

Before I lose my nerve, I caption it quickly:

How I'm spending my Saturday night. #seniors #8isgreat #propertyof #CuddlewithTuttle

And then send to all of my friends.

He's probably going to kill me.

"Mandy." Someone shakes my shoulder. "Hey. Come on. Wake up."

I sit up straight, blinking my eyes open to find Jordan perched on the edge of the bed, an indescribable look on his too gorgeous face. His eyes are still dark and he looks tired. There's this dangerous air around him, like he's simmering just below the surface and about to blow.

I push my hair out of my face and rub my eyes with my fists before remembering I still have lots of makeup on.

Great. Now I probably look like a raccoon.

"What time is it?" I ask groggily.

"Almost eleven. Sorry that took so long." He doesn't look sorry, though. He still looks angry. Maybe even angrier than before.

Unease trickles down my spine. "Should I go?"

"Do you want to?" His hostile tone is too much for sleepy me to deal with at the moment.

"I can, yeah. Clearly you don't want me here." I realize I'm lying under the covers. And I'm still in his jersey, which is going to be super-awkward in about two seconds, but screw it. I throw the covers off and climb out of his bed, note the shock on his face when he catches sight of me in his jersey and nothing else, but I ignore it.

I need to find my shoes, put my dress back on, grab my purse and get the hell out of here.

"You're really going to leave?" he asks incredulously.

"I probably should, don't you think?" I call over my shoulder as I make my way to his closet. My dress is still in a heap on the floor, and my sandals are in there too. I grab the dress, ready to change, but he's standing in the doorway, watching me. "Um, do you mind?"

"Do I mind what?"

"I want to change." I hold the dress up.

He leans against the doorjamb, his arms crossed. "Go ahead."

"Privately?" I wave him away, but he doesn't budge.

"Why are you wearing my jersey anyway?" he asks, sounding genuinely confused.

I shrug, my cheeks hot. "I wanted to wear something to bed."

"You should've just taken off your dress."

"I'm not going to lie in your bed half naked while you're talking to your mom downstairs."

He drops his arms and takes a step into the closet. "You've done it before."

"When your mom wasn't here."

Jordan shrugs like it's no big deal. "I saw your Snapchat."

Oh. Crap. "Yeah?" My voice cracks and I clear my throat.

"Cuddle with Tuttle?" He raises a brow.

My entire body flushes hot. I am such an idiot. Seriously. "Uh…"

"And hashtag 'property of'? Really, Mandy?"

He's now standing directly in front of me, handsome as ever in that pale blue button down shirt I want to slowly unbutton myself. God, being in his presence leaves me feeling so weak, when I should be mad at him. Mad at the way he acted tonight, how he ignored me.

How his parents almost ruined everything for us. He's still angry, and because I'm a sick, *sick* pervert, his anger only turns me on. Leaves me weak and flushed and my blood runs hot. I'm restless and needy and there's a deep, low throbbing between my legs that makes me want to attack him.

Clearly I have issues.

"Please don't be mad," I whisper. "I can explain."

"You think I'm mad?"

"I know you've had a bad night," I start, and he laughs, though there is not one ounce of amusement in the sound. "And my night hasn't been that great either."

"Is that my fault?"

I shake my head, not wanting to blame anyone.

Okay, fine. I want to blame Lauren Mancini for that stupid photo she posted, like she has the right to post shit like that about the boy I am currently with. The boy who I'd like to think is really mine.

"I did the Snapchat thing because of Lauren Mancini," I finally admit, feeling so incredibly lame.

Jordan frowns. "Lauren Mancini? What does she have to do with this?"

"She posted a photo of you and her at the Homecoming dance, dancing in each other's arms and wearing your stupid crowns," I mutter, shaking my head. "She's trying to make it seem like you two are a real couple. She even hashtagged the photo 'Jordan and Lauren.'"

"And...what?" He almost looks amused. "You fell for her trick? Who am I with right now? Isn't that the most important thing?"

I ignore his question. "I got—mad." And jealous. I have no photos of Jordan and me together. None. And in this social media driven world we live in, if there's no photographic proof, then it didn't happen.

"I danced with her because I had to. The homecoming king and queen always have to dance together after they're crowned. It's tradition. The second the song was done, I was out," he explains.

"Until you showed up at Yo Town with her."

"It was a group of us getting frozen yogurt. I just went along with it." He shrugs. Jordan Tuttle is not one to go "along with it". So why did he?

"Did you know I was working at Yo Town when you went there?"

He looks the slightest bit contrite. "Maybe."

"Oh. My. God!" I shove at his chest, wishing I could pull him in closer to me. But I'm still mad at him.

Sort of.

"You were spying on me," I say when he remains quiet. And he still remains quiet, which makes me uneasy. "Were you trying to make me jealous?"

"Never. I just." He hesitates, his gaze locking on mine. "I just wanted to see you."

Now it's my turn to remain quiet. He's stunned me silent. He has this way of making me feel special with just a look, a few choice words. And we're having this crazy conversation-slash-argument in his giant closet, with me still wearing only his jersey and my dress clutched in my hand. I just need to get dressed and get out of here.

But where would I go? Who would drive me? I guess Jordan could take me home, but then I'd have to explain why I wasn't spending the night at Liv's. I could go back to Liv's house, but I don't think she's home. She's still with Ryan most likely. And no way am I going to Ryan's house. They're probably banging at this very moment.

The pang of envy deep inside me doesn't go unnoticed.

"So Amanda." Jordan's voice breaks through my thoughts, and I meet his gaze once more.

"Yeah?"

"Got anything else on under my jersey?" he asks.

Oh. I lift my chin, hoping for confident. Probably failing miserably. What's the point of arguing when we're just going to end up tangled together anyway? That's what I want. I think he wants it too.

"Maybe you should do a little exploring and find out for yourself."

His expression turns thunderous and he grabs hold of my waist just as I try to get away from him. He pulls me in, his hands immediately diving beneath the hem of his jersey and grabbing hold of my butt.

"Still got your panties on," he murmurs as those big hands grab hold of both cheeks and gives them a squeeze. A shuddery sigh escapes me, and when he slips his hands underneath my panties and touches bare skin, I close my eyes. Press my lips together to contain the moan that wants to spill out.

"Jordan," I whisper, but he kisses me silent. It's an aggressive kiss, full of tongue and heat and we're only a few seconds in before he breaks away from my eager lips and hauls me over his shoulder, carrying me caveman-style out of his closet and straight for his bed.

Now I'm yelling his name in protest. Pounding on his back with my fists. He ignores me, his hand coming up to smack me lightly on the butt, and I hiss out a breath, nearly fainting at the way he gently caresses my backside right after he slapped it.

This is getting weird.

He tosses me on the bed and follows me down, so he's hovering above me, his face in mine, my back flat on the mattress. "You're loud," he tells me. "My mom might hear you."

My eyes go wide. I would die if she barged in here to see what was going on. Just…die. "I-I'm sorry."

"Gonna have keep your mouth covered if you can't keep quiet," he says with a smirk, those expert hands of his tunneling up the inside of the jersey, touching me in all the right places.

I close my eyes, a little moan escaping me when he traces my lacy bra, and he lightly clamps his hand across my mouth, silencing me. My eyes flash open to find him watching me carefully.

"Shhh," he whispers, his thumb gently stroking my cheek. "Quiet, baby."

I melt at him calling me baby. This entire situation is weird yet hot. He's using a little force on me—just enough to scare me, but not enough to make me run screaming from his room. I try my best to calm my breathing, my racing heart, our gazes never straying from each other's. When he slowly lifts his hand away from my face, he leans in and kisses me. Surprisingly, it's gentle. A mere brushing of lips on lips, and I feel that simple kiss all the way to my curled toes.

He keeps kissing me, and it's nice, more than nice. But I want more. I become restless. I lift my hips against his knee and he shifts away, breaking the kiss to slowly shake his head. "No grinding on my knee tonight. I want to touch you."

My insides tremble. I want him to touch me too. Jordan shifts away from me and takes off the jersey I'm wearing, his fingers sliding over my stomach, between my breasts, along my collarbone. When he undoes the front clasp of my bra, he takes it off, sliding the scrap of lace down my arms and tossing it on the floor. And then he's kissing my chest, cupping my breasts, stroking and sucking and doing all sorts of wondrous things that make me want to scream.

I must get close to screaming because his hand is back on my mouth, keeping me mute. I let him keep it there, closing my eyes when his other hand drifts down, caressing my stomach, smoothing over one hipbone, then the other, just before he dives his fingers down the front of my panties.

And that's almost all it takes. He touches me there, so carefully at first, so tentatively that I almost want to shout at him *more*. But I remain quiet, his hand still loosely covering the lower half of my face, his other hand in my panties. I squirm against his touch, spreading my thighs, inviting him in, and he takes the invitation. Stroking me, testing me, slipping one thick finger inside me…

"Oh God." The words are muffled behind his hand and he removes it, kissing me again, before he slides his lips down to my throat, behind my ear. I wince when his fingers fumble, a distressed noise leaving me, and he pauses. Goes completely still.

"Did I hurt you?" He sounds worried.

I shake my head. Shift my hips. "Not really."

His mouth is at my ear. "Tell me what you like."

I absolutely cannot answer that. *Please.* I am way too new at this sex thing and he is Jordan Tuttle, the sex god.

"Tell me, Mandy." He kisses my ear. Nibbles it. Makes me squirm again. "I want to know what you like."

"I don't know," I finally tell him, mumbling so low I hope he doesn't hear me. Which is dumb, but I'm feeling so inept. So inexperienced compared to him. He's been with so many girls. A countless list of girls I don't want to think about. They've been with him like this, wrapped up in his arms like this, his mouth on theirs, his hands…everywhere.

I hate to think about it. So I push all of those negative thoughts out of my head and focus on right now.

Jordan is persistent. He touches me in different spots, asking if I like it. And when he touches one spot in particular that makes me see a few sparkly stars in my peripheral vision, I tell him *don't stop*. I might've even begged him. He increases his pace and, with his other hand, tugs my panties down past my hips, to my thighs, until I'm helping him and kicking them off myself. I am completely naked with Jordan in his bed, his fingers between my thighs, and I am so close to exploding I'm afraid I might fall completely apart.

I've never felt so alive.

chapter twenty-two

Tuttle

Amanda clings to me, her long legs tangled with mine, her arms wrapped around my neck as she breathes hard. My head rests on her chest and the wild thump, *thump* of her beating heart calms me. Reminds me that this moment is happening. That what I just did to her is one hundred percent real.

Being with her is like nothing I've ever experienced, and it's... terrifying. That quick encounter with my father tonight reminded me that spending time with her is wrong. Stringing her along, stringing myself along. Pretending I believe in relationships and that what Amanda and I could have could ever be healthy and strong. It's all lies.

We won't work out. Something—me—will screw it up. I am my father's son. And I am my mother's son too. That conversation with my mother earlier had been downright painful. She'd been drinking, and after popping a few anti-anxiety pills, that combination always sends her into near hysterics.

She ranted on and on about her cheating husband. How I should turn my heart to stone to prevent it from ever being broken. She claimed I have a more sensitive heart, that I'm more like her than my father, who's cold and calculating and flat out heartless.

Maybe she's right after all. I've been trying to convince myself otherwise for years. I'm not sensitive. I don't care about anyone. I don't have real friends and I definitely don't need a relationship. Girls are nothing but trouble.

Amanda changed everything. Even when I was twelve, she scared me. And not in a bad way—more like in a good way. It scared the shit out of me how much I actually *liked* her. And the more time I spent watching her, listening to her, seeing her every day in various classes over the years, the more I liked her.

The more I eventually knew I had to make her mine.

And now here she is. Lying in my arms completely naked. I just made her come and damn, she is beautiful when that happens. I don't think I could ever get tired of making her come again and again.

"I want to touch you," she murmurs into my neck. She shifts closer to me, her naked body brushing against mine, and I smooth my hand along her hip, trying to keep myself under control.

"You're tired."

"Not too tired to keep this going." She kisses my jaw once. Twice. Three times. Sweet little kisses that bring her lips closer and closer to mine. "It's your turn."

I turn my head and kiss her fully, effectively shutting her up. When I pull away she's watching me with flushed cheeks and stars in her eyes. "This is ridiculous. I'm completely naked and you're completely clothed."

"I like you this way." I squeeze her ass because it's perfect and I can't stop touching it. "Don't worry about me."

"I want to worry about you." She reaches for the front of my shirt and starts unbuttoning it. "This moment rates high in my fantasies."

"You have fantasies? About me?" That's intriguing. Wonder if she'll tell me them someday. I have a few I could share with her too.

She bats at my chest. "Stripping you of your clothes is a pretty fine fantasy to have, don't you think?"

"As long as I'm the one benefitting from this fantasy, then hell yes."

Her fingers brush against my skin with every button she slips undone, and then my shirt is open and she's spreading the fabric away from my chest, trying her best to tug it completely off. I sit up and get rid of it, tossing the shirt on the floor before I rejoin her.

"Not good enough." She's reaching for the fly of my jeans and it's my turn to bat her hands away. She accidentally brushes her fingers against my dick, and I'm done for. I'll probably come in my jeans and that would be all sorts of messed up.

"It's either we do this or talk about your dad," she tells me, sincerity glowing in her pretty brown eyes.

And there goes my erection.

I fall onto the mattress right next to her, exhaling loudly. "You want to talk about my dad right *now?*"

She shrugs and pulls the comforter over us, then snuggles in close to me. "I just want to make sure you're okay. I know that what happened at the restaurant wasn't—pleasant for you."

The mildest way she could've put it. I'd barely looked at the man and became enraged. My behavior was completely over the top.

But my family is pretty fucking ridiculous, so…

"I'm here for you, Jordan, if you ever need to talk. Or even if you don't want to talk, you know?" She hugs me. Kisses my chest with those lush, beautiful lips.

I say nothing. How can I answer her? I love that she wants to be there for me, but I can't rely on her. I can't rely on anyone.

"I have no idea what I'm doing," she whispers against my chest before she lifts her gaze to mine. "I don't want to mess this up."

"Mess what up?"

She shifts so she's now kissing my stomach. Again and again, her lips soft and damp and making me shiver. Her fingers fumble over the front of my jeans and she hesitates.

"Do you want this?"

Fuck yes, I want to shout, but I remain calm. Neutral. I don't need to act like a crazy man when I'm with her.

But Amanda makes me want to lose my mind.

She starts undoing the front of my jeans and I help until I'm as naked as her. Her slender fingers slip around my erection and I close my eyes. Grit my teeth. Tell myself I need to keep my shit together.

"Tell me what you like," she whispers, a direct copy of what I asked her earlier. "I want to make you feel good, Jordan. Tell me. Show me."

So I tell her. I show her. And she's hesitant at first. A little puzzled yet fascinated, and it's the fascination that gets me. She just wants to make me happy. She's not using me for my money or my status. Amanda likes me. And I don't get why.

I don't.

When she puts her mouth on me, it's nothing like those other times. With those other girls, girls whose names I forget, girls who meant nothing to me. It's so much better with Amanda. Everything's better as long as she's part of it.

And that's the scariest part of all.

chapter twenty-three

"We need to talk."

The four worst words in the English language, spoken by my father. My day couldn't get any shittier than this and it's only just begun. I'm in bed, it's—I look at my phone—almost ten o'clock in the morning and here he is, bringing me down. Ruining everything.

Like usual.

"What about?" I snap as I sit up in bed, then run a hand through my hair. My respect for him went out the window a long time ago. I can't hardly look at him. After what happened at the restaurant between us last night, I'm done. Yet here he is, strutting into my bedroom on a Sunday morning like he has every right.

I guess he does, since this is his house. But it's like he's a stranger. An imposter. A man that doesn't belong here—and who isn't wanted here. His showing up like this has ruined my good mood. Being with

Amanda last night soothed me. She's good for me.

Too good for me.

"Your mother and I have been talking." He looms near the door, as if prepared to leave if he needs to. The way I'm glaring, I guess I can't blame him. "You need to get serious about college."

"How am I not serious about college?" I ask incredulously. "I play football. I'm in honors classes. I get good grades. I'm doing everything I can here to make this shit happen."

He ignores everything I say. "I want to take you to Oregon this afternoon. I've already arranged for a plane, and I've scheduled some appointments first thing Monday morning."

"With who?" This is my opportunity to tell him I don't want to go to the University of Oregon. That's his dream for me, not my dream. I don't want to leave this state. There are better colleges here. I don't understand his fixation.

But he doesn't care what I want. It only matters what *he* wants.

"With the dean of students, and with the head coach and his staff. I know we've toured the facility before, but this time it's serious. We're serious. No more distractions allowed. The parties need to stop. The girls need to stop, especially that one your mother just met. You don't need to break any hearts this year, Jordan. You need to focus." The stern look my father sends me makes most men cower in defeat. Not me though.

I learned from a master. I stare back, not saying a word.

"Take a shower and pack an overnight bag. We leave in a few hours." And with that, he's gone. With that, I'm dismissed.

Grabbing my phone, I roll over on my side and scroll through my notifications. There's a Snapchat from Amanda that came about thirty minutes ago and I open it to find a photo of her in bed, her eyes sleepy, her hair in a messy bun on top of her head, her smile soft.

And so fucking sweet, it kills me to look at her like that. Pretty and open and vulnerable and all mine. The caption tears me apart.

Last night was amazing. I miss you.

She added a few heart emojis and just seeing them totally slays me. I drove her home early this morning, dropping her off down the street from her house before eight. She was worried about my parents finding her in my bed. And if I would've had my way, it could've happened. I wouldn't have cared either.

But she would've. I don't want to disrespect her. I care about her too damn much.

Frustration slides through me and I want to punch something. It's ridiculous. My feelings for her are ridiculous. But they're also real. So incredibly real, she's all I can think about. She consumes me.

Yet I can't have her.

Inhaling deeply, I let it all out and close my eyes. Press my hands over them. I can't do this. I can't keep this up. What Amanda and I have will eventually end. Hell, I can already see the end. I need to let her down gently. I don't want to hurt her, though it'll happen. I know it will. I'll hurt myself too because I can't resist her. Why would I want to?

I don't send her a reply. I don't text her. I don't call her. If I'm going to do this, I need to quit cold turkey. If this is what my dad wants, I need to do it. He'll cut me off. He'll screw me over. Damn it, I need him. I'm not even eighteen yet. He calls all the shots. I have to do what he says.

If I don't, there will be hell to pay.

chapter twenty-four

Amanda

Monday I show up to school and there's no Tuttle. He never makes an appearance.

Tuesday, more of the same. No Tuttle sightings. No texts, no calls, no Snapchats or Instagram posts. No one seems to even notice that he's gone, with the exception of Livvy and Ryan, though they're not saying anything. It's like they're scared to bring it up, especially after what happened Saturday night.

I run into Kyla at lunch Monday and she asks me to come to football practice that afternoon to help her. "I know you have a job after school and I was trying to do it on my own, but I can't," she explained. "So if there's any day you can help me, that would be awesome."

I had to turn her down for Monday and Tuesday. I worked both days after school, covering for Blake since he was sick with some sort of horrific virus. Sonja called me Sunday night asking me to work, and of course I said yes.

I never had to work alone, though. Sonja was there both nights, stuck in her office behind the computer and working on end-of-month accounting stuff. Livvy gave me a ride both days and Dad picked me up once work was finished. Once I got home I stayed up until almost midnight, finishing my homework, checking out stupid Snapchat and getting pissed every time Lauren Mancini made some vague *I wish he was my boyfriend* reference.

For all I know they're spending time together. That's what my envious heart whispers to me late at night anyway.

So yeah. Blake didn't come to school on Monday and Tuesday either. Neither did Mrs. Meyer. It was like everyone was out with some sort of weird virus or whatever, and I started to grow concerned. Was Jordan ill? Was he okay? Where could he be?

But when I want to, I can be stubborn. For some twisted reason, I want him to reach out to me. It should be Jordan who makes the next move. I don't want to look like I'm chasing after him. I don't want to look desperate. I'm sure that's what about a million other girls have done with him in the past. I don't want him to think I'm like all the rest.

I want to be different. Special. Especially after everything we shared Saturday night…

Um, wow. That had been a major moment. We didn't have actual sex, but it was close enough. I've never been that naked—literally—with a boy before. And we were naked. I had my mouth on his…

God. I can't even think it, let alone say it out loud. I tried to do my best, but half of the time it felt awkward, though he certainly never protested. Did I drive him away with my lack of skills? He definitely didn't complain while it happened. Or afterward either. Yet I feel like I messed up, or worse…

I feel like every other girl he's been with. And eventually dumped.

I can't think about it too much, though. If I do, I'll just end up sad.

Depressed.

Devastated.

So yeah. I sent Tuttle a Snapchat Sunday morning and he never replied. I'm worried about him, about us, yet there are so many things I need to focus on right now. I saw my counselor yesterday afternoon and she gave me the fattest packet of scholarship and grant forms I'd ever seen. Plus she handed over a list of website URLs that are full of lesser-known scholarships. My eyes crossed just thinking about all the forms I'll need to fill out. And we're barely into October.

I tell myself I don't have time to worry about Jordan. I don't have time to worry about anything. I need to be on autopilot and just work through one thing after another. Going to class, picking up the pace at yearbook, afterschool water girl duty, Friday night game water girl duty, working, homework, college applications, scholarship applications, helping out at home…

The list is endless. The more I don't see Jordan, the more I realize I don't need a boyfriend. Or even a guy I occasionally see. He's a distraction.

A distraction who will get me off track if I don't watch it.

But I miss him. My heart aches without him around. Without hearing his voice, seeing his rare smiles, feeling his hands on me. I miss everything about him, and it sucks because he doesn't seem to miss me at all.

It's like I don't matter to him. Like I never mattered.

It's Wednesday afternoon right after lunch when I pop my locker open and a note folded into a perfect rectangle falls out, landing on the floor. I grab it and open the note with trembling fingers. It's handwritten instead of typed, and I know from the moment I read the first word it's from Jordan, and it's part of our English assignment. I still haven't shared my entry with him yet.

Where once I said my heart was made of wondrous light, now it is dark. Heavy. Angry. For only she can bring me light, and now that I've lost her, the light is gone. Banished.

She is the only one who can make me feel, but without her, I am numb. We were young and stupid, and if I could go back in time and change my actions, I would.

But I can't. A foolish heart beats like no other, and mine is the most foolish of hearts. The damage has been done. I have lost the girl.

Yet she will never lose me. Not if she looks deep inside her heart.

For now, I hold onto my dreams. For now, I hope for more wondrous light. I hope for my love to come back into my life.

For now, I hold onto Juliet.

My heart breaks at his words. This entry is short but pointed. He writes these things and they feel so real. I've poured my real feelings for him into my diary entries and can't help but think he must do the same.

Carefully refolding the note, I stash it into the front pocket of my backpack and start heading to class. He must be here. He has to be, since I got the note. This means I will see him in English.

The nervous energy starts pouring through my body, making me jittery. And that has nothing to do with the giant Coke I drank during lunch. It's brought on by the mere thought of possibly being with Jordan.

And a few minutes later, when I'm making my way toward the classroom and I actually *see* Jordan, standing to the side and looking down the hall like he's waiting for me, I slow my pace. Try my best to look nonchalant. Like I haven't been anxiously searching for him for days.

When he spots me, the faintest smile curls his perfect lips, his gaze never leaving me as I approach.

Everything comes rushing back. He has that cool, calm Jordan Tuttle aura going on, and all I can see is that one moment when I made him lose control on Saturday night. The way he groaned my name. How he hauled me into his arms when it was over, his body still trembling, his mouth on mine, our naked bodies entwined.

I'm flushed just thinking about it. But I need to remain chill. That is my number one goal.

"Haven't seen you in a while," I say, hip checking him when he falls into step beside me. I hope I sound casual, but it's so difficult. What I really want is to ask him a ton of questions. But that turns me into the needy girlfriend, and I'm positive he doesn't like that sort of thing.

He grabs hold of me, his arm sneaking around my waist. "Missed you," he murmurs as he presses his face into my hair, quickly kissing my temple.

I smile, hoping I seem mysterious. Like nothing bothers me. "Where have you been?"

His gaze goes vacant as he stares straight ahead. "Family stuff. Nothing to worry about, though. I'll tell you about it later."

Naturally, I'm worried. It felt like he just…disappeared, and now he's back, like he was never gone.

The way he's acting, it's weird.

"You're okay?"

"Oh yeah." He glances down at me. "You read my note?"

"Yeah. It was good," I say softly, wondering if he can see all the emotion I feel for him shining in my eyes. I shouldn't show my cards, but being this close to him, having him touch me, it renders me helpless. I think he knows it, too.

"I'm not finished with that entry yet. Have you written yours?"

"I have."

"You should share it with me."

"I will, in class." Ugh, I sort of don't want to, but I will. Maybe I should demand he spill before I let him read my entry. Though that's catty and stupid, and I refuse to act that way around him.

Jordan releases his hold on me as we walk into the classroom, and I'm relieved to see Mrs. Meyer is back. She runs through attendance, coughs a little, pops a Halls and then asks that we quietly work on our projects. "The first part is due this Friday."

A few groans fill the room, but otherwise we're quiet. Well, except for me. I raise my hand.

"Miss Winters?"

I drop my hand. "How many entries should we have by the time we turn in the first part?"

"At least five each," Mrs. Meyer says with a faint smile.

Crap. My heart sinks. I only have three and I want to work on the last one some more. Plus, I have to help with practice after school, and we have a game Friday. Thank God I don't work at Yo Town again until Sunday afternoon, and only for four hours.

Once Mrs. Meyer answers a few slightly panicked questions, we all assemble with our partners. I pull the second diary entry I never let him read last week out of my backpack and hand it to Jordan.

"Please be honest," I tell him. "Tell me if it's awful or not. I really want this to shine and impress Mrs. Meyer."

"You're a good writer," he says, taking the paper from me. "I'm sure it's fine."

I loom over his shoulder and read my words along with him.

Lo, my life is over before it's truly begun. From what passion for him burns so bright to turn so cold overnight. He shone upon me like the brightest star, and I was his ever faithful moon. Until without notice my star was snuffed out, along with the others, one by one. I was left a cold, dark and lonely moon. Faithful and present, yet lost and forgotten.

Will he find me again? Will he shine his light upon me and warm me up? Or am I forever doomed to go this alone?

He's quiet for a moment, as if he's taking the time to absorb my words, and I start to fidget. "Well?" The word bursts out of me like a bullet.

Jordan turns to look at me. "It's sad."

"Romeo and Juliet's relationship is the ultimate in sadness," I remind him.

"I know." He glances at the paper once more, his gaze lingering. "Their relationship was also passionate," he reminds me.

"Passion only lasts for so long, especially with those two. They are a prime example that you cannot sustain a relationship based merely on passion." I sound like I'm totally down on love, and right now, I sort of am.

"You really believe that?" He raises a brow.

I don't know what to believe. Or what to think either. These mixed signals Jordan's sending in my direction are playing havoc on my heart and my mind. I thought what happened between us this past weekend would've brought us closer together, but instead I feel like Jordan has pulled away from me and become almost—distant.

"Yes," I say softly.

He says nothing for a moment. Just busies himself with pulling his iPad out of his backpack and turning it on. I do the same, telling myself

I need to write the next entry, maybe two while we're in class, but I can't help sneaking glances at Jordan. Wondering what he's been doing the last few days. He claims it was family business, but what? I don't know what's going on. I just wish he would tell me something. More than anything, I wish he would include me in his plans and thoughts and hopes and dreams.

Okay, that last statement is over the top, but you get the gist.

"I went with my father to check out a college he wants me to go to," Jordan says out of nowhere.

I look at him. "Where at?"

"Oregon, like I told you about. They want me. He's pushing it hard. Tells me this is my chance."

"Are you going to do it?"

Jordan's gaze meets mine for the briefest moment. "I don't know."

I'm not sure what else I should say. He told me only a few days ago that he didn't want to go. So what made him change his mind? Is that part of the reason why he's acting so distant?

"Maybe we should work on our entries for the rest of class," I tell him, keeping my voice low. All the other groups are chatting loudly, and I wish we were too. But everything feels so serious between us right now. I don't like it.

Things aren't right between us, and I don't know how to fix it. I'm a fixer. It's what I do. But this feels completely out of my control.

Truly? It's pretty damn terrifying. What if he dumps me? Before we even had a chance to really become something?

"If that's what you want," he says, his gaze never straying from the iPad. I wish he'd look at me. I wish he'd talk to me.

But he won't.

We remain quiet as we work, our arms occasionally bumping

against each other's since I'm a lefty and he's a righty. I apologize so many times he finally tells me to stop, and because I'm PMSing and a little moody and miffed at his neglectful treatment, I get pissed.

I never claimed I was rational in Jordan's presence, so none of you can hold my stupid behavior against me.

I look up Romeo and Juliet quotes on the web on my phone and highlight them, adding them to my notes section for future reference. Mrs. Meyer isn't bothered by all of us using our phones and iPads as we work. She encourages us to use them most of the time, unless she catches one of us texting.

Of course, Livvy chooses this exact moment to text me like crazy.

You will not believe what happened.

Brianne Brown talked to me at lunch. Like chattered on and on as if we were best friends.

I couldn't believe it. I had no witnesses either. None.

Where were you anyway?

She told me thank you for leaving Dustin alone so she could finally have a chance with him.

Can you imagine? Like I left him alone for her? Please.

He's the one who avoided me.

I hate her.

A few minutes later…

Ryan and I had sex this weekend and guess what?

The condom broke.

I am freaking. OUT.

What if I get pregnant? I will DIE, A.

Die. Die. Die. I don't care if Ryan makes cute babies.

Cuz you know he could. Look at him!!!

But seriously. The last thing I want is a baby.

She is so dramatic. And why didn't she lead with the broken condom story? That's way more dramatic than Brianne Brown thanking Livvy for letting her have at it with Dustin.

I'm about to text her back quickly, but she sends me another one.

I don't even like kids. Having one of my own? Puke fest.

I don't want them.

Like EVER.

I decide to answer her back and calm her down.

You're not pregnant. Chill out. Screw everyone else and what they think, especially BB.

"Who you texting?" Jordan asks casually.

I glance up from my phone. How he can figure out I'm texting someone is beyond me. I shut off my phone. "Livvy."

"Uh huh." He nods, his expression full on doubtful. Does he think I'm lying? Seriously?

"Whatever," I mutter under my breath as I see another text come in from Liv.

I need to get on the pill. I need to go to Planned Parenthood this week.

You should come with me.

My cheeks go hot and I glance over at Jordan, but he's bent over his iPad and engrossed with whatever he's doing. I should be working too. But now Liv has taken the conversation into an interesting turn and I don't want it to stop.

I don't need to go on the pill.

                    Why not? You and Tuttle ARE doing the nasty. Right????

Sort of. Not really. Not in the very real sense of the word. Kind of.

                                    How do you kind of do it?

We are currently doing everything but IT. You know what I mean.

                                          Ohhhh.......!!!!!!

Now she gets it.

You still need to go on the pill. You don't want a pregnancy scare. Condoms + the pill is the best way to go. You're doubly safe.

My mom is pretty open and explained all that I needed to know about the birds and the bees when I was younger. Plus, we had those special movies and discussions starting in the fifth grade. They were embarrassing, yet oddly fascinating. Plus, I've read plenty of romance novels in my life, so I know what's up. I get the romantic stuff, the sex stuff. Heck, most of those romance books I read I stole from my mom's secret stash in the hall closet.

But if I went to her right now and asked her to hook me up with her gyno so I could get on the pill? She would lose her freaking mind.

I have a sudden thought and decide to ask Liv.

Do you give Ryan a BJ with him wearing a condom?

Ha! What a question. I'm on a roll.

> **Um, no. I thought only hookers did that.**

Where do you come up with this stuff?

I watch HBO. They have all of those old Hookers on the Point documentaries. I've watched a few.

I have no idea what she's talking about, so whatever.

IMO, giving a blowjob is a sign of trust. He's trusting you to put your mouth on his dick. You're trusting him by putting your mouth on his dick. Cuz seriously, it's weird when you think about it. If he can't trust you or worse, he asks you to use a condom while you're blowing him, that is just odd. Time to move on to the next one, you know? You deserve better than some guy who acts like that.

That was the longest text Liv has ever sent me.

Where are you anyway?

> **Study hall. Where are you? English with Tuttle?**

I check on him again. He's still staring at his stupid iPad.

Yeah. Working on our project.

And you're talking about BJs with him sitting next to you? So brave.

I'm trying to come up with a good response when she sends something else.

Did that happen with you and Tuttle? Did he ask you to use a condom before you blew him!!??

No, not at all. But the BJ part...

> **OMG spill woman!**

Let's just say I gave him a BJ and I haven't really talked to him since.

Until now.

Ummm, I hate to say this.

NM.

You can't leave me like that. Tell me.

I don't want to hurt your feelings or worry you Amanda, but that's totally his MO.

What do you mean?

He gets a BJ and then he disappears like a ghost.

But he would never do that to you! At least, he better not.

Or I'm going to kick his ass.

Oh! I'll have Ryan kick his ass for me. For YOU.

We're here for you babe. Promise.

Her texts only confirm my worst fears.

chapter twenty-five

I'm about to go to out to football practice when I hear someone call my name. I turn to find Liv running toward me, her cheeks pink from exertion or making out with Ryan, I'm not sure which.

"I made an appointment for us," she tells me once she catches her breath.

I frown. "An appointment for what?"

"Planned Parenthood!"

Wow, she said that *extremely* loud. I give her a stern look and she winces, realizing her mistake. "Tomorrow at four. Well, I'm at four, you're at four-thirty," she says at a much lower decibel.

"What exactly are we going to, uh, *PP* for?" I told her I didn't need to get on the pill. There's no point. I'm not having sex, so I won't get pregnant. And after the way Jordan treated me in class, how he bolted out of his seat the moment the bell rang, completely ignoring me, I have a sinking feeling that whatever we had, whatever we'd been working toward?

It's all over.

My heart aches. So does my head. I'm so confused. I want to chase after him. I want to kick his ass. I can't make up my mind which way to go.

But I plan on soldiering on. I don't really have a choice, do I? "Please, cancel my appointment," I tell her. "I gotta go. I'll text you later."

"Amanda." She grabs my arm, preventing me from leaving. "Come with me, okay? I need—I really need the support. And I'll support you, I promise. You may as well go to the appointment and get on the pill. Then you'll be safe. We'll both be safe."

I see the fear in her gaze and I realize she is truly freaked out over the condom breaking with Ryan. And she really wants me to be there for her. "I have football practice tomorrow. And I have it right now. I'm gonna be late."

She makes a face. "What? You've joined the team now?"

"Kyla asked me to help her with the hydration station. She doesn't like working it alone."

"Please, Amanda," Livvy says, sounding desperate. "I really need you to go with me. Can't you tell her you have an appointment and you can't make it tomorrow?"

I feel like that's all I do lately. Make excuses to please someone else. I'm doing this water girl thing for Tuttle. Well, I did it for myself to get closer to Tuttle, but look how well that worked for me. We're back at square one. No, it's worse than square one. We started to advance and make real, actual progress, but now we've ended up in this weird limbo place where it's awkward and uncomfortable and we look at each other like we've seen each other naked because, oh yeah, we *have* seen each other naked before. And now it's just weird.

And awkward.

And awful.

"Hey, did you ever talk to Em like you said you would?" I ask her.

Liv lets go of my arm, her expression turning distant. "No."

"Why not?" She is so frustrating. Everyone is frustrating. And no, I'm not being the asshole here. Fact: I surround myself with frustrating people on a daily basis. I must like being tortured.

She shrugs. "I haven't had time, okay? And honestly, I don't really miss her from my life."

"What? Seriously? Come on, Liv. Don't be so cold-hearted."

"Please, *she's* the cold-hearted one, trying to sabotage my relationship every chance she gets. Being mean to me, pushing Brianne Brown on Dustin, the photos with her hanging all over Ryan, all the tricks and constant bullshit. I really don't need that in my life anymore, you know? Without her around, everything's become a lot easier."

"Is that how you really feel, Olivia?"

I freeze. Close my eyes. *Crap.* I know that voice. It's Em. And she's standing directly behind me.

The cool expression on Liv's face betrays nothing. She's like a statue, cold and unmoving. "I didn't mean for you to hear all of that, but…yes. That is exactly how I feel."

I glance over my shoulder and see Em. She looks heartbroken. Her eyes fill with tears and her lower lip trembles, like she's barely holding it together. I want to offer her comfort, but I know that'll make Liv mad. And ultimately, I'm Liv's friend first.

So I need to stick with where my loyalty lies.

"I was hoping we could become friends again. I was really hoping we could forgive each other and move on, but I guess not." Em sounds so lost and sad, I want to go to her and offer her comfort. But I don't. I just give her a sympathetic smile, though she's not even looking at me.

"Even after everything that happened, you really believed that?" Liv asks incredulously.

"Of course I really believed that. We all believe what we want, right? But I guess my beliefs were too crazy to be real." With a shake of her head, Em stalks off, never once looking back.

Liv blows out a harsh breath. "Well. That was surprisingly easy."

I whirl on her. "You *wanted* her to hear that?"

"Maybe not all of it, but I've definitely wanted to tell her how I really felt. I just didn't know how." She sighs. "I didn't have the guts."

I stare at her, shocked that she doesn't feel even remotely bad for what she said. When I don't say anything, I witness Livvy's immediate slide into defense mode.

"Things are so much better now, Amanda! You've seen how I am. How Ryan and I are doing. We're getting along great. We are closer than ever. Plus, I have you in my life. I've made some friends in Yearbook. I don't need anyone else, and I definitely don't need Em stirring the pot and screwing things up."

Maybe Liv's right. Maybe she is better off without Em in her life. Em just seemed so lost, so sad. I really wanted to give Liv back Em, and maybe that's my own guilt seeping in, I can't help it. I wish they could get along.

I'm truly starting to believe that'll never happen. And I need to accept that.

"So." Liv's face turns plaintive. "Will you go with me to PP tomorrow? Please? I really need you there. I can't ask Ryan to go with me."

"Why not?"

"He'll freak out. I assured him I could never get pregnant, even if the condom broke, but I don't know about that. What if I *can* get pregnant? He will die. He might even…" Liv's face starts to fall and I reach for her. Grab her by the shoulders and give her a solid shake.

"You're not—" My voice lowers. "—pregnant. I can feel it in my bones. And my bones never lie."

Liv giggles, but only for a moment before she's somber again. "I won't feel better unless I go and get checked tomorrow. And get on the pill. I need to do this, Amanda. For peace of mind, more than anything."

Sighing, I curl my arm around her and haul her in close to me. "Fine. We'll go. But right after you'll need to bring me back here so I can work on with the team during practice." Practices can run until six sometimes, and maybe if we get out of our appointments early enough, I can help for the last half hour or so."

"What exactly are you doing for them anyway? I just thought you were the water girl at the games."

"Apparently now I'm the water girl during practice too. Staying hydrated doesn't ever stop, you know."

"You sound like a commercial." Livvy rolls her eyes then draws me into a hug. "I need to get home. My mom's expecting me. I'll text you later, okay?"

"Bye."

I walk out to the football field alone, my mind filled with too many thoughts. Thankfully, a lot of those thoughts aren't my own and don't involve Jordan Tuttle, which is nice. It feels like a little reprieve, worrying about someone else's problems. I have enough, and really don't want to add more to the mix if I can help it.

But as I draw closer to the field and see the boys out there, I can't help but think of Tuttle. And how he cut me off.

And how mad that makes me.

Kyla spots me approaching and waves me over. She shows me the elaborate hydration station with all the brisk efficiency of someone who's been at this for a long time. She is in her element here on the sidelines. The boys all treat her like she's their little sister or adopted mascot.

She takes it all in stride, laughing and teasing, sometimes flirting, though not too much. She's very professional. I can't help but envy how easy she makes everything seem. Working with the boys, organizing the water, jumping to it when Coach Halsey screams her name. There's never a hair out of place, her placid expression proving she's unflappable. I wish I were that confident.

The coaches are running the boys through endless drills, though I don't really pay attention. I'm too busy working the hydration station, trying to figure it out as I fill one empty water bottle after another. Kyla's taking care of an injured player and most of the JV team is milling around the hydration station, including one Eli Bennett, Ryan's younger brother.

"I know you," he says, pointing his index finger right at me.

"Anyone ever tell you it's rude to point?" One of the other guys slaps Eli's hand down and a few of them chuckle.

Eli glares at the kid before resuming his examination of me. "You've been at my house."

Oh man. I so do not want to go down this road. "Want some water?" I offer him a water bottle.

"Nah." He shakes his head, his sweaty hair flying, then spits on the ground. Gross. "What's your name?"

"She's a senior, Bennett," another one of his teammates yells at him.

"Save it for a girl who'll really go for you."

"Maybe I like older women." He directs a dazzling smile straight at me, and I can't lie—the boy is gorgeous, just like his brother. He has the same golden brown hair and the strong jaw, though his eyes are more of a hazel color versus green like Ryan's. He's the JV team's quarterback, and while he's not extraordinarily tall, Eli is lean and muscled. He can throw the perfect spiral and he's led the team in a big way this season.

And what? Now he's showing interest in…me? This has to be a joke.

"You were with Tuttle," Eli says as he saunters toward me. "At my house, for Ryan's party. You were sitting on the bus together Friday night. You two a thing, or what?"

I want to say *or what* so bad, but I keep my mouth shut. I shrug instead. I don't want to say we're something when we're not. And I don't want to say we're nothing when we could be.

Meaning, I'm a confused mess and I don't know how to answer Eli's question.

"If she's with Tuttle, you need to leave her alone, bro. Remember what he said?" The other guy leans over and whispers in Eli's ear, resulting in the both of them cracking up.

Remember what *he* said? What did Tuttle say? About *me*?

"Leave her the fuck alone, Bennett." The growly voice is none other than Jordan Tuttle himself. I should've known he'd show up in my time of supposed need. I don't bother looking at him because damn it, I'm still pissed. And I don't want him always running to my defense.

"I've got this," I say, smiling sweetly at Eli. He gives me a questioning look in return, and I take a few steps toward him, trying to get my flirt on. "I'm with no one," I tell Eli. "And while freshmen usually do nothing for me, I might take *you* under consideration."

All the guys start making noise, even Eli, who's laughing and getting plenty of slaps on the back. The only one who's quiet is Jordan. I can feel the anger rising off of him, like a living, breathing thing. But I still won't look at him. I just flash Eli a giant smile before I resume my hydration station duties.

The JV boys run back onto the field, yet Jordan remains. Kyla is nowhere in sight. It's just the two of us, and I know I'm going to have to face him sometime. Slowly I turn to look at him, and the hurt I see in his gaze takes me aback.

"You're really interested in Eli?" He sounds incredulous.

I sigh. Guess I'm not any good at this making Jordan jealous thing. "No. I was just…playing around."

"With that kid? He's a total punk." He stares out at the field. "Damn good player, though."

"Kinda like you?"

He faces me once more. "I'm not a punk."

I muffle a laugh. "Please."

"I think I've grown out of that stage."

"Explain to me then the radio silence these last few days." I cross my arms, waiting for his answer.

Jordan blows out a harsh breath and squints into the sun. Of course he looks amazing when he should really look ridiculous. He's wearing this dark blue cotton Nike headband that girls normally wear, keeping his hair out of his face. He's got his navy blue practice jersey on, and white uniform pants that mold to every part of him. He's a little dirty and a little sweaty and a whole lot sexy.

I could slap myself right now for thinking this way.

"I've had some shit go down. With my parents," he finally says, still not looking at me. "College crap. Life crap. You don't want to hear it."

His words are like a slap in the face. "You don't know what I want," I snap. His surprised gaze meets mine. "I told you I would be there for you if you want to talk, or even if you don't want to talk. Whatever. I *will* be there for you, Jordan. You just have to trust me." I pause. "Maybe that's the problem. You don't trust me."

He stares at me, his mouth opening and closing a few times, like he's trying to find the right words to say. But he says nothing. Just looks at me one last time…

And then he walks away.

chapter twenty-six

My new norm is Tuttle and I not really talking to each other, unless it has to deal with school. Our group project for honors English has been reduced to us working on it on our own. I tend to write the best diary entries late at night, when I'm tired and sad and missing him. I let the emotion flow from my fingertips onto the page, curled up in bed with my laptop. We don't even send them to each other anymore. Instead, we email them separately to Mrs. Meyer. She doesn't say a word, doesn't ask us what's going on.

I'm thankful she leaves us alone.

I went with Livvy to Planned Parenthood. She did a pregnancy test—negative. Got an exam, got on the pill, and now she and Ryan are, and I quote, "boinking like bunnies."

At least someone is getting laid.

I had an exam too. Got a prescription for birth control and went and filled it. I've been dutifully taking the pills for over two weeks, which means I'm fully covered.

I'm also still a virgin, so…that was pointless.

I've been working a lot, both at Yo Town and the hydration station. School is kicking my butt. So is work—Mom always drives me and sometimes Livvy takes me or picks me up. Being at the football games with Tuttle so close, yet so distant, is killing me.

Oh yeah. I'm back to calling him Tuttle again. I don't want to call him Jordan. Feels too intimate, and we're not on that level anymore. I don't think we'll ever be there again.

Late at night, when I'm alone in my bed and I can't sleep, I think about what happened. Wonder endlessly where exactly it went wrong—where *I* went wrong. Did I do something? Say something stupid? Irritate him beyond belief and now he can never forgive me?

I don't know.

And it's slowly killing me.

That last night we were together was…life-changing. He'd shared a side of himself I'd never witnessed before, and I wanted to know more. See more. Experience more. But he cut me off. Denied. That's what it felt like. He took a stamp and punched it on my forehead.

DENIED.

At least Lauren Mancini isn't flaunting their so-called relationship, because they don't have one. She's given up, moved on to someone else, I have no idea who. Em has been hanging around Lauren lately, along with Brianne Brown, who is still with Dustin. Now there's a weird triangle, though I say nothing. Em and I talk a little bit, but it's all surface. I think she's mad at me over the entire Livvy thing, even though I'm not the one who said all that mean stuff.

Yet I feel like I've let everyone down.

It's almost Halloween and the yearbook staff has put together a fundraiser so we can help lower the cost of our yearbooks, which is outrageous. I haven't been able to participate much in the planning, but I am taking part in the weekend festivities. We're hosting a haunted house at the fall carnival this Saturday at school and I'm one of the designated haunters, along with Livvy. She bought a ton of makeup at the Spirit Halloween Store and we found our costumes there too, which luckily weren't too expensive.

She's come over to my house tonight—Ryan dropped her off—and we're practicing our makeup and costumes. It's Thursday and we knew we couldn't get together tomorrow. I have hydration duty and she has girlfriend in the stands duty, since the boys are playing a home game.

Another torturous night spending time with Tuttle so he can ignore me tomorrow—I can't freaking wait.

"How should I do my hair?" I stare at myself in the mirror, frowning. We're in the middle of my room sitting on the floor, and I have my own light up mirror while Livvy brought hers. They're both double-sided and I'm looking at myself five times closer, which is sort of freaky. I can see every flaw, every tiny zit and scar and a weird hair growing out of my forehead that's nowhere near my hairline. I need to pluck that thing like yesterday.

"Long and flowing and straight, parted right down the middle. Like Elvira," Livvy answers me as she lines her eyes repeatedly with black kohl eyeliner. If she keeps that up, I won't be able to see her eyes at all.

"Who's Elvira?"

Liv sends me an exasperated look. "Google her."

I grab my phone and do as she says. Immediately I find Elvira, Mistress of the Dark, who does *not* part her hair in the middle. She has bangs and a big poufy bouffant thing on the back of her head that looks crazy, along with the biggest boobs *ever.*

"I look nothing like Elvira." I thrust my phone out toward Liv, showing her the photo. "Look at her hair! And her giant boobs!"

Livvy starts giggling, and soon both of us are laughing, sprawled out on my floor, makeup surrounding us, our mirrors between our knees. I finally sit up and wipe the tears from beneath my eyes, thankful I still have Livvy when I've felt so down and out these past few weeks. She's been a good friend. Has even ditched Ryan a few times so she could hang with me.

That meant a lot.

"Let me work on you," she says, staring at my very blank, makeup-less face. "I can make your skin really pale and your eyes super dark, then give you blood red lips."

"Should I wear fangs?"

"No." She shakes her head. "Let's keep it simple. Besides, aren't you supposed to be a witch?"

"I don't know what I'm supposed to be. I don't think anyone really cares." I glance over at my costume, which is hanging from the open door of my tiny-yet-still –a-walk-in closet. It's black and long with flowing sleeves and an equally flowing skirt. The edges are jagged and the neckline dips to a low V, meaning I'll have lots of skin on display but no cleavage since…you know. I don't have any.

But whatever. I'm going full on in character this Saturday night, and I'm excited. This is the first time I've been excited about anything in a while. Halloween has always been one of my favorite holidays. I'm helping decorate the haunted house—aka the cafeteria—on Saturday morning before I go to my four-hour shift at Yo Town, which ends at three. Then I'll come right back to the school, get into costume, have Livvy do my face, and we'll be ready to scare by the time the carnival starts at five o'clock.

Livvy grabs my mirror and pushes it away, then sets in on creating my mask. She slathers on a blend of regular foundation mixed with white face paint, then works on my eyes. She slicks so many layers of mascara on my lashes I eventually ask her why I don't just wear fake eyelashes, but she tells me to shush.

So I let the artist work her magic commentary-free.

When she's finally done, she hands me the mirror and I blink at my reflection, stunned. She did an amazing job. My eyes are dark and scary. My skin is so pale I look like a ghost. My lips are an arresting shade of red, and she even drew faint, thin black lines coming from the corners of my mouth.

"Think we should do light black shading for blush on your cheeks?" she asks as I contemplate my face.

I meet her gaze. "Will that look good?"

"It can't hurt," she says with a shrug. She grabs her own mirror and starts lightly streaking black face paint onto her cheeks. "Maybe we need spiders drawn on our cheeks too."

"We shouldn't overdo it," I warn.

Livvy rolls her eyes. "It's Halloween. We're working in a haunted house. Of course we should overdo it."

I stand and go to my closet, grabbing the costume before I hide myself inside. I carefully take off my T-shirt, shuck off my yoga pants and slip the black dress on before I reemerge and twirl around for Livvy. "What do you think?"

Livvy looks away from the mirror, gaping up at me from where she sits on the floor. "Wow, you look great! I love that dress on you."

"I'm not showing too much skin?" I glance down at my chest. The neckline on this costume is so freaking low I'm not sure if I can wear a bra, but it's not like I have much to support, so what's the big deal?

"You're showing the perfect amount of skin" She smiles. "You look hot."

Ugh. Ever since the whole thing happened with Tuttle, she's been holding back, but I know she's dying to hook me up with someone. Possibly Eli Bennett, who has asked his big brother about me multiple times. Ryan has mentioned this to both Livvy and me, and I never know how to respond. It'd be one thing if Eli was at least sixteen, but he's not. He's almost fifteen. Meaning he's *fourteen.*

I can't do it. I don't care how cute he is or that he's taller than me, and that he looks pretty much like a grown man. He's a *kid.*

"I should've brought my costume." Livvy mock pouts. "We could've taken photos together."

Her costume is prettier than mine, but she spent more money, so that's expected. The dress is similar in style, but hers is made out of alternating panels of black velvet and red satin, and came with a sparkly red rhinestone choker. The collar rises high around the back of her neck too, which makes me think she really is supposed to be a vampire.

"You're going to have blood dripping from the corners of your mouth, right?" I ask her.

"I guess I should. I think I am a vampire. Maybe I could be a redheaded Elvira." She makes a weird face, her teeth sticking out over her bottom lip. "I vant to suck your blood!"

We start laughing again and it feels good. It feels normal. And I haven't felt normal in a while. Not since the beginning of summer.

"We're gonna be busy Saturday night," Livvy says as she starts drawing a spider on her face as she stares into her mirror.

I watch her. "It'll be fun." It'll keep me occupied so I don't think about the boy who so cruelly cut me out of his life.

"I hope you really mean it. That you'll have fun." Livvy's gaze meets mine and I see the concern there. Uh oh. "I'm worried about you. After what Tuttle did, you haven't been the same."

"I've been down and out lately, I can own it." I sit up straighter. "He walked out of my life without an explanation, so I think I have a right to be upset."

"Well, yeah. Of course you do." Livvy frowns, ready to say something else, but I hold my hand up, stopping her.

"But I don't want to talk about him anymore, okay?" I try my hardest to keep my voice gentle. "It's just—pointless. There's no reason for me to try and get his attention. And I really don't want to include him in any of our plans. What we had is over. Done."

She smiles faintly. "Good. I'm glad you feel that way. I wasn't about to suggest you try to get Tuttle's attention again, because I am so ready for you to move on. That guy doesn't deserve you crying any tears over him. Forget that. Forget *him*. He's a jerk."

"Right." I nod, trying my best to believe it. "You're so right. I'm over this. Over him."

"Awesome. Perfect. I love it." Livvy's eyes are sparkling and she looks awfully pleased with herself. "And I know just the guy to help you get over Tuttle once and for all."

I frown, wariness easing down my spine. "Who?"

If she says...

"Eli." Now it's her turn to hold up a hand to stop my protest. "Hear me out. Yes, he's young."

"Olivia." I never call her by her full name, and that definitely gets her attention. "He is only fourteen years old."

"He'll be fifteen next week!"

"He's a baby."

"A baby with a sexy smile and a great butt."

"Gross! You're into his brother, not Eli."

"I can appreciate the ultra fine genes in both of those Bennett boys, can I not?" Liv bats her eyelashes, and we both start laughing. There's been a lot of laughter tonight.

"There are only two years that separate you," she says.

"I'll be eighteen in March."

"That's a long time from now!" A sly smile curls her lips. "Maybe he's the rebound guy, you know? He's not looking for anything serious. He doesn't even understand the word serious. He just wants to have a good time."

"If a good time is code for sex, I'm not interested in having sex with a fourteen year old boy."

"*Fifteen.* He'll be fifteen next week, don't forget that," she stresses. "Besides, I don't think he's looking for full on sex. Fairly certain he's still a virgin, at least according to Ryan."

I make a face. "Ryan discusses his brother's sex life with you?" I can't imagine George having sex—*ew*—let alone talking about it with Livvy. And if she had a crush on my brother, that would be even worse.

Yes, I am a total child. So maybe Eli and I *would* hit it off...

"Ryan and Eli are constantly talking about dicks and asses and tits and banging and hand jobs and munching boxes. All of it." Livvy sighs and I can barely keep in my laughter. "They're boys and they're absolutely disgusting. Yet they're both oddly attractive when they talk like that."

"You're crazy." I grab a ruffled pillow that fell off my bed earlier and throw it at her, smacking her right in the face. She throws it back at me, but I dodge it in time and it hits the wall instead.

"No, *you're* crazy for not giving Eli at least a chance. He's totally into you."

I don't understand why. First I have Tuttle chasing after me, now I have Eli. They could have anyone they want yet they both choose me. I seriously don't get it.

"Why would he be into me? And I'm not looking for sympathy either. I just..." I shake my head, throw my hands up into the air. "It's weird."

"Here's the truth—you're really pretty and nice. You're not stuck up, like so many of those other girls who chase after him—them. Oh, and that's another thing. You don't chase. Ever. I think guys find that attractive."

"It's not game-playing strategy," I tell her. "It's just something I—don't do." Because I never believe I have a chance, so why bother?

"Yeah, well, they like it. I think Tuttle liked it too." She winces. "Sorry, scratch his name from this conversation. I know *Eli* likes how elusive you are, how you always tell him no when he's dying for you to say yes. I don't think any girls deny him, with the exception of you."

Huh. Interesting.

"And I think that's what the other one liked too. Everyone tells him yes. They fall over themselves for the chance to get with him, and you never did. Ever. They like the challenge." She points her index finger at me. "You, Amanda Winters, are a challenge."

I cover my face with my hands. "I don't mean to be," I whine from behind my hands.

"Oh, stop." Liv reaches over and pries my hands from my face. "Just run with it. Let Eli talk to you a little bit tomorrow at the game. See what he has to say. Flirt with him. He'll love it."

"I don't want anything to happen in front of Tuttle," I whisper, immediately wishing I could cram my words back into my mouth. Too late now. We're too intertwined still. What happened between us is still so fresh. And damn it, I miss him. I want him back in my life. But he doesn't want to be a part of it, so I have to suffer and watch him and wish for him and…

God, I *really* can't wait for football season to be over.

"Please, you *should* flirt with Eli in front of him! Screw Tuttle! He's the one who dissed you and shut you completely out of his life with no explanation! He's a total asshole for doing that. If he doesn't want you, then someone else will. You should go for it with Eli! Have a little fun. He's completely harmless."

"Is he really harmless?" Why am I even considering this? He's too young. Way too young.

"You want my prediction? I believe Eli is a little handsy and probably uses too much tongue, but that can be controlled, you know what I mean? Be the wise older woman and mold him into the perfect boy. The one who can kiss and touch a girl just right." The grin on Livvy's face is huge and she wags her eyebrows at me like some sort of perv.

I grab the pillow and toss it at her again, laughing when it bounces off of her head. "I can't do that—and you can't make me."

"You so can. What's a little innocent making out? There is nothing better than a boy who's an excellent kisser." The dreamy look on Liv's face tells me that Ryan is a most excellent kisser.

And so was Tuttle. I can't deny it. His kisses were dreamy. Too dreamy. My fear of never finding a guy who can kiss as well as Tuttle can is about to come true.

I can almost count on it.

chapter twenty-seven

I survive both the JV and varsity game, too busy to talk to anyone, let alone flirt with Eli Bennett. He comes around the hydration station a few extra times, but I can only smile helplessly at him when we make eye contact.

What's funny is that I am seriously considering Liv's suggestion to make out with Eli and get Tuttle out of my system once and for all. Maybe she's on to something. Maybe I really do need to find a rebound guy to make out with for an hour or three. Eli's not bad looking. In fact, he's really gorgeous, with the golden skin and hair, and the hazel eyes and the nice mouth. His lips are full and his jaw is a sharp edge, just like his nose. He has a nice smile and sometimes he reminds me of an overeager puppy, but puppies are sweet. I like puppies. So I'll probably like Eli too.

Tuttle doesn't say one word to me during the game. Not a single one. He barely looks in my direction, and I tell myself that's the way

I prefer it. I let Kyla have him for the night. I even tell her I won't work with Tuttle during this game, and while she gives me a weird, questioning look, she doesn't say anything. Instead, she keeps her eye on Tuttle so I don't have to.

It's a total relief.

Now the varsity game is almost over and we're killing them in a total shutout, forty-five to zero. It's embarrassing, how badly we're beating them. The backup players are out on the field, thankful for the chance to play, and I can hear Tuttle and his friends talking. Of course, I'm totally eavesdropping.

"Party at your house tonight, dude?" Ryan asks him.

Tuttle nods, his gaze locked on the field. "Sounds good to me. Everyone's gone, so we can do whatever we want."

"What else is new?" Ryan slaps him on the back. "I can find some booze if you need it."

"Nah, we should be good, but call me if you go home first. I might need a backup plan."

What does he mean by that?

"Can I go?" This is the enthusiastic Eli asking. He's somehow snuck onto the bench, sitting on the other side of Ryan, and his brother doesn't look too thrilled that he's there.

"Everyone's invited." Tuttle glances over his shoulder, his gaze meeting mine for the briefest moment. I refuse to be the one to look away first, and thankfully, I don't have to. "Everyone," he stresses, when he looks away from me.

I pull my phone out of the back pocket of my jeans and send a quick text to Liv. She answers almost immediately.

Hell yeah we're going to Tuttle's house! Whoooo!!!!

I turn to Kyla. "Are you going to Tuttle's party?"

"No way." She shakes her head. "I never go to his parties. I always feel so left out there."

"You should come with Liv and I. Hang out with us." I smile. "It'll be fun."

Kyla shakes her head some more. "I don't think so. That's really not my scene, Amanda. Thanks for including me, though."

Dang it. I'm trying to include her and get closer to Kyla.

Once the game is over, we start to clean up. I'm almost finished when Eli makes his approach, a cocky smile on his face when he stops directly in front of me. "You going to Tuttle's? Or are you afraid, since you two used to be together or whatever?"

"Afraid? I'm not afraid." Nothing like getting right to the point. "And yeah, I'm going to his party."

Eli's brows shoot up. "Seriously?" His voice squeaks a little and he clears his throat. It's sort of cute.

"Seriously," I deadpan. "I'm guessing you'll be there?"

"Oh yeah." He nods eagerly, his face lighting up. "I'll see you there."

"See ya," I say to his retreating back. Smiling, I turn to find Kyla watching me with her arms crossed. My smile immediately fades. "What's wrong?"

"Bouncing from one football player to the next isn't the best idea," she says, her voice dry.

Yikes. Who crowned her Queen Judgey McJudgey Pants? "There is absolutely nothing going on with me and Eli."

"Right. That's why he just high fived all of his friends after talking to you."

I glance over to where Eli is standing with his circle of friends, and they are *still* giving him high fives. That's sort of embarrassing. "I have no idea what that's about."

"I'm sure I can tell you *all* about it. I'm guessing some of the guys made a bet with Eli that he couldn't get in your panties tonight. And I'm pretty positive Eli said he could. To make the bet even more interesting, they put a little money on it. Just to liven it up, you know?" The hostility in Kyla's voice is cluing me in that something like this might've happened to her. And that's just…awful. "Don't fall for their shit, Amanda. You'll only end up getting hurt."

Before I can utter a word or ask her a question, she turns and walks away.

By the time we're entering Tuttle's house, the party has been going on for a while. The place is packed. In some weird almost twist of fate, at one point I was supposed to ride in the same car as Eli and go to the party with him, and I was freaking out over it with Liv.

But that didn't happen. Liv took too long getting ready and one of Eli's teammates stopped by the Bennett house and got him. Ryan eventually came by Liv's place and picked us up. I'm starting to feel like a total third wheel in their relationship, but most of the time they act like they forget I'm even with them. Meaning, they say things to each other in front of me that are kind of embarrassing—and intimate.

Ugh.

I'm still trying my best to forget the over the top things Liv and Ryan said to each other as I make my way to the kitchen, where I know the booze is. I grab a beer can and crack it open, guzzling it down as fast as possible. I'm tired and stressed over everything I've been trying to do the last few weeks. Now I just want to get a good buzz on and forget my troubles for a little while.

"Don't get drunk," Livvy says as she wags a finger at me. She grabs a beer too. "This is for Ryan. I'm the sober driver tonight."

"How responsible of you."

"I'm trying to turn a new leaf. After the—" She lowers her voice to a loud whisper. "—pregnancy scare, I realized I'm the only one responsible for my own actions. So no babies, no DUIs and no getting into drunken car wrecks!" She clinks the unopened beer can against mine. "Gotta go find Ryan. I'll catch up with you in a few, okay?"

She ditches me before I can say anything, which feels like a common theme tonight. And now I'm thinking about Kyla and what she told me earlier, how angry yet sad she seemed. Did some of the football players try to trick her? I can't imagine it happening now. She seems so in charge and sure of herself. Maybe when she was younger, did one of them—or a bunch of them—take advantage of her?

God, I hope not.

"Hey, you."

I turn to find Em standing there, with Brianne Brown on one side of her and Lauren Mancini on the other.

I hate my life sometimes.

"Hi Em." I aim my smile at her, barely looking at the other girls. They've always been mean to me, so why would they change now? "How are you?"

"I'm okay." She cocks out a hip and I take her in. She's wearing a cropped baby blue T-shirt that shows off the flat expanse of her belly, and a low slung pleated black miniskirt. Her hair is sleek and tucked behind her ears, and her lips are this deep, glossy pink. She looks like the typical schoolgirl gone bad.

If Livvy were here right now, she'd be mocking her hardcore.

"What's going on with you?" Em asks.

"Not with Jordan anymore, huh?" Lauren asks sweetly, her expression pure innocence.

I'm not falling for it. She's a total snake, just waiting to sink her fangs into me. I ignore her question and focus on Em.

"Not much. Been super busy lately."

"Right, have to keep those boys hydrated," Lauren says. The matching smirks on Brianne's and Lauren's faces make me want to smack them both.

"I'm sorry we haven't talked much," Em says, and she actually sounds sincere. "I, uh, figured you didn't want to, considering you took Liv's side."

My mouth drops open. "I didn't take Liv's side." Well, I sort of did.

"It's okay, I get it. You were friends with her first. I can appreciate your loyalty."

"God, this conversation is so boring," Lauren says just before she fake yawns.

"I want to go find Dustin," Brianne whines.

Em shoots me a look, then rolls her eyes.

"And I want to find Jordan." Lauren hooks her arm through Brianne's. "Let's go."

We watch them leave and Em sighs. "They're so annoying."

"Why do you hang out with them then?"

"I really don't have anyone else," she says with a shrug.

I actually feel sorry for her, and Livvy would probably yell at me if she knew that. "They're total bitches."

"I know. But their bitchiness protects me in a way."

I sort of get it, though I don't want to. "You need new friends."

"I'd hang out with you if Livvy would let me." Em's expression turns sad. "But she's still pissed."

What can I say? Em is one hundred percent right. Instead of talking, I slam back the rest of my beer and then grab another one, cracking it open.

"It really sucks, because all Brianne does is talk about Dustin," Em says. "And he barely talks to me anymore. He's still mad at me too. I know he hates that Brianne and I are friends. I think he's afraid I'm going to do something to ruin their relationship."

I should tell her that's everyone's fear when it comes to her, but I keep my mouth shut. "You should tell Liv you miss her."

"Why? She won't even look at me, let alone talk to me. Telling her that would be completely pointless." Em's gaze sweeps the kitchen. "Is she here?"

"Yeah."

"Did you come with her?"

"Yeah, her and Ryan."

Em rolls her eyes. "That guy is a total douche."

"They're getting along right now," I say in their defense. "They make a really cute couple."

"Whatever. Just wait. He'll grow tired of her eventually and then dump her ass." Em sounds bitter. I remember that once upon a time, she went out with Ryan too. "Though I will admit, he's been sticking with her for a while."

I really don't want to get caught up in this conversation. I came to Tuttle's—oh, the irony—to have a good time, not get embroiled in some more drama. I'm about to bail when Eli Bennett magically appears, clutching a red cup, a giant smile on his face.

"Amanda," he breathes, his gaze drinking me in. "You came." He sounds surprised.

"I did." I smile at him. "What's going on?"

"Nothing." He chugs from the cup like he's nervous, then crushes the empty cup with a squeeze of his fingers. "You look pretty tonight."

Oh. "Thanks. You're so sweet."

He flashes me a lopsided smile. "I bet you are, too."

Is that supposed to be a pickup line?

"Um, what the hell is going on here?"

Crap. I forgot Em is still standing with us. "Em, do you know Eli?"

"Ryan's brother." She smiles coolly. "Nice to see you again."

"Yeah," Eli mumbles, looking away from her.

"Please don't tell me you two are a thing," Em says to me in disbelief.

"No, no," I reassure her. "We're just friends."

"With benefits," Eli tacks on, grinning wildly.

"Not even," I mutter.

Em laughs. "You two are an—odd couple. But I'm kind of liking the possibilities. Revenge sex against Tuttle?"

"What? *No.* There's nothing happening between us," I say again. "Seriously."

"Whatever you say," Em drawls, wiggling her fingers at us as she starts to walk away. "See ya later."

The moment she's gone, Eli is shifting closer to me, as if he's trying to invade my space. I take a step back. "Trying to play it cool with your friends?" he asks.

"Um, I guess so."

"So you wanna keep this on the DL?" He nods before I can give him an answer. "I'm cool. I'm down."

"Uh-huh. Listen, Eli, it probably *is* better that we not make a big deal out of this, you know?"

"This?" He raises a brow. "What are you talking about?"

"Don't pretend you don't know." I hesitate. "You want to…hook up?"

"And you don't?"

This is ridiculous. "You're only fourteen."

"Almost fifteen. Next week."

"And a freshman."

"Quarterback of the JV team. Next year I'll be stepping in for Tuttle since he'll finally be gone. Then I'll be the fucking star."

I'm sure he will. His easy confidence will take him far. "So Livvy said you have a thing for me."

"Jesus," he mutters, then takes my hand and drags me out of the kitchen.

"Where are you taking me?" I yell at him, dodging people as he tugs me through the crowd.

"I'm not having this conversation in the middle of the kitchen where everyone can hear." He pulls me down the hall—the hall that leads to the secret back staircase, and he's opening doors, one after another. He finds a supply closet, a linen closet, an empty bathroom—bingo—and drags me inside, shutting the door behind us. "Now what did Livvy say?"

"She said you…liked me."

"I'm going to kill her," he mumbles, running his hand through his hair, messing it all up. He looks adorable. What's up with cute boys with messy hair? "Listen, you're fine as *hell*. And you're a senior. If you were into me and we hooked up tonight? I'd be a freaking legend."

Seriously? "You probably shouldn't tell me that."

He frowns. "Why not?"

"You only want to hook up with me because I'll give you legend status." He just blinks at me. "That's not really cool, Eli. You're just using me because I'm a senior?"

Well, I'm supposedly only using him because he's interested, so I guess we're even.

Now he's full on grinning. "But that's a good thing. An honor. You're hot, Amanda. And the best thing? It's like you don't even know it. You wear those tight jeans and we're all staring at your ass out on the field while you're handing out water bottles or bent over one of us, taping up our hands. We're all trying to catch a look, or even better, cop a feel."

"Cop a feel?" I'm dumbfounded.

"You don't even notice, huh?"

"No." He's got to be exaggerating a little. "I had no clue."

"Oh yeah. None of us would touch you, though. Tuttle made his claim and we weren't allowed to hardly look at you."

So freaking primitive. What is he, a caveman? I ignore the warm feeling that washes over me at the thought of possessive Jordan Tuttle. When he acted like he cared about me. When I believed I was the most important person in his life.

I shove the thought out of my head before I start to cry.

Eli takes a step closer, then another. I back up, until my butt hits the edge of the counter and a wave of Axe body spray washes over me when he looms. "But now you two are done. So I called first dibs."

He says the worst things. "You did not just say that."

"I did." He is all up in my business, his hands braced on the counter on either side of me, caging me in. The boy may say stupid stuff, but he has a few moves. And he's rather persuasive. "I know you were all about that Tuttle life, but hopefully you've moved on."

I can't stop myself from laughing. I've never heard such cheesy lines, not that I've had much practice. Eli starts laughing too, and I appreciate his cheesiness because it's a total distraction. Tuttle's rejection still stings.

"Amanda."

Glancing up, I find Eli leaning into me, his head tilted to the side, like he's coming in for—what?

Oh God. A kiss.

I can't do it. I can't do it.

I turn my head away at the last second and his lips collide with my cheek. It was sweet, a missed chance, and I felt…

Nothing.

Not a damn thing.

Eli pulls away and licks his lips, his gaze laser focused on my mouth, like he can't wait to taste it. "Can I touch you?"

"Um…"

He goes ahead and touches me anyway, one hand resting lightly on my waist. He studies me intently and it's like I can see the cogs turning in his brain, trying to come up with a plan.

"This isn't going to happen, Eli," I say softly.

He frowns. "You're not even going to give me a chance?" The disappointment in his voice rings clear.

I slowly shake my head. "I'm sorry."

"Is it because of Tuttle?"

Being with Eli like this, in Jordan's house, I can't help but think of him. His smell and his taste and how he knew just how to touch me.

The last time we were together in this house, in his room, naked and on his bed. The memories come one after another. Quick and intense and unavoidable, and then I'm pushing Eli away, a gasp escaping me when the door slams open and I see who's standing in the open doorway.

Watching us.

It's Jordan.

chapter twenty-eight

Tuttle

"What. The. Fuck." I bite the words out, my fingers curling against my palms, my blood running so hot I feel like I'm about to burst into flames.

Eli Bennett backs away from Amanda, holding his hands up in front of him and scared shitless. His eyes are wide and he can't stop shaking his head. "It's not what you think, bro."

"I'm not your bro, asshole." I flick my head. "Get the fuck out of here."

He sends Amanda a quick look before he's scurrying out of the bathroom like the scared little rat he is. I make a disgusted sound as I shut and lock the door, pressing my forehead against the cool wood for a moment so I can gather my thoughts. Gather my emotions. My anger.

I count to five, take a deep breath, and turn to face her.

She's perched on the edge of the bathroom counter looking like a goddamn queen. Her back and shoulders are straight, and there's a haughty look on her face. Her eyes are a little dazed and her lips are parted. Lips I've kissed so many times, and I miss them. I miss her.

But she let Eli Bennett *kiss* her. In my bathroom.

I can't believe it.

"Let me out," she says, the slightest catch in her voice, like I scare her.

Good. She scares me too. She fucking terrifies me. That's why I've been avoiding her the last few weeks.

"No." I lean my back against the door and cross my arms, contemplating her. "We should talk."

"We have nothing to talk about," she snaps.

"I think we do." I remain quiet and so does she. I'm trying to outwait her, but she's stubborn and I give up fast. When I'm pissed, I lose patience. "Eli, Amanda? Really?"

"You have no room to judge." She flicks her hair over her shoulder, her eyes full of anger.

"He's a kid."

"At least he likes me. He's into me. And he has no problem letting everyone know about it either."

That was a direct hit. "Get real. Being with you gives him bragging rights. That's it. He only wants to bag you because you're a senior and he's a lame ass freshman."

She recoils and looks away, her normally lush lips forming a thin, straight line. "*Bag* me?"

Bad choice of words. But I'm in too deep now, so there's no going back. "Hook up with you. Fuck you. Whatever you want to call it."

Amanda turns that angry glare back on me, her dark eyes blazing.

"You really think I'd—*fuck* him tonight? Seriously?"

"I don't know." I shrug. When I'm jealous, I lash out. That's what I'm doing right now. Lashing out like an asshole because she let some other guy put his hands on her. Put his lips on her.

It's killing me. Tearing me apart. But I deserve it. I pushed her away. I acted like she meant nothing, when she means *everything* to me, and I was too scared to face it, face *her* head on like a man.

I'm a coward.

"Nice to know you think so low of me." She hops off the counter and stalks toward me, determination in her every step, looking sexy as hell, too. "Move out of my way."

"No."

"Open the door." She's standing so close to me, her body almost brushes against mine. Tilting her head back, she glares. "Open it."

I study her beautiful face. Memorize every little detail. I've missed her. So damn much. "No." I switch tactics. "Did you kiss him?"

"Who?"

"Eli Bennett! Did you, Amanda? Did you kiss him?"

"No, of course I didn't!"

Relief floods me, heady and strong, and she notices. For some reason, that sends her into a full on rage.

She reaches out and pounds on the door, right by my shoulder. "Let me out!" She's yelling at the top of her lungs, and I wince. "Please! Somebody!"

I cover her mouth with my hand, silencing her. Bending down, I thrust my face in hers. "Stop yelling, okay? I'll let you out. Just—be quiet."

Slowly I uncover her mouth and she starts beating on my chest. Pummeling me with her fists, one hit after another. She keeps saying something again and again, the words falling from her lips so fast, I can't make them out at first. Until I can.

"I hate you, I hate you."

I grab hold of her wrists to stop her from hitting me. "Amanda."

"I hate you, Jordan. I really do. I hate you so much." She's crying. Tears are streaming down her face and her mascara is running. I've seen plenty of girls cry before. I've seen my mother's tears countless times. They always make me uncomfortable. Tears in general put me on edge.

Seeing Amanda cry breaks my heart.

I pull her into my arms and hold her close, letting her cry all over the front of my shirt. "You don't hate me."

"I do! God, I do. I swear. I really, *really* hate you, Jordan."

Her words are like tiny knives, carving into my already fucked up heart. She's blubbering against my shirt, soaking it with her tears and I feel helpless. I can't make the tears stop. How do I make the damn tears stop?

"Amanda." I cup her cheeks and tilt her head back, forcing her to look at me. She glares, her eyes glittering with unshed tears, her lips red and swollen, her cheeks flushed pink.

"Please don't cry," I whisper, my throat raw. My feelings, my insides, my emotions, all scraped raw.

Her face crumples at my words, like I just made it worse. I lean down and press my forehead against hers. Close my eyes and inhale in her sweet, delicious scent. My heart pounds, and my breaths come fast. She's killing me. Ripping my heart to shreds with every shuddery breath, every soft cry.

She slowly pulls away, her head bent, like she can't look at me. "I trusted you, Jordan. I told you that you could talk to me about anything, that I would be there for you no matter what, and you still dumped me after the blowjob. Just like you do with all the other girls."

"It wasn't like that—" I start, but she cuts me off with a look.

"It was *exactly* like that. I gave almost everything to you, and in the end, you dumped me. I'm just like the rest of them. You discarded me as if I was trash and never really talked to me again. Not even for our project." The tears start back up. "Who does that? What the hell is wrong with you? Don't you care about anyone?"

"No!" The word explodes out of my mouth and I pull away from her, run my hands through my hair in frustration. "I don't. I care about no one. Not my parents, not my so-called friends, not anyone. Okay? Is that what you want to hear?"

She stares at me like I'm some sort of freak. Unshed tears fill her eyes and I want to go to her, catch the tears with my thumb, kiss her pain away.

But I can't. I'm the one who caused her so much pain. I have to leave her alone.

"Why are you like this?" Her voice is a harsh whisper. "Why?"

I shrug. "I don't know. I can blame my mom and dad. They're fucked up, Amanda. More fucked up than I am."

She grabs my hand and laces her fingers with mine, and that is my undoing. That I can be so awful to her and she still cares, she still wants to help me...

I can't resist her. Instead, I pull her into my arms.

Having her like this, holding her like this, relaxes me. It's been too long. The past few weeks have felt like years. My entire body sways toward her, like it's desperate to get close and I have no control.

Amanda curls her hand around my nape, her fingers tightening into my skin. When she angles her head slightly to the right...

We're kissing. Our mouths drawn to each other like we can't fight it, fight this, whatever we have brewing between us. The kiss turns hot and deep in an instant and I pull her in close, whirl her around so she's the one pressed against the wall as I continue to devour her sweet mouth. She grabs hold of me, a whimper sounding low in her throat, and I slip my hands around her, under her, gripping her ass and hauling her up so her legs go around my hips.

I pin her against the wall with just my body and unleash my everything on her. We kiss like we never plan on coming up for air, and my hands wander. Search and explore. Reacquainting myself with her body. This body that feels like it belongs to me.

Only one word pounds through my head, throbs with my heart.

Mine. Mine. Mine. Mine.

She's mine.

And I'm never going to let her forget it.

chapter twenty-nine

Amanda

It's both a relief and pure torture, being in Jordan's arms again. My back is against the door, his hard body pressed to mine, my legs wound around his hips. We kiss and kiss, and sometimes it feels like a battle. Like he's trying to conquer me. But then the kiss softens, his lips lingering on mine, his tongue doing an achingly slow sweep...

I don't ever want this to stop. But it has to. And when it stops, the pain will come again.

Just like before.

I break away from his lips first and he tries to kiss me again, but I turn my head away. "We can't keep doing this."

He touches my cheek, forces me to look at him once more. "Yeah, we can."

His mouth settles on mine gently. Slowly he works his magic, his lips and tongue persuasive, until I'm a moaning, writhing mass of hormones. He rocks against me and I can feel him, hard and long and rubbing me in just the right spot. Our bodies fit perfectly; our mouths fit perfectly too. But we aren't perfect. We are far from it.

How could something that feels this good end up hurting us so bad?

"Jordan." I whisper his name against his lips, but he ignores me. I say it again, shoving at his shoulders, and finally he withdraws, his expression wondrous, a little dazed.

"What?"

"Put me down." My voice is firm. My emotions are everywhere, but I need to keep it together. Remain strong. Remain in control.

He does as I ask, setting me on my feet, and I stare at his chest, see the tear stains soaked through his T-shirt. I release a shuddery breath and lift my gaze to his.

"We can't keep doing this," I repeat.

Jordan frowns. "Doing what?"

"Kissing each other. Ignoring each other. Arguing with each other. You can't have it both ways, Jordan."

His frown deepens, but he remains quiet.

"I need to know." I take a deep breath and exhale loudly, trying to calm my tumultuous emotions, but it's impossible. "How you feel. If you're serious about this—about us. About me."

His silence feels like an answer, and I tilt my head to the side, so very weary of the constant game playing. "Just let me out of here. Please."

"I want to be," he whispers, and I step back, confused.

"You want to be what?"

"Serious. About this. About us. About you." He hesitates. "But I don't know how."

I shake my head. "That sounds like such a bullshit answer—"

He cuts me off. "It's not. I don't know how to be real with you. I don't know how to be real with *anyone*. How to share myself with someone, how to show someone I—I care. I just can't do it."

His words make me hurt for him, but this isn't my fault. I refuse to feel guilty for his past, for his lack of emotion. "I can't be with someone who won't tell me how he feels," I whisper.

Again, his answer is silence.

He's killing me.

"If you don't know how to share yourself with me, then I don't think this is ever going to work. I need you to trust me, Jordan," I say quietly, speaking to my feet. I don't want to look at him anymore.

I can't.

"I don't know how." His words sound like an excuse.

And I'm done with excuses.

He shifts away from the door and opens it, silent permission for me to leave. So I take it, bolting out of that bathroom so fast, I practically trip over my own feet. I stagger down the short hall, end up in the kitchen, which is crawling with all sorts of people. I see Ryan sitting on a chair in the breakfast nook and Livvy is perched on his lap. They look cozy, like a real couple, and I'm taken over by a sudden wave of envy.

I wish I was sitting on Jordan's lap, talking and flirting and letting everyone in the whole damn school know that we're together.

But it will never be that easy with him. And while I'm all for fighting for love and that kind of stuff, it's hard when the one that I want doesn't seem to know what *he* wants.

It feels like I'm fighting a losing battle.

"Amanda! Come here!" Livvy waves me over, and I go to her and Ryan. "Eli is telling *everyone* you kissed him," she says when I reach them.

Oh, God. I completely forgot what we did—or more like what we *didn't* do. What does that say about me? I go from almost kissing one boy to actually kissing another in a matter of minutes. But that last boy, I care about. A lot. "Um, well. We didn't."

"So he's lying," Livvy says, sounding pissed.

"No, not exactly. We—sort of kissed." That's a nice way to put it, though why I'm trying to make it seem like more, I don't know.

Livvy's jaw drops open. And so does Ryan's. "Seriously?" she squeaks.

"So he didn't lie," Ryan mutters, looking shocked.

"He kissed me on the cheek. It wasn't a big deal." Pretty underwhelming actually, not that I'd ever say that out loud.

"Well, it was a big deal to him," Liv says, worry filling her eyes. "He's telling everyone he made out with Tuttle's ex in Tuttle's bathroom."

"Crap." I rub my forehead and glance around the kitchen. They're all watching me, looking away quickly when I catch them staring. They're probably all talking about me too.

This is…not good.

"I can kick his ass for you if you want me to," Ryan volunteers. "I'll gladly do it."

"Thanks, but I'll pass," I say sarcastically, then reconsider. "For now."

This makes Ryan laugh, and Livvy too.

"There she is. Where'd you go, babe?" Eli is beside me, slipping his arm around my waist, like we're a couple. "I missed you."

"Cut the shit Eli," I tell him, making him immediately drop his arm. "This is not a thing."

"But the kiss…"

"It was nice." I spare his feelings and reputation by not bringing up that the kiss was on the cheek. I'm setting myself up for countless rumors, but I don't care. I'm over all of this. "You know it would never work out between us," I tell him softly. "We're too different."

"So you're breaking up with me?" He's shouting. I guess he wants everyone to hear our conversation?

"I'm afraid so," I tell him.

The entire kitchen has gone quiet. As in, they're all listening. This is nuts. And by the wild look in his eyes, Eli is loving every minute of it.

"Well, that fucking sucks, Amanda. I thought we had something real between us, but I guess not." He grabs hold of me one last time and presses his mouth to mine in a fierce, quick kiss. "See ya," he murmurs with a smirk and a wink.

Yes. He just kissed me. And *winked* at me.

Eli saunters out of the kitchen and I swear, ten girls follow after him, every one of them calling his name.

"You just gave him tremendous street cred," Ryan says, shaking his head. "Now all the girls will want him."

"I don't get boys. At all." This I tell Livvy, who's totally laughing at the spectacle Eli just made.

"Join the club," she says, offering her hand up for a high five. I give her a weak one, but this time, I can't muster up the energy to laugh with her.

It's either I laugh or burst into tears though. And I definitely don't want to cry. Then everyone will think Eli was the one who made me cry, when he had nothing to do with it.

It was all Jordan. Jordan and his bossy demands, not letting me leave the bathroom, acting like such a complete jerk I started hitting him and telling him I hate him.

I don't hate him.

God, I think I'm in love with him.

Yes. That's my problem. I'm in love with Jordan Tuttle. I'm madly in love with him, and he doesn't love me back.

"What's wrong?" I jerk my head up to find Livvy climbing off of Ryan's lap and coming over to grab hold of my arm. She's frowning, her eyes full of concern. "You all right?"

"Why do you ask?" My voice is shaky and my knees are wobbly. I need to sit down.

"You look like you just saw a ghost. Or got sucker punched."

"The last one. Definitely," I mumble, feeling faint. "I think I need to sit."

She leads me over to a chair and I fall into it, leaning my head back so I can close my eyes. I cover my face with my hands and sit like that for a while, running over everything that just happened in my head.

"You look traumatized over the entire Eli scene," Livvy says. "I hope you know you're just making him look that much more desirable."

I lift my head and start laughing. I can't help it. "This night is surreal."

Liv grabs a chair and sits in front of me. "Tell me what happened."

So I do. I tell her about Eli dragging me to the bathroom. How we really didn't kiss, it was just on the cheek—and then how Tuttle interrupted us.

"And he thought you were kissing Eli, right?" Liv's eyebrows practically shoot up into her hairline.

I nod. "He was so pissed."

"I'm sure," she murmurs, her gaze growing distant. "Not like he has any room to feel anything, considering how he's been ignoring you."

That exact thought ran through my head again and again. It still does. Worse, I feel guilty for what happened between Eli and me—and *nothing happened.* I didn't do a thing, yet it feels like I somehow cheated on Tuttle.

I absolutely, one hundred percent didn't. *He* rejected me. *He* kicked me to the side like I meant nothing to him and he forgot all about me. No explanation, no nothing. Just…one night he's got me naked in his bed and a few days later, we're acting like strangers.

His rejection still hurts. It hurts so much.

"What happened after that?"

"He kicked Eli out, and then we—got into a fight."

"Oh my God, Amanda! He didn't hurt you, did he?"

"No! He would never do that. It was a stupid argument. I totally overreacted." I shake my head. "And then after I overreacted and cried all over his shirt, he—he kissed me."

"Oh. Wow." Livvy leans back in her chair, staring at me. "He *kissed* you?"

I nod, the tears threatening to spill again. I press my lips together, desperate to keep it together. "And then I told him we had to stop."

"You made him stop."

"I had to. He won't commit to me, Liv. I can't be with someone who runs so hot and cold. He doesn't trust me, and that means I can't trust him either." I don't tell her everything Jordan said to me. That's private.

"You're never going to get over him if you two keep doing this. Trust me, I should know." Yeah, she should, what with her Ryan and Dustin love triangle. "Once Dustin and I stopped doing whatever it was we were doing, I was able to focus on Ryan. And that's exactly what I needed."

"You're not telling me to forget about Tuttle so I can focus on Eli, are you?" I am horrified at the thought.

"No." Livvy shakes her head, laughing a little. "Absolutely not. He's not the right distraction for you. But you do need to move on from Tuttle. He's only hurting you, Amanda. I hate to see you in pain. As hard as that is to hear, you're never going to get over him if you don't eventually meet someone else."

"I don't want to be with someone else." *I want to be with Jordan.*

Okay, that thought makes the tears flow. I wipe at my cheeks, frustrated at my lack of control, and when I glance up, I catch sight of Tuttle standing near the refrigerator, frozen in place as he watches me.

I stare back, letting him see me in all of my pitiful glory. Maybe he'll come running over to me. He'll pull me into his arms and tell me it'll be okay and then we'll be back to normal. He'll say he trusts me and I'll trust him, and then eventually I'll admit I love him, and he'll repeat the same words to me. He can be my first, and we'll be the perfect high school couple.

But none of that happens. I'm living in a complete fantasy world. Tuttle turns away and exits the kitchen, his retreating back reminding me that I'm a fool.

A total fool.

chapter thirty

I spent the night at Liv's Friday and while we groaned and bitched at getting up so early this morning, we did make it to the caf by nine. Both of us are clutching venti PSLs in one hand and a warmed croissant in the other, surveying the mess that is the cafeteria.

"We are total clichés living the high school dream," Liv mutters just before she takes a big chug of her coffee. "Who the hell is in charge of this nightmare anyway?"

That would be yearbook editor Elaine Kingston. She's barely five feet tall, but she is a powerhouse of organizational skills and a take-no-bullshit attitude.

And she is nowhere to be seen.

"Don't tell me we're going to have to take over this project." I'm still half-asleep, and it feels like no amount of Starbucks coffee is going to get me going. I didn't sleep that great. Kept having weird nightmares with Tuttle in the starring role. The last one was the worst. Would you like to hear about it? I know people telling you their dreams can be kind of boring, but this is a good one.

I promise.

I'm at the Halloween carnival, and I'm wandering lost among the rows of games and food booths. There are all of these familiar faces, but not one of them is a real friend. I finally spot Tuttle, and when I run up to him, he grabs hold of me and kisses me. Right in front of everyone, and they all start cheering.

But when I pull away, it's not Jordan holding me any longer—it's Eli. He has this evil grin on his face and then he starts laughing at me. They all start laughing. It's all I can hear, the echo of their laughter as I try to struggle out of Eli's arms. He's holding on too tight, though, and I can't get away. No matter how hard I struggle, I can't get away…

And then I woke up, a sweaty, trembling mess. I glanced at the clock, saw that it was five a.m.—we stumbled into bed around one—and I couldn't go back to sleep.

Yeah. That nightmare is still clinging to me.

"Hey girls!" Elaine's perky voice breaks through my thoughts and I'm so relieved she's here, I almost hug her.

"You're late, Elaine. Sure you're feeling okay?" Liv teases.

"I've been here since eight," Elaine says with a scowl. She's holding a clipboard and there's a pen stuck behind her right ear. She's wearing a black T-shirt with a witch on a broom on the front and it says, *Yes, I can drive a stick.*

"Nice shirt," I tell her.

The scowl disappears and she smiles. "Thanks, Amanda. How long are you girls staying today?"

"I'm here as long as you need me, though I have to drive Amanda to work," Livvy answers.

"I have to leave around 10:45," I tell Elaine.

"Less than two hours for you, then. Hmm." She grabs the pen and taps it against her lips. It's black with tiny orange pumpkins scattered all over it. Girl has some serious Halloween spirit going on. "I'm going to have the boys start hanging the black tarps right away. Help direct them and then come see me when you're done."

She bustles off to go boss someone else around.

"Let's go, soldier." Liv snaps her fingers, and we're off.

Surprisingly, the haunted house is really coming together by the time Livvy and I leave so she can drive me to work. The yearbook staff is huge and almost everyone is there to help out. Under the efficient command of our leader, we are seriously getting stuff done.

It's the perfect distraction I need, after what happened last night with Eli and Tuttle. I'm kept busy at the cafeteria, and by the time Livvy's dropping me off at the shopping center, I feel pretty good. When I walk into Yo Town, I'm happy to see it's busy there, too. Sonja is in the back working at her computer, and she calls me into her office when she sees me pass by.

"Have a seat." She waves at the chair on the other side of her desk.

I settle in, trying to fight the unease that threatens to grab me. "Everything okay?" I ask.

"Everything's fine. You're doing a tremendous job, Amanda. I'm so glad we have you as an employee. You're such a hard worker and you never complain." She shoots me a sympathetic look. "But I'm afraid I'm going to have to cut your hours after November 15th."

Blake warned me this was coming, and now the moment is here. "By how much?"

"Well, currently I schedule you anywhere from twelve to fifteen hours a week. After the fifteenth, though, I'm probably not going to be able to give you any more than ten hours a week." She gives me a bleak smile. "I know that's not much, and I'm so sorry I have to do this. But business slows way down once the cold weather is upon us, and we're pretty much there."

It's a clear, sunny day, but it's brisk outside. Everyone's over frozen yogurt, I guess. "I get it. I do."

"If you need to find more hours elsewhere, I completely understand, but if we get to keep you through the winter, that would be great too. Just know I will respect your decision no matter what."

"Thank you for the heads up, Sonja. I really appreciate it." I stand. "I don't plan on going anywhere, but I might have to find another part-time job once football season is officially over." I really don't want to, but what choice do I have? I can't do much with ten hours a week. That's barely four hundred dollars a month after taxes, and I need more if I want to save up for my future.

"I understand," she says with a nod. "Just keep me posted."

I go into the bathroom, quickly change into my Yo Town shirt and then clock in before joining Blake out in the store, which is now empty.

Blake's cleaning up the topping station and he glances up when he spots me. "My mom already give you the bad news?" he asks.

"Yeah." I go to stand beside him, noticing that the frosted animal crackers are black and orange and white. Halloween colors. Everyone's got the Halloween spirit. Sonja put up decorations in the window a few weeks ago. "Kind of sucks."

"I know, sorry. I warned you, though." He tries to cheer me up by saying, "We only opened an hour ago and we've been pretty steady, so that's good."

"I'm glad. I don't want the shift to drag. I need to go back to school once it's over." At Blake's confused look, I explain further. "The

Halloween carnival is tonight. The yearbook staff is hosting a haunted house. Aren't you coming?"

"Nah." Blake's cheeks turn ruddy. "That's kids stuff."

"No it's not. It's fun." I nudge him. "Have you ever been?"

"Only during my freshman year, and I hated every minute of it."

"Aw, you should give it another chance and go, Blake. Won't some of your friends be there?"

"I don't know. Maybe—maybe Kyla's going," he mumbles, turning away from me to straighten up the cup display.

My ears perk up. "Wait a minute, did you say Kyla?"

He keeps his back to me. "I don't think so."

Liar pants.

"Um, I do think so." I tap him on the shoulder and he whirls around, looking defensive. "Are you talking about Kyla the water girl? Short, medium-length brown hair, pretty brown eyes?"

He says nothing, but he doesn't have to speak. The answer is written all over his embarrassed face.

"I know her, we're friends!" Well, a slight exaggeration, but we're getting there. "I'm a water girl too, remember? We spend a lot of time together at the games and at practice. How do you know her?"

Blake shrugs, his expression pained. "We have a couple of classes together."

"Is she going to the carnival tonight?"

"I don't know." He heads to the back of the store without another word.

Clearly he doesn't want to talk about it, so I let it go.

Customers stream in steadily throughout my shift, a lot of them people from school. I see Lauren Mancini and her posse, which isn't a surprise because remember, she just loves this place.

But what is a surprise is her demeanor. She approaches me as I stand behind the register, and there's almost a—shy expression on her face.

Say what?

"So, hey, Amanda. What's up?"

"Nothing much," I say warily. "How are you?"

"I'm good, I'm good." She pauses, then leans in closer. "Um, can I ask you a question?"

I calculate the weight of her frozen yogurt cup and then key in the price on the register. "Four dollars and sixty two cents." I hesitate when I catch the expectant look on her face. I don't know what her plan is, but I'm not in the mood to be messed with today. "As long as it has nothing to do with Tuttle, then sure. Ask away."

She looks slightly taken aback but she forges on. "What's the deal with you and Eli Bennett?"

Okay. That was unexpected. Where's the punch line? I'm waiting for her to accuse me of poaching a freshman. Or being a cradle robber. Whatever mean thing she can say about Eli and me, I'm prepared.

But I see nothing on her face but genuine curiosity. Which of course, leaves me curious too.

"There's no deal with me and Eli," I tell her. "We're just friends."

"Really? He said you two broke up last night, and that you were really upset over it."

"Did he tell you that himself?" I'm half tempted to beat that kid up, I swear. Again with the violence, but I guess when you're dealing with idiots, you can't help it.

"Well, I wasn't the one who actually talked to him." She shifts her feet, clearly uncomfortable.

"Who did then? One of your friends?" Was he at the party

spreading rumors to everyone or what? Stupid Eli. I knew he would run with this, but I didn't realize just how far.

"I heard a rumor, okay?" Her voice is full of irritation and she shakes her head. "Nothing confirmed."

"Oh." This entire situation is only getting weirder and weirder. "Okay, fine. Eli and I were kind of hanging around." *For approximately thirty minutes.* "And yes, we had some good times." *They lasted three minutes, tops.* "Before everything fell apart." *Thanks to his running away from Tuttle. Heaven forbid he risks getting his ass kicked.*

Why am I covering for him again? I have to admit—there's something about Eli Bennett that's charming. He's crass and overeager and he says really dumb things, but he's also really cute and kind of sweet. He's harmless.

"Short and sweet then."

"That's all you need with Eli," I assure her. *Listen to me.*

What am I doing?

Lauren wrinkles her nose and lowers her voice. "He's kind of cute, though, don't you think?"

"He's really cute," I stress. Not a lie either. The boy is hot, but definitely not for me. I'm in love with someone else. "So tall too."

"Taller than his brother."

"And Eli's a great kisser."

Lauren's eyes go wide with surprise. "You really did kiss him?"

I give a short nod, but say nothing. Let her imagination run wild. It makes the story that much more interesting.

"How do you catch all of these elusive hot guys, Amanda? I don't get it."

"I don't get it either," I say with a soft laugh. Her other friends approach and she shoots me a look that tells me to be quiet.

So I am. I don't reveal her interest in Eli, and she's not mean to me, so I guess we've come to some sort of truce.

"Going to the carnival tonight?" I ask them as I'm handing over their change.

"You know it," Lauren says with an arrogant little smile. "We're running a kissing booth."

Figures. "A kissing booth during Halloween? Isn't that more appropriate for Valentine's Day?"

"Kissing is appropriate year-round. Besides, we're dressing up as sexy witches. It'll be fun!"

They grab their yogurt and leave the shop in a whirlwind of whispered words and not so discreet giggles.

"I hate those girls," Blake says the moment they're gone.

"Have they been mean to you?"

"Nah. They don't even know I exist. They're just so self-absorbed."

He's right. I think we all become self-absorbed. It's like we can't help it. We're in our own little world, surrounded by our friends and family and interests, and after a while, we don't even notice anyone else.

"They're not so bad if you know how to deal with them." I smile at Blake. "Maybe I can give you lessons on how to deal with bitchy cheerleaders."

He cracks a smile. First one I've seen from him all day. "Sounds like a plan. Though I'd rather you give me a lesson on how to talk to Kyla."

Now we're talking. I rub my hands together greedily. "I need more details first before I can start teaching. You ready to talk?"

"Not really." Blake swallows hard. "But I can try."

"That's all I can ask for."

chapter thirty-one

"You need to hurry," I tell Liv as she carefully attaches fake lashes we decided to go with after all to my right eye. "We have to be out there soon."

"Shush, I'm almost done." I already have fake eyelashes on my left eye and my lids feel extra heavy. "You are going to look so amazing. I hope Tuttle dies a little inside when he sees you."

I snort. "He won't even be here tonight. He's not social, remember."

"True. He *should* be here, though. Let's make sure and take lots of photos tonight and plaster them all over Snapchat. You are the sexiest witch ever." She steps back and beams.

"I don't even know if he follows me." Lies. He does follow me. The #cuddlewithTuttle memory still lingers.

Still hurts.

"Ugh, he makes me nuts. Forget him." Livvy is still smiling at me. "You look amazing."

"So do you."

She bats her false eyelashes. "Why thank you, my spooky witch friend."

I turn to look at myself in the mirror and I have to admit, I look pretty damn good. Even better than the trial run on Thursday night, and we were pretty smokin' hot and spooky then too. My makeup is on point—scary without being hideous. My hair is parted in the middle and flowing past my shoulders, straightened to perfection with Livvy's extra-hot straightener. I'm still a little self-conscious about the low neckline on this costume, but screw it. I'm performing tonight. I get to be someone else for a little while.

May as well enjoy it.

Livvy grabs my shoulders from behind and leans down so she's in the mirror with me too. Our gazes meet in the reflection. "We look so freaking great! We better head over to the caf before Elaine kicks our asses."

We leave the auditorium where we got ready, via the back exit, which is also the long way, since we don't want anyone to see us in costume. It's not quite five o'clock, but the quad is already full of people milling about. And there's a decent-sized line to get into the haunted house.

The Halloween carnival at our high school is an annual event, and it's a huge deal. It's a great way for organizations and clubs at the school to raise money. It's always fun, and who doesn't love Halloween? Well, there are more than a few people who don't love it, and during our freshman year, a few disgruntled parents from the PTA threatened to shut it all down, but the students and faculty eventually prevailed. The Halloween carnival lives on.

This is our last year to attend, so it feels bittersweet. It's hard to believe all of these things we've experienced the past three years are our lasts this year. Our last first day of school, last homecoming—which I missed—and now it's the last Halloween carnival.

I need to make the most of this tonight. I know Livvy wants to as well.

Usually I'm participating in the band fundraiser, which, naturally, always involves music. This year's theme is a haunted band performance. I heard they set up the band room to look like an old time bar with a tiny stage where various band members perform. They're all dressed up as ghosts from the Wild West. I see more than a few girls dressed like they walked straight out of a saloon, but their faces are white and their eyes are black. It's pretty cool.

"Everyone looks so great," Livvy says as we head toward the back entrance of the cafeteria. One of the staff members is standing guard in front of the doors, and when he sees it's us, he lets us in.

It's dark inside, with the black tarps hanging and the majority of the lights are off. We created a haunted maze within the cafeteria and there are little alcoves scattered throughout, where different "scenarios" are set up. Livvy's in the vampire scenario while I'm in a witches and warlocks scene, but I have no idea where I'm supposed to go.

"There you two are!" Elaine miraculously appears in front of us, dressed in a devil costume with a pointy red tail and little red horns sticking out of the top of her head, plus she's carrying a pitchfork. It's scarily accurate, what with the way she ran all of us ragged this morning. Livvy told me she never let up either.

This is why the cafeteria looks so amazing. Elaine wouldn't accept anything less.

"Hey, boss!" Livvy waves, extra cheerful on purpose. We know it drives Elaine nuts. "Where do you want us?"

Elaine briskly walks us through the maze, pointing to where each of us should go. The vampire section comes up first, so Livvy's out, blowing kisses at us and laughing when Elaine takes my hand and drags me deeper into the maze.

"Here's your station." Elaine gives me a little shove and I'm in an alcove with a small round table where three other witches sit. "Be scary and freak them out, but remember, don't touch the houseguests!"

"Oooh, you look extra scary," one of the witches says as she takes me in. She's wearing a sexy witch costume, and her boobs look like they're ready to pop out at any moment. She kicks out the last chair for me. "Sit at the front of the table."

Scary music kicks on and people start trickling in. We sit at the table at first, hissing and cackling and saying goofy stuff as people pass by. But eventually we get bored, so we hide behind corners and randomly jump out at different times, scaring our so-called houseguests. People shriek and scream and run from us, but there's lots of laughter too.

It's so freaking easy, and we are having way too much fun with this.

I see a few people I know and they call out my name and wave, or say silly stuff, trying to get me to break character. But I hold up as best as I can, calling everyone, "my pretty" and wiggling my long, black press-on nails at them as they walk by.

At one point I see Tara and Thad pass by our alcove, holding hands and looking very couple-y. I feel a pang in my heart for the briefest moment. Then I wonder why they're not working at the band fundraiser.

About halfway through my shift, Em walks right up to me, fully decked out in a *Suicide Squad* costume. Tiny booty shorts, a tight-fitting top that shows off her stomach, and a little heart painted just below her right eye—she makes a most excellent Harley Quinn.

"You don't scare me," she drawls, her bright red lips stretching into a huge smile.

I wave my nails at her. "Where's your baseball bat?"

"They wouldn't let me bring it on school property. They considered it a dangerous weapon." She mock pouts and I can't help but laugh.

She just shakes her head at me and walks away.

Eli Bennett walks through with his friends and they all stop and stare at me while Eli just stands among them and nods. I can only imagine what he's told them about me. He's got the biggest shit-eating grin on his face, and I glare at him, hoping he'll leave.

He doesn't. So I steadily approach, until I'm standing just in front of him. So close I could touch him. They all freeze, their eyes wide, matching horrified expressions on their faces. The other witches rally behind me, and they also remain quiet. I'm thrilled they're cooperating without my having to even ask.

"She's freaky, man," one of the boys whispers, and another one shushes him.

I twist my red lips into a wicked smile, tapping one long black nail against my lower lip as I contemplate them. They're just waiting for me to do something outrageous, so I go for subtle instead.

"Boo," I whisper, and they all scatter like leaves in the wind.

Ah, silly freshmen boys.

We start doing this for all the witches' friends—and enemies. Whenever one of the girls leaps to the front, we fall in behind, following her cues. Every time we chase someone away, we collapse against each other in giggling fits. I've never had such a good time scaring people in all my life.

We keep up this pace for a solid two hours until an announcement is broadcast over the cafeteria sound system.

"Attention, houseguests. We ask that you please exit the house within the next ten minutes. The house is closing for a fifteen-minute break, but fear not! The house will reopen soon. Thank you, boos and ghouls." The announcer sounds off with an evil laugh.

My shift is over after those ten minutes, and then the second crew will come on duty. I seriously need to pee and I'm desperate for something to drink. My throat hurts from all the witch talk and yelling. Plus I'm starving, and I bet Livvy is too. We'll have to go check out the food booths and grab something to eat.

People start leaving the cafeteria in droves, so I cut out early and head to the bathroom in the back near the kitchen, which is closed off to the public. I handle my business, wash my hands, fix my smeared makeup as best as I can, then exit the bathroom, intent on finding Livvy so we can go get something to drink and eat.

But I stop short when I see who's standing there. Like he's waiting for me.

Tuttle.

"Hey." His voice is soft and he keeps his distance, as if he's afraid I'll run. Or attack him.

"Hi." I stay where I'm at, not wanting to get close for fear I might do something. Like run. Or attack him.

"How are you?"

Why are we making pointless small talk? "How did you get in here?"

He smiles sheepishly. "I bribed Elaine King."

My mouth drops open. "She's not bribeable."

"Trust me. Everyone is bribeable. We all have a price." His expression turns somber as he cuts his gaze away from mine.

His words make me fume, and I know he's not referring to me, but still. I don't like that he believes I have a price and that eventually, he'll be able to meet it if he needs to. "Well, I can't be bought. Not by you."

Now he looks pained. "I know, Mandy. I'm not talking about you. It's just..." His voice drifts and he thrusts his fingers through his hair, thoroughly messing it up. I wonder when was the last time he got it cut. It's longer than usual, curling against his neck. I remember how soft it is...

And I am becoming completely distracted by his hair, which is ridiculous. I need to focus.

He makes it hard to focus, though. Not like the boy has to try too hard to distract me. All he has to do is stand there, wearing jeans and a black pullover hoodie, and I want to drool.

It's seriously not fair.

"It's just what?" I ask when he still hasn't said anything.

"I'm already messing this up." He blows out a harsh breath and flicks his gaze up to the ceiling before he looks at me again. "Can I just talk to you for a few minutes? Somewhere private?"

"I have plans to meet up with Livvy right now." I'm not going to give in. He'll just walk all over me again. Reel me in only to reject me, push me away, and I'll be left behind a sobbing mess. I gave him too much power over me before. I can't do that again.

"After the carnival then? Can I pick you up?"

"You're not going to the carnival?"

"I'm here, aren't I?" His gaze sweeps over me, lingering on my chest. "You look amazing, by the way."

"Thank you." I want to say no. Yet I also want to say yes. Saying yes will result in me getting hurt. I'll listen to what he has to say, he'll feed me a line or two of complete crap, I'll fall for it, we'll spend time together, I'll get my hopes up and then...

My hopes will come crashing down in a blaze of shame and low self-esteem and Livvy will tell me, "I told you so."

I can't go through that again.

"I don't think I can meet with you after the carnival, Jordan," I say, my voice soft. I see the hurt on his face, the pain in his eyes, and it makes me feel terrible. "I'm sorry, but I can't go through this again. Have a good night." I turn on my heel and walk away.

He follows after me. "Amanda, wait!" He grabs hold of my arm and stops me before I can get too far away. "Could we maybe talk tomorrow?"

"What else is there to talk about?" I jerk out of his hold and throw my hands in the air, wishing I could throw a punch at him instead. When I don't want him to be persistent is, of course, when he actually is.

I can't win with him. I just…can't.

"What do you mean?" Jordan frowns, taking a step back.

"You don't want to be with me. You've already told me that. Is that what you want to talk about? How it'll never work out between us? Well, I got the message loud and clear yesterday, okay? We're done. Over. Just the way you want it." I glare at him, breathing so hard my chest rises and falls rapidly, and I swear I feel faint. It's probably because I'm hungry.

That I can even still be hungry gives me hope. Maybe I am over Tuttle after all…

"I never said I didn't want to be with you." His voice drops and his gaze is intense as he watches me.

"You didn't have to," I whisper just before I turn and walk away.

And never once look back.

acknowledgements

First up…I'm so incredibly sorry, readers. I didn't mean for this book to end in a cliffhanger, I swear. But as I wrote Amanda and Jordan's story, I realized he's a lot more complex than I originally thought. Truthfully, so is Amanda. So yes, I'm writing another book about them, and it will conclude their story, I promise.

Before I thank everyone, I want you all to know that Tuttle was only going to be a walk on character in Just Friends. A throwaway kind of guy who appeared every once in a while just to be a jerk or to be that extra friend Ryan and Dustin needed to talk to. Instead, Tuttle took over my brain and demanded his own story. So did Amanda. She became the girl so many readers rooted for—and so did I. So their story is not only for me (because it was a total joy to write, let me tell you), but for all of you too.

All right, now for the thanks…

A big, huge, sloppy kiss-filled thank you to my publicist and friend Nina, who has been such a loyal supporter of this series from the start and who will cut a bitch if anyone tries to take Tuttle away from her. Another big, huge, sloppy kiss-filled thanks to my assistant Kati. We've been together four (!!!) years now, and I don't know what I'd do without you. Plus you make great graphics that every raves over. Huge thanks also to Jenn Watson for her advertising skills and general awesomeness. And to Gelytaz, who also makes beautiful graphics and trailers—thank you for all that you do.

To my daughter who is currently experiencing Just Friends-type drama, only it's the eighth grade version (seriously – the inspiration is constant). Thank you for being so open with me, thank you for making smart choices and thank you for choosing such good friends. I love you.

I must always thank my critique partner, my friend, my wifey Katy Evans for always taking care of me in the best way possible. Big shout out to my cover designer for this series Hang Le – these covers are so gorgeous, I can't stop staring at them! Plus, thank you to my editor Mackenzie Walton and my proofreader Dana Waganer—you ladies keep me in line and make sure the story is the best that it can be. Also, thank you to my formatter E.M. Tippetts—the interior of my books always look fabulous thanks to you and your team.

Last but not least, thank you to the readers, reviewers and bloggers who've read the Friends series so far and given me so much support. I know Livvy made a lot of you nuts. I know many of you couldn't stand the majority of the characters in Just Friends. So thank you for enjoying their story anyway, and I hoped I changed your minds with Amanda and Jordan's story. I adore these two. I hope you did too.

CPSIA information can be obtained
at www.ICGtesting.com
Printed in the USA
LVHW04s1604250718
584895LV00002B/214/P

9 781682 308790